"Tonight's not the night to press your luck."

Short hooked his thumbs in the armholes of his vest. Courtright stiffened, his eyes suddenly alert. "Don't you pull a gun on me!"

"Take it easy." Short fanned the lapels of his coat aside. "I'm not heeled."

"Like hell you're not!"

Courtright was primed for a fight. He knew Short habitually went armed, and when the gambler spread his coat, that was all the pretext needed. His arm a blur, Courtright reached for his right-hand gun, smoothly performing the reverse draw. The barrel cleared leather.

Short was a beat behind. His hand dipped to his rear pocket and came out with the stubby Colt. The men were not three feet apart, and he saw the long barrel of Courtright's pistol swinging into position. . . .

St. Martin's Paperbacks by Matt Braun

Wyatt Earp

Black Fox

Outlaw Kingdom

Lords of the Land

Cimarron Jordan

Bloody Hand

Noble Outlaw

Texas Empire

The Savage Land

Rio Hondo

The Gamblers

Doc Holliday

One Last Town

The Brannocks

The Last Stand

Rio Grande

Gentleman Rogue

GENTLEMAN ROGUE

Matt Braun

St. Martin's Paperbacks

GENTLEMAN ROGUE

Copyright © 1999 by Matt Braun.

ISBN: 0-312-96827-2

Printed in the United States of America

St. Martin's Paperbacks edition / March 1999

St. Martin's Paperbacks are published by St. Martin's Press, 175 Fifth Avenue, New York, NY 10010.

10 9 8 7 6 5 4 3 2 1

To CHRISTINE and E.J.
Who hear the sound of the written word

Author's Note

Gentleman Rogue is based on a true story.

Luke Short was preeminent among professional gamblers on the Western frontier. From a Texas cowhand, herding longhorns up the Chisholm Trail, he went on to become one of the foremost gaming impresarios of his time. He traveled the gamblers' circuit from Tombstone to Deadwood, and he was a major figure in the wild-'n'-woolly days of Dodge City. A legend himself, he numbered among his closest friends such luminaries as Wyatt Earp, Bat Masterson, and Doc Holliday. Like them, he was deadly in a gunfight, and killed several men during his years as a gambler.

Yet the most intriguing aspect of Luke Short's life began in 1883. Upon leaving Dodge City, he bought a partnership in a prominent gaming club in Fort Worth. There, he quickly became embroiled in the struggle underlying the transition of the Old West into the modern era. A man of foresight, shrewd in his judgments, Short allied himself with the movement to reform the notorious district known as Hell's Half Acre. He incurred the wrath of the sporting crowd, and ultimately, the personal animosity of the town's reigning gunfighter. They were to meet in one of the most fabled shootouts in Western history.

Gentleman Rogue chronicles the life of a man who adapted to changing times and survived to take his place in our national folklore. The tale told here is a blend of fact and fiction, with sufficient literary license to present the legend of Luke Short. A tale of how the Old West rode kicking into the sunset.

All else is a storyteller at work.

Chapter 1

The engineer set the brakes with a racketing squeal. A moment later, belching clouds of steam, the train rocked to a halt before the station house. Dusk was settling over the land, and lamplights glowed like columns of fireflies across the town. Passengers began debarking the train.

Luke Short gathered his valise from the overhead luggage rack. He moved to the end of the coach and went down the steps onto the platform. A raw November wind whipped off the prairie, and he tugged at the collar of his topcoat. He stood for a moment staring at the broad expanse of Fort Worth.

The town was situated on a rolling plain, bordered on the north and west by the Trinity River. Originally an Army outpost, established in 1849, it had provided a line of defense against warlike tribes who preyed on Texas settlers. But now, late in 1883, it was a bustling metropolis, rivaling Dallas, which lay some thirty miles to the east. The population was pushing twenty-two thousand, and the community was served by two railroads, the Missouri Pacific and the Texas & Pacific. Town boosters fondly touted it as the "Queen of the Prairie."

Short waited outside the station house while the baggage car was unloaded. He signaled a porter, who claimed his steamer trunk and muscled it onto a hand-cart, along with his valise. The porter led the way around the corner of the depot, where carriages for hire waited in line out front. After the trunk and valise were stowed aboard the rear of a carriage, Short slipped the porter three dollars. He gave the driver the name of an uptown hotel.

The immediate area around Union Depot was known locally as Hell's Half Acre. Located at the south edge of town, it was the heart of the sporting district, operating wide open day and night. The streets were lined with saloons, gaming dives, dance halls, and whorehouses, devoted solely to vice and separating working men from their wages. Over the years, as Fort Worth had doubled and doubled again in size, the district had grown to encompass the entire southern part of town. Today it was referred to simply as the Acre.

The carriage turned north onto Main Street. Short watched as throngs of men crowding the sidewalks made their way from dive to dive. He was reminded that several generations of Texican cowhands had given the Acre its reputation as a hellhole. For more than twenty years, herds of longhorns had been driven up the Chisholm Trail, passing through Fort Worth on the long trek to distant railheads in Kansas. In large degree, all that had ended when railroad lines crossed the Red River and laid track deeper into Texas. Herds were now driven to the stockyards on the outskirts of town.

Fort Worth itself had been transformed from a dusty cowtown into a thriving center of commerce. With the advent of the railroads, business and industry had replaced cattle as the mainstay of the economy. The streets were paved, brick buildings dominated the uptown district, and the town was home to one of the finest educational institutions in the state, Texas Wesleyan University. Yet there was an odd mix of the old and the new, with spurred cowhands still jostling along the sidewalks among laborers, railroad men, and factory workers. The town itself may have changed, but some aspects of life were seemingly immutable to change. The Acre had simply grown larger.

A knot of cowhands burst from one of the dance halls. Their raucous laughter intermingled with the strains of a rinky-dink piano accompanied by a banjo. Watching them from the carriage, Short reflected that the Acre was his reason for being there. By profession a gambler, he had spent the last five years in Dodge City operating a gaming parlor for wealthy Texan cattlemen who had trailed their herds to the railhead. But with the railroads moving ever southward, the cattle trade had begun to dwindle off over the past year. Dodge City was no longer the mecca for high rollers.

To compound matters, a reform element saw opportunity in the gradual decline of the cattle trade. The reformers put together an unholy alliance of clergymen, straightlaced businessmen, and crooked politicians. The purpose of their campaign was not the outright ban of gambling, but rather to winnow out those who refused to knuckle under, particularly those without political connections. Short fell into that category, and a month ago he had set out to find himself a new home. Before returning to Dodge City, his trip took him to various parts of Colorado, and finally to Texas. He thought he'd found what he was searching for in Fort Worth.

For all its growth, Fort Worth was one of the few wide-open cities left in the West. Though the county seat of Tarrant County, the community was still largely controlled by local politicians. The city government imposed so-called occupation taxes on saloons, whorehouses, and gaming dives, and the revenues generated kept the town treasury afloat. The politicians placed a discount on morality and a premium on economic stability, and rarely tried to enforce the letter of the law. A truce was maintained with the sporting crowd, with occupation taxes acting as the buffer, and everyone benefited. So long as the Acre held violence to a minimum and confined immorality to the south end of town, the law was tolerant.

Not quite a fortnight ago, Short had spent almost a week in Fort Worth. His presence aroused curiosity, for he was known and respected among the gambling fraternity throughout the West. But he had kept his own counsel, avoiding questions as to the reason for his visit, and devoted considerable time to inspecting the town. The Acre interested him only in the sense that it was a sinkhole of iniquity overlooked, and therefore condoned, by City Hall. He had nothing in common with tinhorns and grifters, and even less with bawdy whores and those who operated rotgut saloons. His interest was in monied high rollers, and establishments that catered to a select clientele. He found an abundance of both in Fort Worth.

A mule-drawn trolley car clanged along the tracks on Main Street. Short recalled from his visit that the trolley ran the length of the town, a mile from the southern edge of the Acre to the northern frontage of Courthouse Square. As his carriage rolled through an intersection, he recalled as well that there was a line of demarcation between uptown and downtown. The corner of Main and Seventh established a boundary separating the sporting district from the rest of the town. Below Main and Seventh, where the Acre started, a blind eye was turned to virtually all forms of vice. Anything went.

Uptown, where the better class of people lived and conducted their business, nothing unseemly was tolerated. There were gambling clubs, and saloons, and variety theaters, but none of the depravity to be found in the Acre. As though the town fathers had drawn a line in the sand, everything above Main and Seventh was held to a different standard. There the streets were free of violence and whores and anything that smacked of disorder. The law worked, and worked well, uptown.

Short thought it made imminent good sense. Below the line, cardsharps and Soiled Doves plied their trade with virtual immunity. Yet above the line, a man was assured of a straight deal and honest cards. He was impressed, eager to get on with his plan.

Fort Worth seemed made to order.

The carriage rolled to a halt before the Mansion Hotel. A porter appeared from inside, bobbling his head in greeting, and began unloading the luggage. Short paid the driver from a wad of greenbacks, waving away the change. He walked toward the entrance.

The Mansion was an elegant hotel, widely regarded as the finest in Fort Worth. A four-story brick structure, it occupied half a block on Fourth Street, just off the corner of Main. The lobby was appointed with leather chairs and couches, grouped before a fireplace ablaze with logs. Several well-dressed men sat conversing in low tones.

George Harper, the night clerk, waited at the registration desk. "Good evening, Mr. Short," he said effusively. "Welcome back to the Mansion."

"Thank you, George," Short replied. "You got my wire?"

"Yessir, we certainly did. We reserved the streetside suite, just as you requested."

Short had stayed at the hotel on his previous visit. The clerk's obsequious manner was somewhat overdone, but hardly more than he expected. He was accustomed to deferential treatment.

A man of medium stature, five seven and a solid 140 pounds, he was a dapper dresser, attired in the latest fashion. His features were square, with slate-gray eyes, dark hair, and a brushy mustache. Yet it was his bearing, a steely force of character, that commanded respect. He seemed somehow taller.

Harper swung the registration ledger around. "How long will you be staying with us, Mr. Short?"

Short glanced at a wall calendar behind the desk. He marked the date as November 18, and scrawled his name in the ledger with a pen. "I'll be here indefinitely," he said with an enigmatic smile. "Tomorrow, I'll talk with the manager about a long-term rate."

"That would be Mr. Orcutt. John Orcutt. Are you planning to make Fort Worth your home, Mr. Short?"

"Time will tell, George. Why do you ask?"

"Pardon the curiosity," Harper said, aware that he'd overstepped himself. "I didn't mean to pry. It's just that you're . . ."

Short waited when the clerk's voice trailed off. "Go ahead, speak up, George. What were you going to say?"

"Well, you're a man of some reputation, Mr. Short."

"Am I?"

"Oh, yessir," Harper said quickly. "Last time you were here, everybody in town was talking about it. All the gamblers, I mean."

"And what were they saying?"

"Why, they thought you might be looking for a game. Guess they wanted to test their luck."

Short nodded. "Are you a gambling man?"

"Just a little faro, now and then, Mr. Short. Strictly small time stuff."

"A wise decision, George. The house always wins."

Harper laughed. "Sure seems that way with me."

A bellman led Short to the steam-powered elevator. The suite was on the fourth floor, with a view looking north toward the river. By the time the bellman had the gas lights turned up and the fireplace blazing, the porter arrived with the luggage. Short dropped his hat and coat on a chair, waiting until they were through. He tipped them on their way out the door.

Afterward, Short wandered through the suite, pleased with his accommodations. A lush Persian carpet covered the sitting-room floor, and grouped before the marble fireplace were several chairs and a chesterfield divan. The bedroom was appointed in the Victorian style, connected to a bathroom with hot and cold running water. A series of handsomely draped windows overlooked the city.

Short halted before a window in the sitting room. Flickering streetlamps marched into the distance, lighting the square farther uptown and the dome of the courthouse. Looking out, his thoughts drifted back to a time when there was no courthouse, and Fort Worth was a crude collection of wooden buildings. A time when he was younger.

In 1870, when he was seventeen, he'd left the family ranch in Grayson County. A day later, at Fort Worth, he signed on as a cowhand and went up the Chisholm Trail to Kansas. The cowtowns proved to be a lure, and he quit the cattle outfit, determined to make a new life for himself. For four years he operated a traveling saloon for buffalo hunters, wandering the Western plains by wagon. He discovered gambling in the buffalo camps, drawn by the excitement of wagering it all on a card. More often than not he went broke.

By 1876, in league with a partner, he was operating as a whiskey smuggler on the Sioux Reservation in Dakota Territory. All the while he continued to gamble, honing his skills, blessed with quick hands and a mathematical instinct for the odds. Along the way he killed two men who tried to rob him, got himself arrested for whiskey smuggling, and managed to escape. Finally, in 1877, he landed in Denver with a fat bankroll. He set about transforming himself into a professional gambler.

For the next year he traveled the gamblers' circuit, with stops in Leadville, Cheyenne, and Deadwood. Unable to abide card cheats, he killed his third man in a dispute over a poker game. Then, in 1878, he returned to Kansas, settling at last in Dodge City. By 1880, he was a partner in the fabled Long Branch Saloon, and close friends with Bat Masterson and Wyatt Earp. During the winter of 1881, he took a brief sojourn to Tombstone, Arizona, where the Earp brothers were involved in a struggle for political control of the county. There he killed yet another man in a gunfight, and was exonerated on the grounds of self-defense. He spent the next two years in Dodge City, battling crooks in the guise of reformers. The battle won, but strangely lost, his gaze again turned to Texas.

Staring out the window, Short felt as though he'd come full circle. Over the course of thirteen years, afflicted with wanderlust, he had traveled the mountains and plains, never once returning to Texas. In that time, his mother and father had died, and his only sister had married and moved to California. He often thought he should have returned, but there had always been another gold strike, another boomtown, the lure of the cards. His one regret was that he had come home too late.

Yet he was here, and he meant to stay. At thirty, he had already lived several lifetimes, and all to a purpose. He was in his prime, at the top of his game, the equal of any gambler who cared to test his skill at cards. Even more telling, he was schooled by years of experience in operating a gaming emporium, and making it profitable. A large part of his reputation was founded on a square deal, no tricks and nothing underhanded, an even chance. But the house always won.

High in the sky, he caught the twinkle of the North Star. Whether or not it was his lucky star seemed a moot point, for skill was far more certain than luck. What mattered most was that he had a bank draft in his pocket for fifty thousand, and in the money belt beneath his shirt, another ten thousand in cash. He operated on the motto that money made money, particularly in tandem with a still stronger axiom. Hard cash spoke the loudest of all.

Tomorrow he meant to put it to work.

Chapter 2

Late the next morning, Short came out of the bathroom. He was freshly shaved, his mustache trimmed, his hair neatly combed and slicked back on the sides. His underwear was hand-stitched Egyptian cotton.

Last night, he had devoted most of the evening to putting his home in order. His suits now hung in an armoire that occupied a corner of the bedroom. The suits were properly somber in color, each one hand-tailored, cut from the finest of fabrics. His shirts, imported from New York, and his underclothing were arranged in a dresser opposite the bed. A row of some twenty books stood wedged together atop the dresser.

Short was a self-educated man. Early on, when he'd become a professional gambler, he realized that wealthy high rollers, usually businessmen with formal educations, judged a man by his manner of speech and his ability to converse in polite society. He began an omnivorous reading program, and soon discovered a taste for classic literature and anything historical. Among other works, he was partial to Dante's *The Divine Comedy*, Voltaire's *Candide*, and Gibbon's *History of the Decline and Fall of the Roman Empire*. His favorite, apart from Shakespeare, was Cervantes' *Don Quixote*.

A man's attire, he'd found, was no less important than his manner of speech. To look the part, a man had to dress the part, and Short studied fashion and style with the same zeal that he devoured books. In time, he became an impeccable dresser, fastidious to a fault, particular about every aspect of his appearance. The select clientele in any city, those with the most money to squander over a gaming table, were bankers, merchants, and prominent landowners, men who conducted themselves as gentlemen. He transformed himself into a gentleman gambler.

Today, he selected a dark-charcoal suit tailored from a rich, imported worsted. He chose a patterned cravat, knotting it beneath his shirt collar, and topped it off with a deepwater-pearl stickpin. His vest matched the suit, with a gold watch tucked in one pocket and an intricate chain and fob draped across the front. The last item of apparel was a Colt Peacemaker, chambered for .45 caliber, with gutta-percha grips and a four-and-three-quarter-inch barrel. The right hip-pocket of his trousers was tailored with an insewn holster of sueded leather. The pistol slipped into the pocket with a snug fit.

In a very real sense, Short was a diamond in the rough who, over the years, had buffed off the rough edges and emerged a man of polish and élan. Which in no way tempered his refusal to suffer insult or an affront to his personal dignity. He was a gentleman who carried a gun and occasionally put it to deadly use.

Short looked upon the pistol as a tool of the trade. He considered himself an honorable man, and he never resorted to underhanded methods. Yet one of the first lessons he'd learned all those years ago was that every game was assumed to be crooked. A boomtown served as a lure to cardsharps and grifters, and their ability to cheat was more art than science. There was less likelihood of marked cards or a crooked deal among high rollers; but he had discovered that even the wealthiest of men would sometimes rig the game. The pistol was his punctuation mark to any argument.

The door of the armoire was fronted with a full-length mirror. After shrugging into his suit jacket, Short studied his reflection with a critical eye. He adjusted the knot in his cravat and tugged the bottom of his vest into a smooth line. Then, turning sideways to the mirror, he inspected the drape of his jacket over the pistol. The tailoring concealed any unseemly bulge, eliminating the slightest hint that he carried a gun. Finally, satisfied that he passed muster, he took a high-crowned hat from atop the armoire and moved through the bedroom. A noonday sun lighted the windows as he walked from the suite.

Downstairs, he ordered a late breakfast in the hotel dining room. A gambler's life was one of long nights, and years ago he'd grown accustomed to having breakfast when most people sat down for their midday meal. The waitress brought bacon and eggs, with fluffy biscuits and an assortment of jams. Over a second cup of coffee, he took a slim, black cheroot from his inside pocket and lit up in a haze of smoke. Idly, savoring the coffee and the cheroot, he considered his plans for the day. He thought the first stop would be the bank.

Outside, he walked to the corner of Main and turned uptown. The weather was brisk but comfortable, with a warm sun, and he strolled along at a leisurely pace. Fort Worth was laid out on a checkerboard grid, with the numbered streets running east to west. At the north end of town, Main Street opened onto the courthouse square, which encompassed two city blocks. The courthouse was constructed of native stone and stood like a domed monolith in the center of the square. Around the square were an array of shops and business establishments, the commercial heart of the city. A block farther north were steep bluffs dropping off to the Trinity River.

Uptown and downtown were all but separate worlds. Downtown, with its fleshpots and the hurdy-gurdy atmosphere of the Acre, was home to the sporting crowd. The respectable people of Fort Worth lived west of Courthouse Square. A section to the northwest, overlooking the river, was a residential enclave for the wealthier class, far removed from the Acre. Unless the need arose to catch a train, some of the uptown crowd had never ventured south of Seventh Street. There were nine churches and sixty saloons within the city limits, and for most people, it was a case of never the twain shall meet. They kept to their own kind.

On the square, Short turned east and entered the First National Bank. The president of the bank was Karl Van Zandt, one of the movers and shakers of Fort Worth. A couple of weeks ago, during his previous visit to town, Short had heard that Van Zandt fancied himself a poker player and frequented the uptown clubs. He thought it only good business to bank with a banker who was considered a high roller. There was often an advantage to be gained through the personal touch.

Short requested a moment of Van Zandt's time. After mentioning the matter of a substantial deposit, he was ushered into a private office dominated by a massive walnut desk. Van Zandt was an imposing man, on the sundown side of forty, with sharp eyes and an affable smile. He offered a firm handshake.

"Have a seat, Mr. Short," he said, gesturing to a leather wing-back chair. "Are you new to Fort Worth?"

"I arrived last night," Short informed him. "Given the right business opportunity, I plan to make my home here."

"Well, you've certainly come to the right place. How may I assist you?"

"I wish to open an account."

Short extracted the bank draft from his pocket and slid it across the desk. Van Zandt took it in both hands, noting that it was drawn on the Dodge City Grover's Bank. He glanced up with an inquisitive look.

"Fifty thousand dollars," he said. "Not an inconsequential sum, Mr. Short. May I inquire the nature of your business?"

Short smiled. "I am a professional gambler."

"Indeed!" Van Zandt remarked, tapping the draft

with a finger. "I daresay a successful one, as well. What is your game?"

"I have a fondness for poker."

"And where do you plan to conduct your business?"

"Somewhere uptown," Short said easily. "I expect to know more this afternoon."

"Be sure to let me know, won't you, Mr. Short? I'm partial to the game of poker, myself."

"I would count it an honor to have you at my table, Mr. Van Zandt."

"Well then, allow me to welcome you to Fort Worth."

"Thank you most kindly."

Short dipped a pen in the inkwell and endorsed the draft.

The deliveryman walked to the rear of the ice wagon. A leather apron covered his back and he carried a set of steel tongs with sharp points. He hooked the tongs into a hundred-pound block of ice, turning and stooping, and hefted the block off the wagon onto his shoulder. He lugged the ice into a restaurant.

Short hesitated until the deliveryman went past. Then he continued along the sidewalk to the corner of Second and Main. He waited for a buggy to rattle by on the street, and crossed the intersection to the opposite corner. A few doors down, he saw a man raise a rifle to his shoulder and take deliberate aim. The crack of gunfire racketed along the street.

The Acme Shooting Gallery occupied a narrow space between two buildings. At the rear of the gallery, some thirty feet from the sidewalk, were a series of metal targets mounted on spinning wheels and horizontal trolleys. Short paused, interested in any display of marksmanship, and watched the man reload. He nodded approvingly as a slug sent one of the pinwheels flying.

A woman stood behind the counter. She was heavy-set, with doughy features, and Short gathered that she was the operator. The rifles being used were Colt Lightning pump-action, chambered for .22 caliber, and sandbags at the rear of the gallery easily absorbed the slugs. From the muted sound of the report, Short suspected the shells were loaded with a low powder charge. The woman gave him a sassy smile.

"Try your luck, mister," she said. "Only two bits for five shots."

"Another time."

"No time like the present."

Short waved, moving off as the rifle cracked. He turned into the entrance of the White Elephant Saloon. The name belied the elegance of the establishment, one of the finer restaurants and gaming clubs in the city. A two-story structure, the ground floor housed a forty-foot-long mahogany bar, crystal chandeliers, and linen-covered tables for fine dining. Toward the rear, a carpeted stairway led to the upper floor, where a handsomely appointed clubroom offered games of chance. The White Elephant catered to the uptown crowd.

The noon rush was over and the place was all but empty. Jake Johnson, the owner, was talking to one of the bartenders. He looked around as Short walked along the bar. "Well, Luke!" he said jovially. "Back again so soon?"

Short accepted his handshake. "I couldn't stay away, Jake. How are things with you?"

"Things got any better, I'd have to turn 'em away from the door."

Johnson was a large man with florid features and the good-natured humor of a raconteur. But he was a poor liar, and the skittering cast to his eyes betrayed his boast. Short knew full well that the White Elephant was losing business and hard-pressed to turn a profit. From his last trip to town, simple observation of the nightly crowd, supported by growing rumor, told him that Johnson was in trouble. He nodded pleasantly.

"I'd like to talk business," he said. "How about your office?"

"Why, sure, Luke—follow me."

Johnson's office was off an alcove opposite the kitchen. He got Short seated across the desk and dropped into his chair. He grinned like a frog.

"Looking for a game, aren't you? I knew it when you were here last time."

"Not the way you mean," Short told him. "I plan to buy into a club. I've narrowed it down to your place and the Centennial."

"The Centennial?" Johnson echoed. "You'd get in bed with Lowe?"

The Centennial Theater, located across the street from the White Elephant, was owned by Joe Lowe. A man of brutish character, he operated out of his uptown club and controlled several dives in the Acre. He was widely acknowledged as the vice czar of Fort Worth.

"I'd rather go partners with you," Short said in an offhand manner. "But I could learn to live with Lowe."

Johnson stared at him. "What makes you think I'd want a partner?"

"Your club's in trouble, Jake. Lowe's stolen half your business with high-stakes games and a snazzier operation. Everybody in town knows it. You need new blood."

"And you think you're the man?"

"I've got the name and I bring the game. Think of me as an attraction to high rollers."

Johnson considered a moment. He knew, as did everyone in the business, that Short was an impresario of gambling. The recent blowout in Dodge City had, if anything, added to Short's fame. According to newspaper reports, the mayor of Dodge City, in league with Short's major competitor, had enlisted the aid of misguided reformers. In a smear campaign laced with dirty tactics, they had attempted to run Short out of business and out of town. The upshot was what was widely publicized as the "Dodge City War."

Short imported Bat Masterson and Wyatt Earp, along with four other gunman associates, from Colorado. The conclave of gunfighters dubbed themselves the "Peace Commission," and challenged Short's opponents to make good on their threats. Faced with such formidable adversaries, clearly spoiling for a fight, the mayor and his self-styled reformers quickly conceded defeat. The war ended before it began, and Short, though victorious, decided to put Kansas behind him. Word spread throughout the sporting crowd that he'd sold his gaming parlor for a fortune in cash.

"All right, let's talk," Johnson said at length. "I'm willing to go partners on the club, but not the restaurant. Does that interest you?"

Short laughed. "So long as my meals are on the house."

"Then let's get down to brass tacks. What do you bring to the table besides your name?"

"Ten thousand now . . ." Short unstrapped his money belt and tossed it on the desk. "Thirty thousand more when we put it in writing. Have your lawyer draw up a contract."

Johnson's eyes were glued to the money belt. "I call the shots."

"Sorry, Jake, no dice. You tend to the restaurant and I'll run the club. That's not negotiable."

There was a prolonged silence. Finally, with a rueful shake of his head, Johnson chuckled out loud. "Looks like I've got myself a partner. When do we start?"

"Tonight," Short said crisply. "Let the word get around there's action to be found at the White Elephant."

"Luke, I have to say it, you jump right in. I like your style."

"How would you like Bat Masterson at our tables for a week or so? Think that might draw a crowd?"

"Jesus H. Christmas!" Johnson blurted. "Are you serious?"

"Dead serious," Short said. "I wired him before I left Dodge City. He'll be here a week from tomorrow."

"You were awful damn sure of yourself. How'd you know I'd go for the deal?"

"Why, that's the simplest thing in the world, Jake."

"How so?"

"I'm a gambler."

They signed the contract late that afternoon.

Chapter 3

Courtright pushed away from the table. The children stopped talking, their usual chatter at supper stilled by a sudden tension. They glanced from their father to their mother, who sat at the opposite end of the table. Her features were cloudy.

"I've got to go out," Courtright said, nodding to the children. "Help your mother with the dishes and do your homework. I don't want any bad reports."

"Yes, Pa." Sarah, who was fourteen, tried to defuse the situation with a bright smile. Timothy, who was eleven, and Ellen, the youngest at nine, avoided their father's gaze. He turned out of the dining room.

Elizabeth followed him into the parlor. She was a small woman, plumper from time and childbirth, but still quite attractive. By contrast, her husband, who was thirty-nine, looked years older than his age. He was tall, with a thatch of wheat-colored hair, pale blue eyes, and a soup-strainer mustache. His face was cast in a perpetual squint.

Courtright paused by the front door. He took a gun belt off a wall peg and strapped it around his waist. Two holsters were fixed on the belt, reversed in a cross-draw manner, the gun butts jutting forward. The pistols were silver-plated Colts, with ivory grips and seven-and-one-half-inch barrels. He cinched the buckle, glanced at his wife.

"Don't start, Betty. I don't want to hear it."

Elizabeth sniffed. "You'll hear it anyway, Jim. You're going to the Acre, aren't you?"

"What of it?"

"You're out all night and you sleep all day. The children are lucky if they see you for ten minutes at supper. That's what of it!"

Courtright gathered his hat and coat off the wall pegs. "I don't have time for this. I've got business to tend to."

"Some business!"

"Keeps clothes on your back and food on the table."

"Maybe it does," she snapped. "But I'm ashamed to tell my children what their father does for a living."

"You've turned into a hard woman."

"And who gave me reason?"

Courtright left her at the door. Their house was a modest frame dwelling on Second Street, just off Calhoun. Located on the east side of town, it was a respectable neighborhood, if not one of the more desirable. But it was what he could afford, and he made no apologies to anyone, least of all his wife. He walked toward Main Street.

The situation was getting worse. Courtright remembered a time when his wife was pretty and animated, a woman of spirited laughter. That was before their return to Fort Worth, and since then, she had become a whiner, forever badgering him about the life they led. But he had to admit that it wasn't entirely her fault, for he was no longer the man she'd married, either. He sometimes didn't like himself.

Courtright felt life had played him dirty. After the Civil War, and four years' service under the Union flag, he'd drifted west, working as a buffalo hunter, and later as an Army scout. Once he married Elizabeth, he tried to settle down, homesteading a farm outside Fort Worth. But he was a rough man with rough tastes, and he didn't last long behind a plow. They moved to town, and what

he found there was work for a man who was handy with
his fists and even better with a gun. He caught on as a
peace officer.

From 1876 to 1879, Courtright served as city marshal
of Fort Worth. A quick gun and a tough attitude enabled
him to keep a lid on the Acre, and the voters elected
him to three successive one-year terms. Some people
likened him to Wild Bill Hickok, and he reveled in the
comparison, for he was unbeatable with a gun. By the
latter part of 1879, he was riding high, one of the most
popular figures in Fort Worth, destined for great things.
But then, brought low by scandal, he and his deputies
were accused of extorting money from gambling dives
and whorehouses. Disenchanted, the voters turned him
out of office at the next election.

Still, there was always work for a man with a reputation. An old Army comrade offered Courtright the job
of foreman of a ranch in New Mexico. The job had less
to do with cows than with intimidating squatters who
were encroaching on the cattle spread's open range. A
year later, two sodbusters who refused to be scared off
were killed, and Courtright was charged with murder.
He fled New Mexico, returning to Fort Worth with his
family, only to find that the law had a long reach. After
an extradition warrant was issued, and Texas Rangers
took him into custody, Courtright managed to escape.
He fled the country.

For two years, Courtright found refuge in South
America. But then, weary of living on the dodge, he
returned to New Mexico and surrendered himself to the
authorities. Whether witnesses were frightened off, or
simply suffered a memory lapse over the years, the prosecutor was unable to produce anyone with firsthand
knowledge of the killings. Courtright was acquitted of
murder charges, and after the trial, he rejoined his family
in Fort Worth. There, too soon, the joy of being reunited
turned to bickering and recriminations. His rough ways
had at last taken a toll on his marriage.

Just as quickly, Courtright discovered that Fort Worth had changed during his long absence. The Acre was still there, and the sporting crowd was still tolerated; but the townspeople were determined to outdistance the tarnished image of their burgeoning city. Wherever he called, even among friends from the old days, Courtright found there was no gainful employment for a gunman with a shady past. Yet he was nothing if not resourceful, and within a month or so, he opened the Commercial Detective Agency. He thought there was more than one way to make a living.

Tonight, still smarting from Elizabeth's waspish manner, he hopped aboard the trolley car at Second and Main. He paid the driver the nickel fare and took a seat, trying to push their running squabble to the back of his mind. There were more important matters that required his attention. Matters of a financial nature.

He had business to conduct in the Acre.

The corner of Main and Fourteenth was a gathering spot for cowhands. Located two blocks north of the railroad line, it was within easy walking distance of the stockyards. The Buckhorn Saloon, the favorite watering hole of cattlemen, occupied the northwest corner. Even on a crisp November evening, it was a beehive of activity.

Marshal Bill Rea stood talking with one of his policemen outside the saloon. Though he was attired in civilian clothes, his twelve-man police force wore blue uniforms and black helmets, and went armed with revolvers as well as billy clubs. The Buckhorn was one of the more troublesome dives in the Acre, for cowhands juiced on rotgut whiskey were prone to fight just for the hell of it. Rea generally stopped by to check it out once or twice a night.

Courtright stepped off the trolley car as Rea turned away from the uniformed officer. Their meetings were infrequent, and invariably disagreeable, much like two dogs circling the same tree. Rea thought Courtright was a holdover from the past, still trading on a reputation eroded by time and age. Courtright considered Rea a political hack, elected to office as a lawman, but known to be the bagman for City Hall. The worst-kept secret in town was that money exchanged hands between the dives and city officials.

Four years ago, Courtright had lost his badge for accepting bribes. He felt it ironic that Rea was on the take and still managed to present a legitimate front. As he stepped onto the curb, the bitterness showed in his voice. "How's tricks, Marshal?" he said with a satiric smile. "Out fighting the good fight for law and order?"

Rea was a head shorter but solid as a stump. His eyes slitted with anger. "I manage to keep the peace, Courtright. That's more than can be said for your racket."

"Careful now, Bill, you're liable to hurt my feelings. I'm just a detective with generous clients."

"How long's it been since you solved a crime, Mr. Detective?"

"Not as long as you, Marshal."

Courtright moved past him, crossing the sidewalk. He thought he'd won the exchange of insults, but only at a steep price. For all his dodging and weaving, he could never escape the allegation leveled by the lawman. The sole business of the Commercial Detective Agency was operating a protection racket in the Acre. Ostensibly, the service he provided the dives was protection against their rivals. His clients were assured that a competitor would not disrupt their business.

In actual fact, the dives were buying his good will. Courtright was still considered a dangerous man, and no one wanted to incur his wrath. The sporting crowd paid him off to avoid the veiled threat that he himself would cause trouble. They routinely made payoffs to City Hall, and Courtright's shakedown racket was viewed as just another cost of doing business. Some paid on a weekly basis, and others by the month, and either way, Courtright was not greedy. His top fee was a hundred dollars a month.

Courtright always walked into a joint as if he were foreclosing on the mortgage. There was a swagger in his step, his manner bold, and the butts of his pistols were openly displayed. Tonight, the Buckhorn was packed with cowhands, three deep at the bar, and a crowd gathered around a pool table at the rear. On the wall overlooking the bar was a painting of voluptuous nudes romping through a field of flowers in gossamer scarves that did little to hide their charms. The cowhands never tired of commenting on the breastworks of nymphs so vividly etched in a pastoral setting.

The owner of the Buckhorn treated Courtright to a drink, and slipped him a five for the week's fee. After finishing his drink, Courtright left the saloon and headed uptown. At the corner of Rusk and Twelfth, he entered the Two Minnies, one of the more risqué bawdy houses in the Acre. The ground floor was appointed with sofas, scantily-clad girls, and a fully-stocked bar. The ceiling was constructed of thick glass, supported by crosstimbers, and afforded a view of the upper floor. The girls upstairs wore nothing, parading around naked, their jiggling bottoms visible through the glass ceiling. The customers downstairs got an eyeful while having a drink.

Minnie Stover, one of the two Minnies who owned the establishment, greeted Courtright as he moved through the crowd. "Evening, Jim," she said with a slow smile. "Guess I don't have to ask why you're here."

Courtright shrugged. "Funny how the week flies by."

"Yeah, especially when you're having fun. You ever think of taking it out in trade?"

"Never crossed my mind, Minnie. I'm a happily married man."

She laughed. "So are most of my customers."

By eight o'clock, Courtright had made his rounds. He

had thirty dollars in his pocket, and one stop left for the night. His largest client paid by the month, and never haggled. It was like money in the bank.

He walked back to Main and caught the trolley car uptown.

The Centennial Theater was the liveliest spot in town. A two-story structure with leaded-glass doors, it offered diverse forms of entertainment. Upwards of two hundred men might be found there on any given night.

On the first floor were the bar and the theater. The stage, which was centered on the rear of the room, hosted variety acts from around the country. A gallery with private booths circled the theater, and patrons were allowed to entertain actresses when they were not on stage. The upper floor was devoted exclusively to gambling.

Joe Lowe was the proprietor of the Centennial. He owned as well four saloons, three brothels, and a dance hall, all located in the Acre. His holdings made him the kingpin of vice in Fort Worth, and the gang of hooligans on his payroll enabled him to enforce that leadership on other dive owners. He was the undisputed link between the Acre and the political hierarchy in City Hall.

In years past, Lowe had been a prominent fixture in the Kansas cowtowns. A burly man with a hot temper and a violent streak, he had survived several gunfights. At the time, he was known as Rowdy Joe, and his wife, a scrapper in her own right, was known as Rowdy Kate. But their outward behavior, if not their methods, had undergone a transformation upon settling in Fort Worth. They maintained the appearance of respectable club owners, part of the uptown crowd.

Courtright found Lowe and his wife watching a new variety act. A team of acrobats, with a shapely female as the centerpiece, gyrated around the stage to modest applause from the audience. Lowe, who was smoking a thick cigar, finally tired of the performance and turned to Courtright. He nudged his wife.

"Well, look who dropped around! Say hello to our friend Jim."

"Hello, Jim," Kate said in a bored voice. "Here for your usual handout?"

"Now, that's not nice," Lowe said with feigned good cheer. "Jim renders a valuable service to our little enterprise. Don't you, Jim?"

"No complaints yet," Courtright said. "I take care of my clients."

"Why, of course you do." Lowe peeled off a hundred dollars and passed it across with a wide smile. "What's your game tonight, Jim? Faro or poker?"

"Thought maybe I'd buck the tiger. Got a hunch I'm due to hit at faro."

"That's the ticket. Get a hunch, bet a bunch! Good luck to you, Jim."

"Lady Luck owes me a turn. I might just break the bank tonight."

Lowe clapped him on the shoulder. "I like your spirit. Let me know how you come out."

Courtright nodded, moving off through the crowd. As he mounted the staircase to the gaming room, Kate glanced around at her husband. "I don't know why you tolerate that bum. He's a joke!"

"Two reasons, my dear," Lowe said, wedging the cigar in the corner of his mouth. "You never know when you might need a man who's good with a gun. Courtright hasn't lost his touch."

"We've got men on the payroll who can use a gun."

"Not like our friend Jim. He's in a class by himself. A natural-born shootist."

Kate humphed. "Still sounds like charity to me. What's the other reason?"

"That's the kicker," Lowe said slyly, puffing a wad of smoke. "At cards, he's a natural-born loser. Worst I've ever seen in my life."

Lowe called the turn. By ten o'clock, Lady Luck deserted Courtright at the faro table. He lost the hundred, and then digging deeper, he lost the thirty he'd collected earlier that evening. His hunch proved to be just that.

He walked out of the Centennial stone broke.

Chapter 4

Late the next morning Short emerged from his hotel. Under a cloudless sky, with a sharp tang in the air, he set out at a brisk stride. He turned uptown toward the Courthouse Square.

The square was the commercial hub of the city. The courthouse was a three-story stone structure, with four wings extending off a central building constructed in the shape of an octagon. A tall cupola rose skyward from the dome, the flag of the Lone Star State snapping on a sturdy flagpole. All manner of wagons jammed the square, and horses lined the hitch racks outside business establishments. The sidewalks were crowded with people who seemed in a rush to get somewhere.

On the west side of the square, Short turned into a shop. A black-and-gold sign on the plate-glass window was lettered J. B. WELLS—TAILOR. As he entered the door, a gnomish man with wire-rimmed glasses glanced up from a sewing machine. His wrinkled features were crowned with frizzy gray hair, and he looked something like an organ grinder's monkey. He slowly got to his feet.

"Yessir," he said, the glasses perched on the bridge of his nose. "May I help you?"

Short nodded amiably. "I'm told you are the best tailor in Fort Worth, Mr. Wells. I require your services."

"I appreciate the compliment," Wells said in a piping voice. "Might I ask who gave you the recommendation?"

"Jake Johnson," Short replied. "I am the new partner in the White Elephant. My name is Luke Short."

"You've made a wise investment, Mr. Short. Jake's a good businessman, and honest, too. I've known him since he came to Fort Worth."

"So he told me."

Wells openly inspected the cut of his suit. "I see you have a taste for fine clothes."

"I've always felt a man should indulge himself, Mr. Wells."

"Oh, definitely, definitely. How can I assist you today?"

"I thought I might order a couple of suits. I prefer matching vests."

"Naturally."

Wells began spreading bolts of cloth on a large table. As he prattled on about the quality of the goods, Short fingered the fabrics, pausing to study various weaves and patterns. Finally, after some consideration, he selected a muted herringbone in dark gray and a solid worsted in midnight blue. Wells set the bolts aside.

After a brief discussion of style, the tailor collected his tape measure. He asked Short to remove his suit jacket, and stepped back, clearly startled, when he saw a pistol butt protruding from the right hip-pocket. His eyes narrowed in an inquisitive frown.

"Most unusual," he said, peering closer. "Do you have a holster sewn into all your suits?"

"Yes, all of them," Short affirmed. "I have some extra holsters back at the hotel. Will that be a problem?"

"No, no," Wells assured him. "Just that I've never seen that particular . . . arrangement."

"I find it's the easiest way to carry a gun. You'll have to adjust the drape of the jacket so it's unnoticeable."

"Oh, don't worry yourself about that. No one will be the wiser when I'm finished, Mr. Short."

Wells began taking measurements. As he worked, Short stared out the window at the Courthouse Square. The throngs of people, and the sheer jumble of freight wagons, reminded him again that he'd made the right choice. Fort Worth was booming, a center of commerce and trade, and there was no end in sight to the town's growth. Opportunity was everywhere, and to a large extent, the money was there for the taking. Last night seemed to prove the point.

The gaming tables in the club were only moderately active. The take on faro and roulette was respectable, though nothing to brag about, and the two dice tables were quiet all evening. But Jake Johnson quickly spread the word that the White Elephant had a new partner, a resident high roller. By nine o'clock Short had himself a poker game, and men ganged around waiting for an empty chair. The play was fast, cutthroat poker in a table stakes game, and by the end of the night, he'd won slightly more than a thousand dollars. Not bad at all for his first night in town.

"That should do it," Wells said, breaking into his ruminations. "I wish all my customers were so easy to measure. Nothing out of kilter on you, Mr. Short."

"Glad to hear it, Mr. Wells." Short slipped into his suit jacket. "When should I came back for a first fitting?"

"Would a week from today be satisfactory?"

"You must work nights. That's sooner than I expected."

"For a first-time customer, nothing's too good."

"I'll see you a week from today, then."

"Certainly." Wells hesitated, fiddling with the tape measure. "Mr. Short . . . ?"

"Yes."

"You haven't asked the price."

Short smiled. "Your price is your price, Mr. Wells. I'm sure it's fair."

J. B. Wells was too surprised to respond. Short bid him good day and turned to the door. The tailor idly rubbed his jaw, watching his new customer through the window. He considered the question he'd dared not ask.

He wondered why a man went to such pains to conceal a gun.

That afternoon Short put the next step of his plan into motion. A lifetime spent in boomtowns had taught him an essential lesson. Gamblers were a fraternity but not a brotherhood, and good will was never to be taken for granted. All the more so when it came to the sometimes fierce competition in courting high rollers.

The new man in town was obliged to get the lay of the land. In part, that meant determining who the key players were, and more importantly, where they stood in the hierarchy of the local gambling fraternity. Today, he set off in the guise of paying a courtesy call on the uptown club owners. But the underlying purpose was to deliver a message. There was a new player in town.

Short's first stop was the Cattle Exchange. The club was owned by Nat Kramer, who was something of an icon among professional gamblers. A seasoned veteran of the trade, Kramer began his career as a riverboat gambler on the Mississippi. Following the Civil War, he migrated to Fort Worth and opened his own club, establishing a reputation for honesty and integrity. He was a shrewd operator, perhaps the most respected club owner in town. Which was the reason for Short's call.

Kramer was in his late fifties, a man of impressive bearing with a leonine head of white hair and an impenetrable gaze. He and Short had met a few times in the past, once over a card table, and their relationship was one of mutual respect. He rose from behind his desk, hand outstretched, when Short entered his office. His smile was cordial.

"Good to see you again, Luke. I heard just last night that you've bought into the White Elephant. Let me offer you my congratulations."

"Thanks most kindly, Nat." Short accepted his handshake and took a seat on the opposite side of the desk. "I think maybe I've found a home in Fort Worth."

"Indeed so!" Kramer said with a knowing chuckle. "From what I'm told, you found a game your first night in town. You never were one to let grass grow under your feet."

"I suppose that's one reason I'm here. We've never worked the same patch before, not for the high roller trade. I thought it was worth some friendly discussion."

"Well, that certainly gets my attention. I'm all ears, Luke. What's on your mind?"

Short lit a cheroot. "We're competitors now," he said, exhaling a plume of smoke. "But I'd like to think we can keep it on a gentlemanly basis. No need to undercut one another."

"No dirty tricks, you mean," Kramer said, weighing the thought. "No rumors of marked decks or rigged games, plucking the pigeons. Is that the idea?"

"I couldn't have said it better, Nat. Anything less and the uptown clubs would sink to the level of the Acre."

"Have you talked to the other club owners about this?"

"You're the first," Short admitted. "I know the others respect your opinion."

Kramer merely nodded. "For the most part, our clientele are gentlemen. So I agree, we should conduct our business as gentlemen. I believe the other club owners will support that view." He paused, shook his head. "With the notable exception of Joe Lowe."

"I suspect you're probably right. Joe's a graduate of the school of dirty tricks. All the same, I'll still try to bring him around."

"I wish you an extra dollop of luck. You'll need it, Luke."

"Well, like they say, nothing ventured, nothing gained."

By late that afternoon, Short had spoken with the owners of the Pacific Saloon and the Merchant's Exchange. They endorsed the idea of upright competition, for they, too, considered themselves gentlemen gamblers. But they were quick to agree with Nat Kramer.

Rowdy Joe Lowe was no gentleman.

A man on a pinto pony reined to a halt beside a streetlight. He stood up in the stirrups and with a long stick tapped open the vents below the round glass globe. The pilot light ignited the gas line that fed through the post with a sputtering pop. A moment later the globe spread a mellow glow through the quickening dusk.

Short walked past as the lamplighter continued along Main Street. The afternoon seemed to him time well spent, and he was pleased by the spirit of cooperation. There were five uptown clubs, including the White Elephant, and four of them were now aligned by mutual interests. That left only the Centennial, and as he walked on, he considered what might appeal to Joe Lowe. He thought the most persuasive argument might be one of status.

Lowe was a rough and tumble fighter. He believed that force and intimidation, and violence itself, were the tools of everyday business. Yet, for all his vice activities in the Acre, he tried to cultivate an image of a genteel ruffian with the uptown crowd. He routinely wore a top hat and a frock coat, and despite his hardened features and walrus mustache, he adopted a gallant manner when the occasion demanded. His clumsy efforts to acquire status and acceptance seemed to Short the key to the man.

At the corner of Third and Main, a large crowd was gathered outside the Theater Comique. A thin cable was stretched taut between the roof of the theater and the building on the opposite corner. To attract business, the management had a tight-rope walker perform his daring act on the high wire over the street. The crowd gasped whenever he wobbled, struggling for balance, and broke into wild cheers when he finally gained the roof of the theater. Watching the performance, Short thought it was not too different from what he planned for the White Elephant. Bat Masterson, though no tight-rope walker, would still draw a crowd.

Halfway down the block, Short entered the Centennial. The evening was early, but three bartenders were already busy with customers eager for a drink. Toward the rear of the room, he saw Kate Lowe watching a song-and-dance act prance around the stage in the theater. Joe Lowe was nowhere in sight, and he thought the likely place to look was the gaming room. He crossed to the staircase.

The upstairs club was virtually empty. Gamblers were for the most part night people, and trade usually picked up sometime after the supper hour. Dealers nonetheless manned their tables, patiently waiting for the evening rush to commence. Short spotted Lowe at the rear of the room, one of five men seated at a poker table. Courtesy dictated that he not interrupt the game, and he was about to leave when his eye was drawn to a faro layout. The dealer was an attractive young woman.

Short approached the table. The woman appeared to be in her late twenties, with upswept blond hair, a pert nose, and high cheekbones. She wore a rich blue gown that accentuated her slim waist and full breasts. Her eyes danced merrily, watching him as he came closer. She waited until he took a seat.

"Anytime's a good time to try your luck. Would you like chips?"

Short took a hundred off his roll, dropped it on the layout. "You're new here, aren't you?"

"I just started last week."

"That explains it."

She pushed a stack of chips across the layout. "Explains what?"

"You weren't here when I was by last time. Otherwise, how would I have missed you?"

"Aren't you the flatterer?" she said with a salty grin. "Care to make a wager?"

Short bet the king to win and coppered the eight to lose. He watched her hands as she dealt, aware that she was smooth and quick, unusually talented. She was gracious, her hands flashing as she kept up an engaging patter, and she swiftly ground him down. Within minutes, all his chips were on her side of the table.

"I take my hat off." Short wagged his head with an appreciative smile. "You have a gift with cards."

"Why, thank you," she said lightly. "A girl does like to be complimented."

"I'm Luke Short."

"Marie Blair." She arched an eyebrow. "Are we socializing, or would you care for more chips?"

Short laughed. "I'm a partner in the club at the White Elephant. How would you like to come to work for me?"

"What—?"

"I'll double your salary and give you a percentage."

"Are you serious?"

"Say yes and you can start tonight."

Her eyes went round. "How could I say no!"

"What the hell's going on here?"

Short turned to find Joe Lowe at his elbow. "Good evening, Joe," he said genially. "I was just having a chat with Miss Blair."

Lowe glared at him. "You've got no business in my place, Short. I won't have you spying on me."

"No need to get offended, Joe. I actually came by—"

"I don't give a goddamn why you came by. You and me, we've got nothing to talk about. Trot your ass on back where it belongs."

"You're sure?"

"What'd I just say?"

"Too bad." Short rose, nodding across the table. "Time to go, Marie."

"Hold on here!" Lowe barked. "She not going anywhere."

"Yes, I am," she said sweetly. "I quit, tonight."

Lowe glowered around at Short. "You sorry sonofabitch! You're not stealing one of my dealers."

Short's eyes went cold. "Try to stop me."

A turgid silence settled over the room. For a moment, his face the color of ox blood, Lowe stood with his fists clenched. Then he saw something in Short's gaze that gave him pause, a willingness to go the limit. He was staring at death.

"Don't think you've heard the last of this, you goddamn runt. I'll fix your wagon one of these days."

"I sincerely doubt it, Joe."

Short extended his arm. Marie took it and he led her down the staircase. A few moments later, as they went out the front door, she gave him a dazzling smile. Her eyes sparkled.

"God, I feel like I've been rescued. I can't tell you how much I loathe that man and his wife."

"Why did you go to work there?"

"Well . . ." She looked almost contrite. "A girl needs a job."

Short smiled. "Let me show you the White Elephant."

Chapter 5

Bat Masterson arrived in Fort Worth on November 27. Short met the noon train and took him from the depot to the Mansion Hotel. There he was ensconced in a fourth-floor suite, and with considerable ceremony, management treated him like visiting royalty. He was the most celebrated Westerner ever to stay at the hotel.

The two gamblers spent a good part of the afternoon catching up on old friends. Masterson reported that Wyatt Earp was operating a gaming parlor in Coeur d'Alene, the major boomtown in the Idaho goldfields. By all accounts, his operation was quite profitable, and on the side, he dabbled in mining claims. Another long-time friend, Doc Holliday, was still traveling the gambler's circuit. He was currently in Leadville.

"How's his health?" Short asked. "Any change for the better?"

Masterson chuckled. "Doc will probably drink himself to death before he dies of consumption. Still downs his regular ration, a quart a day."

"Has he killed anyone lately?"

"Believe it or not, he hasn't. 'Course, that's not to say his temper's improved to any noticeable degree. Like I always said, Doc could start a fight in an empty room."

Short enjoyed Masterson's trenchant humor. Of all the old Dodge City crowd, he considered Masterson his closest friend. A man of medium height, with dark good looks and a thick mustache, Masterson possessed a quick insight into the foibles of other men. They shared a fondness for games of chance, beautiful women, and a wardrobe of dapper clothes. These days, Masterson habitually wore a derby hat and carried a walking stick.

The rest of the afternoon was spent in discussing their plans for the week ahead. The goal was to promote the White Elephant while at the same time, providing Masterson with a shot at the town's high rollers. Short had invited several of Fort Worth's more prominent businessmen to tonight's game, and all had accepted. No sooner had word got around than a crush of gamblers stepped forward, and there was now a waiting list. The idea was for Masterson to take down a respectable payday without ruffling anyone's feathers. A smart gambler always left high rollers wanting more. He was to win, but not to excess.

In the end, the White Elephant would be the big winner. Masterson, though scarcely thirty years old, was a legend across the West. A buffalo hunter in the early years, he took part in the Battle of Adobe Walls, in which a small band of hide hunters fought off a Comanche war party of more than a thousand braves. Three years later, after settling in Dodge City, he was elected sheriff of Ford County, and achieved nationwide renown as a lawman. After leaving office, he followed the gambler's circuit, quickly establishing himself as one of the top professionals in the business. These days, he headquartered in Denver, but he could find a game anywhere. His name alone was a draw.

Toward dusk, Short and Masterson emerged from the hotel. They were elegantly attired, dressed for an evening in the company of gentlemen. When they entered the White Elephant, an expectant crowd was already gathered at the bar, and every table in the restaurant was full. Jake Johnson played the part of gracious host, popping the cork on a bottle of champagne in celebration of the event. Following a toast, reporters for the *Standard* and the *Gazette* pushed forward, trailed by their photographers. Short, orchestrating a show of sorts, cleared room at the bar for an interview. One of the reporters eagerly took the lead.

"Are you ready for a big game, Mr. Masterson? Any limit on the stakes?"

"I'm here to play," Masterson said agreeably. "As for the stakes, I'll be happy to oblige the gentlemen in the game."

"Do you expect to win?"

"I always expect to win, and you can quote me as saying—I seldom disappoint myself."

The remark brought an appreciative laugh from the crowd. The second reporter jumped in with a question. "Mr. Masterson, you're known as much as a peace officer as a gambler. Is it true you've killed twenty-six men in gunfights?"

Masterson struck a pose as the flash-pan over a camera went off. Short walked toward the staircase, assured now that the newspapers would give it prominent coverage. He was amused by the last question, but he'd heard Masterson's stock reply many times over the years. The former lawman was his own best press agent, and cleverly fostered the notion that twenty-six desperadoes had fallen before his gun. In truth, Masterson had killed only one man, in a shootout over a saloon girl.

Upstairs, Short crossed the club room to Marie's faro layout. She wore a cobalt blue gown with revealing décolletage, and a minxish smile. Her eyes were bright with excitement.

"Sounds like we have a winner," she said gaily. "Has the famous Mr. Masterson charmed the crowd?"

"Like birds out of a tree," Short observed with a quick grin. "Bat missed his calling as a vaudevillian. He's a first-class showman."

"All the better to entertain your high rollers."

"Never a sore loser at Bat's table, and that's a fact. He shears them with a deft touch."

Her mouth dimpled. "Are you sure you're not describing yourself?"

Over the past week, Short had become captivated by his new faro dealer. She was stunningly attractive, with an infectious sense of humor, and a sassy attitude that made him smile. For her part, she found him intelligent and witty, unusually thoughtful, and far gentler than he let on to the rest of the world. Last night, she'd shared his bed for the first time, and she was still gloating at the memory. The fireworks were definitely there.

"I was thinking," Short said with a wry look. "Bat and I will go for a late supper after the game. Would you like to join us?"

"Why, yes I would, thank you very much."

"And after we get rid of Bat—"

"That, too," she said with a sultry smile. "Aren't I a naughty girl?"

"Naughty suits me just fine."

Short was acutely aware of her presence. He wanted to touch her, but he knew the other dealers were watching them. With a little nod, he walked to a poker table at the center of the room, reserved for tonight's game. The table was roped off, ensuring some measure of privacy, but positioned so that everyone in the club would have a view. By tomorrow, the whole of Fort Worth would be talking about the White Elephant.

The high rollers began arriving shortly before seven o'clock. First were two of the largest ranchers in the area, Jack Burke and Will Hudgen. Within minutes, they were followed by Anson Tolbert, a wealthy merchant, and Frank Wilcox, the major liquor wholesaler in the city. Last to arrive was Karl Van Zandt, president of the First National Bank. The seventh man in the game was Short himself.

For all their wealth, the men shook hands with Masterson as though he were an eminent dignitary. There was a certain honor attached to playing with a gambler of note, and whether they won or lost, the men felt privileged to have been invited. The invitations were all the more coveted because of Masterson's reputation with a gun; the players accorded him the deference generally reserved for lion tamers and other intrepid daredevils. Short was privately amused by their subdued manner.

The game tonight was five-card draw. In some Eastern casinos, the traditional rules of poker had been revised to include straights, flushes, and the most elusive of all combinations, the straight flush. The highest hand back East was now a royal flush, ten through ace in the same suit. By all reports, the revised rules lent the game an almost mystical element.

Poker in the West was still played by the original rules observed in earlier times on riverboats. There were no straights, no flushes, and no straight flushes, royal or otherwise. There were two unbeatable hands west of the Mississippi. The first was four aces, drawn by most players only once or twice in a lifetime.

The other cinch hand was four kings with an ace, which precluded anyone holding four aces. Seasoned players looked upon it as a minor miracle, or the work of a skilled cardsharp. Four kings, in combination with one of the aces, surmounted almost incalculable odds.

An hour or so into the game, Frank Wilcox, the liquor wholesaler, was dealt the miracle hand. Masterson, who drew a full house, bet the limit, five hundred dollars. The other players dropped out when Wilcox, unable to restrain his glee, raised the limit. After a moment of deliberation, Masterson merely called the raise. Wilcox proudly spread his hand.

"Feast your eyes, gentlemen!" he crowed. "Four kings with an ace kicker. Can you believe it?"

"I'll be a monkey's uncle," Masterson said, appropriately awed. "Your luck's running strong, Mr. Wilcox."

"There's no beating me tonight!"

Short thought otherwise. There was something to be said for luck, and no seasoned player would argue the point. But in the end, the skill of a professional inevitably overshadowed the vagary of a lucky draw. All the same, he was quietly elated by the turn of events. Frank Wilcox's four kings would be the talk of the town.

So the White Elephant had indeed drawn into luck tonight.

Joe Lowe stood at the window of the Centennial. Across the street, he observed the hubbub at the White Elephant, the crowd spilling out onto the sidewalk. Earlier he'd watched the town's top high rollers arrive for tonight's widely touted game. His temper was high, and his features were set in a tight scowl. He chewed furiously on a soggy cigar.

Word had been circulating for the past week about Bat Masterson's visit to Fort Worth. At first, despite the buzz throughout the sporting crowd, Lowe had thought the excitement would run its course and quickly peter out. But tonight, staring across Main Street, he had to admit that he'd misjudged the attraction of a celebrated figure such as Masterson. The White Elephant was packed and the Centennial was all but empty.

"Some turnout," Kate said, joining him at the window. "Makes you want to cry in your beer."

Lowe grunted. "Have to admit, it fooled me. Never figured Masterson would draw flies."

"Well, honeybun, that just goes to show you. People are natural-born suckers, ripe for a gaff."

"Yeah, but you've gotta give the devil his due. Short called the tune and everybody came to the dance. Look at that goddamn crowd!"

"Dirty little pissant," Kate said acidly. "Stole our hottest faro dealer and now he's stolen our crowd. I'd like to kick his ass."

Lowe silently remarked that his wife was a coarse woman. In the Kansas cowtowns, even in the Acre, she was among her element with the whores and grifters. But with the uptown crowd, she was like a fish out of water, unable to adopt an air of refinement, act the lady. Her penchant for vulgar speech, and a stout figure stuffed into gaudy, sequined gowns marked her for what she was: a product of the red-light district.

Still, in spite of himself, Lowe admired her tough-as-nails attitude. For all his genteel pretensions, the top hat and frock coat, she was his kind of woman. He was quick to admit as well that she was right about the threat to the Centennial. Luke Short needed to have his butt kicked from Courthouse Square all the way down to Union Depot. One look at the theater and the upstairs club room told the tale. Their normal business was off by half.

"So?" Kate demanded. "What d'you intend to do about the little bastard?"

"I dunno," Lowe said, lapsing into old speech habits. "I'll have to give it some thought."

"What the hell's to think about? He ought to be taught a lesson."

"Don't kid yourself about Short. Maybe he's on the stumpy side, but he's nobody to mess with. He's put more than one man in his grave."

"Honest to Christ!" Kate huffed. "You've been hanging around with these uptown swells too long. Where's the Rowdy Joe Lowe that never backed off from a fight?"

Lowe shot her a look. "Watch your mouth or I'll box your ears bloody. Don't get too big for your drawers."

"I'm just saying you gotta do something. You've got a position to uphold."

"Goddamnit, woman, I know that!"

"And—?"

"I'm thinkin' on it."

"Careful you don't strain yourself."

Before Lowe could retort, the lead-glass doors swung open. Jim Courtright pushed through, glanced around, and saw them beside the window. His features squinched in a bemused expression as he moved toward them. He jerked a thumb across the street.

"Looks like Short stole your trade."

Lowe grimaced. "That's what Kate's been telling me."

"Helluva note," Courtright said. "Just come from the Acre and nobody's talkin' about nothing else. You'd think Buffalo Bill hit town."

"They don't need him," Kate said bitterly. "They've got themselves the terror of the plains, Deadeye Masterson."

"Don't believe half of what you hear. Masterson's better with a deck of cards than he ever was with a gun."

"Well, in that case, Mr. Pistolero, why don't you walk over there and call him out? Go ahead, show him up for the windbag he is."

"Why would I do that?" Courtright said blankly. "I got no bone to pick with Masterson."

"You just made me remember I need a drink."

Kate stalked off toward the bar. She wasn't sure who she detested more, Courtright or Luke Short.

Lowe stood as though contemplating the riddle of the ages. Something Kate had said made him take a closer look at Courtright. She'd almost been on the right track.

"I'm not the only loser here tonight," Lowe said pointedly. "Way things look, you're getting robbed, too."

Courtright stiffened. "What makes you say that?"

"How much you been charging Jake Johnson for protection?"

"Let him off for fifty a month. He's only got the one club."

"Maybe so, but Short's changed all that. They're raking in money faster'n they can count it."

"Yeah, they'll likely make a bundle."

"Don't you think you ought to get your share?"

"For what?"

"For more protection," Lowe suggested. "All that business, they need more protection—they can afford it."

"Yeah, you're right." Courtright stared out the window. "Hundred a month ought to cover it."

Lowe merely nodded in agreement, the seed planted.

Chapter 6

Three days later, Short turned the corner onto Main Street. The weather was brisk, with banks of cottony clouds off to the northwest, and he was in a chipper mood. He walked toward the White Elephant.

The past three nights had gone better than anything he might have imagined. As he'd suspected, word of a local man beating the great Bat Masterson with four kings had swept through town. The story even got coverage in the newspapers, reported in the hyperbole normally employed for twisters and other freaks of nature. A circus atmosphere prevailed as the crowds grew larger and the White Elephant became the place to see and be seen. The restaurant and the club were packed every night.

Masterson had won something more than four thousand in three marathon poker sessions. But word of his winnings was a stimulant rather than a deterrent, drawing even more high rollers to the club. Everyone wanted a shot at the visiting king of the pasteboards, and Short had to take himself out of the game on the second night. There was now a long waiting list, and with so many demanding to play, he thought it wiser to accommodate their growing clientele. The general attitude was that it was better to have played and lost than not to have played at all. A certain distinction attached itself to the biggest game in Fort Worth's history.

Short was himself showered with accolades. The high rollers sang his praises, and the newspapers dubbed him the greatest promoter of the decade. Karl Van Zandt and other influential businessmen were quick to compliment him on his civic spirit and the renewed sense of boosterism he brought to the city. The game assumed an aura usually associated with championship sporting events, and Short was lauded for having brought it to Fort Worth. The *Democrat* and the *Gazette*, vying for circulation, ran side-by-side interviews with him and Masterson. He was suddenly the toast of the town, the man who had restored the image of gentlemen gamblers. And the White Elephant became a veritable money machine.

Masterson, who needed to revitalize himself for tonight's game, was still asleep at the hotel. But Short strode along under a midday sun, shy on sleep yet nonetheless eager for his meeting with Jake Johnson. Today was November 30, the last day of the month, and their partnership agreement was structured on a monthly accounting system. Short allowed Johnson to keep the books, though he maintained a personal journal of the nightly take at the club. They had been in business together not quite two weeks, and the last three nights had virtually doubled their gross profits for the entire period. He expected to pull down a windfall.

The noon-hour rush was playing out as Short entered the White Elephant. Among the men still ranged along the bar, he saw Jim Courtright, one boot hooked over the brass rail. He knew Courtright on sight, and recalled hearing that the former lawman now operated Fort Worth's only detective agency. From casual gossip, he was aware of Courtright's sordid background as well, and the scandal involving not just extortion, but allegations of murder. He thought it was an old story, a familiar plot device even in ancient literature. A man's fall from grace.

As he passed by, he saw Courtright watching him in the backbar mirror. Whether it was real or a trick of the imagination, it seemed that Courtright accorded him a small, cursory nod. He moved on, wondering why he'd never seen Courtright in the place before, and rounded the end of the bar. Halfway down the corridor, across from the kitchen, he turned into Johnson's office. He closed the door on the noise from the kitchen.

Johnson looked up from an accounting ledger. His features spread in a chipmunk grin. "Just now finished the tally from last night. Guess what?"

Short smiled. "We struck the mother lode."

"Partner, I have to say it, you're an absolute genius. We're rolling in green!"

"Show me."

Johnson swung the ledger around. As Short pulled up a chair, he began tracking the rows of figures with his finger. Their joint accounting began on November 19, and there was a marked increase in the daily receipts from that date. The last three nights indicated a dramatic spike upward in gross gambling receipts from the club. At length, separating restaurant proceeds from gaming revenues, Johnson tapped the final entry in the ledger. His chipmunk grin broadened.

"We *cleared* six thousand dollars in nine days!"

"Not bad," Short said, studying the rows of figures. "Not bad at all."

"Not bad?" Johnson exclaimed. "Luke, that would've been a good *month* for me. You're a goldang wizard!"

Short pointed to an entry. "What's this item, Civic Contributions? One hundred forty-eight dollars."

"Payoffs to City Hall. Five hundred a month to keep the wheels greased with the police and the city council. I prorated it for nine days."

"Grease is a way of life with politicians. What's this mean, Commercial Detective Agency? A hundred dollars."

"That's Jim Courtright," Johnson said with a shrug. "Used to be fifty a month. But we're doing so well, he wants it upped to a hundred. I told him I'd have to clear it with you.''

''I saw him at the bar,'' Short said. ''Why do we need a detective agency?''

''Well, it's really more of a protection racket. Everybody in town pays him off.''

''What does he protect us against?''

''Mainly himself,'' Johnson noted. ''When the mood hits him, Jim's a troublemaker. Nobody wants problems.''

''So it's extortion.''

''Yes, I suppose you could call it that. But it's nickel-and-dime stuff. No harm done.''

''I don't agree,'' Short said, shoving the ledger aside. ''Crooked politicians are a necessary evil in our business. I won't be extorted by some two-bit thug.''

''Think of it as charity.'' Johnson spread his hands. ''Look, I've been friends with Jim Courtright for a long time. Helped raise a defense fund when he was brought up on charges in New Mexico. What's a hundred a month?''

''Jake, it just goes against the grain. I won't pay it.''

''Then I'll pay it out of my end.''

''No,'' Short said bluntly. ''We're partners, and that would be the same as me paying it. Let him stiff somebody else.''

''C'mon now, Luke,'' Johnson temporized. ''No need to bow your neck over something so penny-ante. Where's the harm?''

''I'm telling you where I draw the line. I won't agree to it, and that's final. Let's not spoil a good thing over this.''

Johnson fell into a deep silence. He saw in Short's eyes that the matter was not open to debate. Either he conceded the point or he would risk jeopardizing their partnership. There seemed to be no middle ground.

''Christ,'' he said finally, pursing his mouth. ''How do I explain this to Courtright?''

"No need," Short said. "I'll take you off the hook."

"What'll you say to him?"

"Don't worry, he'll get the message. I suspect we speak the same language."

"You watch yourself, Luke. He's got a short fuse."

"So do I."

Short turned out of the office. He walked along the corridor, entering the main room, and saw Courtright still standing at the bar. Courtright knocked back a jigger of whiskey as he approached, setting the glass on the counter. He stopped a couple of feet away.

"Good afternoon, Mr. Courtright. I'm Luke Short."

Courtright pushed off the bar. At six feet, he towered over Short, his expression one of guarded curiosity. "What can I do for you?"

"Nothing," Short said in a neutral voice. "No offense, but I've just had a talk with Jake Johnson. We won't require your services any longer."

"Do tell," Courtright said in an amused tone. "Everybody needs protection—even you."

"I'm my own protection."

"Well, don't you see, I operate sort of like a special officer. I drop by now and then to make sure nobody gets out of line."

"Not anymore," Short told him. "Having you here would do more harm than good. I'll thank you to stay away from the White Elephant."

"That a fact?" Courtright squared himself away, brushing aside his coat to reveal the butts of his pistols. "You talk mighty tough for a little fellow. I'm tempted to stunt your growth more'n you'd like."

Short held his gaze. "I think you're bluffing, Courtright. Why don't you try me on for size?"

A bartender standing nearby scurried for cover. Courtright tensed, his pale eyes studying the smaller man, on the verge of drawing. But then, warned off by some inner voice, his arms went slack. His mouth curled in a wolfish grin.

"We're not finished here yet. You just bought yourself a world of trouble."

"On your way," Short said evenly. "Don't come back."

"Hey, Mr. Gamblin' Man, that's the best bet in town. You'll see me around."

"I'm easy to find."

Courtright walked away with a harsh laugh. Short watched him out the door, wondering if it was yet another bluff. Some visceral instinct told him it wasn't so.

He thought he hadn't seen the last of Jim Courtright.

Masterson ambled into the White Elephant about three o'clock. He looked clear-eyed and rested, jaunty in a three-piece suit and his Derby hat. The chef obligingly put together an elaborate breakfast, even though it was the middle of the afternoon. Nothing was too good for the star attraction of the establishment.

Short joined him at the table. For all his debonair manner, Masterson was a man who ate with gusto. He tore into a platter of ham and eggs, with a mound of freshly fried potatoes sprinkled with ground parsley. Thick slices of toast were larded with butter and jam, and a waiter kept his coffee cup full. He nodded appreciatively over his food.

"Tell you something, Luke," he said between mouthfuls. "You've got yourself a damn fine cook."

"Don't let him hear you say that," Short commented. "He considers himself a *Chef*, with a capital *C*."

"Well, whatever he calls himself, he knows his way around a stove. Tastiest ham I ever cut into."

"Imported all the way from Virginia. Jake prides himself on serving nothing but the best."

Masterson paused for a swig of coffee. "How's things with your new partner?"

"Tip-top," Short said with conviction. "After this week, there's not a club in town to match our style."

"You'll recall that's what started the trouble in

Dodge City. You've always got to put your competition in the shade.''

"I plead guilty on all counts, Bat.''

"Just a friendly reminder.''

Short lit a cheroot. He took a puff and blew a perfect smoke ring. "Are you up for the game tonight? We'll have a full table again.''

"Lambs to the slaughter,'' Masterson said, spearing the last bite of ham with his fork. "When I'm on a roll, I can't be beat. Lead them to me.''

"What with our waiting list, there's no scarcity of lambs.''

As Masterson drained his coffee cup, a bartender approached the table. He nodded to Short, placing a gunnysack full of empty whiskey bottles on the floor. The bottles settled in the sack with a distinctive clink, and Masterson's expression turned quizzical. He glanced from the sack to Short.

"You collecting dead soldiers in your spare time?''

"Pistol practice,'' Short replied. "A man doesn't want to lose his touch. Care to join me?''

"Don't mind if I do, Luke.''

Short led the way through the business district. Some while later, they halted along a deserted stretch of the Trinity River. To their rear the steep bluffs rose skyward, and the dome of the courthouse was visible in the distance. After flipping a coin, Masterson positioned himself upstream, dumping bottles from the gunnysack onto the ground. The empty bottles were corked and airtight, guaranteed to float. The purpose of the drill was to hone their skills with a pistol.

Masterson tossed a bottle into the river. Then, one after another, he lobbed four more in rapid succession. The bottles bobbed to the surface, spaced several feet apart, and floated downstream. Short's hand snaked beneath his suit jacket and came out with the stubby Colt, the hammer cocked. Long ago, he'd come to the conclusion that the victor in a gunfight was not necessarily the faster man. He subscribed to the adage that speed was fine but accuracy was final, and he focused on placing every shot dead-center. He was quick, but deliberate.

His arm leveled and the Colt bucked in his hand. The first bottle erupted in a geyser of water and glass. He swung the Colt in an arc and locked onto the second bottle. His eyes sighted along the barrel—caught within an instant of deliberation—and he feathered the trigger. The second bottle in line exploded. Then the next and the next, and finally the last as the current swept it some yards below his position. Less than five seconds had elapsed from the moment he pulled the gun.

The drill was repeated several times. Short and Masterson alternated between tossing bottles into the river and blowing them out of the water. Masterson carried a Colt six-gun holstered at his side, and he too advocated accuracy over speed. Like Short, he believed the shot that killed an opponent, rather than the first shot, was what counted. Their personal engagements, as well as witnessing countless gunfights, had taught them a vital lesson. More often than not, the man who hurried his opening shot was soon bound for the graveyard.

When all the bottles were gone, they had each fired twenty times. Short had missed once and Masterson twice, and they agreed it was from rushing the shot. Upon finishing, they ejected spent shells and stuffed fresh cartridges into their pistols. As a matter of safety, they loaded five chambers and lowered the hammer on an empty chamber. The Colt six-gun was, for all practical purposes, a five-shooter.

After reloading, Masterson holstered his pistol. He gave Short a curious look. "You seemed a little intent popping those bottles. Why so serious?"

Short related his earlier dust-up with Jim Courtright. He concluded on a somber note. "I've got a hunch he won't leave good enough alone."

"You think he'll force a fight?"

"Depends on how bad I hurt his pride."

"Courtright?" Masterson said, repeating the name. "Never heard of him. Who is he?"

"The local toughnut," Short said. "Dive owners pay him off to avoid trouble. I understand he's killed a few men."

"So you decided it was time for some pistol practice."

"Never hurts to be prepared."

"Maybe you should've brought him along to watch you bust bottles."

"I doubt that would have scared him off."

Masterson laughed. "Then he's dumber than he sounds."

Short nodded. "Let's hope you're wrong, Bat."

They walked back to town in the gathering twilight.

Chapter 7

A line of carriages jammed the street outside the opera house. Everyone who was anyone in Fort Worth was attending the opening performance of *Fidelio*. The house was sold out.

Drivers hopped down to assist their passengers from the carriages. For the gala occasion, the men were dressed in white tie and tails and tall top hats. The women wore fashionable gowns and were adorned with their finest jewelry. One carriage after another disgorged a gathering of the town's elite. They slowly made their way into the opera house.

A block away, Short and Marie approached on foot. Earlier, he'd called for her at her hotel, and they had walked over to Main Street. Opening night at the opera was a special occasion, and he had decided the White Elephant could manage without them. Bat Masterson had departed town four days earlier, and business at the club had slowed only by a small degree. Tonight was their night to celebrate.

"Omigod," Marie said softly, her eyes darting ahead to the crowd. "Look at the way those women are dressed, and all that jewelry! I feel like the scullery maid."

She wore her best gown, silk trimmed with lace, with a fur wrap and a gaily feathered hat. Short thought she was a vision of loveliness, though he could understand her apprehension. Some of the women were dressed in the latest Parisian fashions.

"You'll do just fine," Short assured her. "Besides, with you on my arm, all their husbands will be jealous. I've got the prettiest girl in the crowd."

She squeezed his arm. "I do love a smooth talker. Even if it's not true."

"I never lie to a lady."

"You know something, Luke? I feel like a lady tonight! Maybe because it's my first time at the opera."

Short himself had been to the opera only once before. In Denver, many years ago, he had attended a performance of *Otello*. The evening had left him impressed by the vitality and force of an operatic production. He thought Marie would enjoy the experience.

"I hope I understand it," she said. "I don't speak a word of Italian."

"Neither do I," Short confessed. "You just sort of follow along with the action. The story tells itself."

"Well, anyway, I'm excited. I feel so ... sophisticated."

"Then the evening's already a success."

A few doors down from the opera house was the Knights of Pythias building. The fraternal order occupied a brick structure where men of wealth devoted themselves to charitable causes. On the second floor, positioned in an arched alcove, was a suit of medieval armor, fondly known to the locals as "St. George." Some years ago, a drunken cowhand had galloped past and opened fire with his six-gun. The armor was pocked with bullet holes.

As they walked by, Short glanced up at St. George. He was reminded that Fort Worth, for all its size, was still a city divided by uptown and downtown. A suit of armor riddled with bullets, and an opera house where arias were sung in Italian, seemed to him emblematic of a wild and woolly cowtown rapidly being overtaken by the modern era. The frontier, much like the knights of medieval times, was all but a memory.

The crowd filed into the opera house with a buzz of excitement. Opening night was a major social event, and the lobby was packed with people who paused to exchange greetings. Short checked his topcoat and hat at the cloak room, and turned back to Marie, wending a path through the throng. As they approached the theater entrance, he saw Karl Van Zandt talking with a group of people. A woman in her late forties, dripping in diamonds, clung to the banker's arm. Short assumed it was Van Zandt's wife, and thought it only proper to stop a moment and greet the couple. He caught Van Zandt's eye.

"Good evening, Mr. Van Zandt. A pleasure to see you again. May I introduce Miss Marie Blair."

Van Zandt appeared uncomfortable. "Good evening, Short. Are you a student of the opera?"

"Hardly that," Short admitted. "But I like the spectacle of it. The pageantry."

"Yes, well, you'll have to excuse us. Enjoy the performance."

Neither the banker nor his wife acknowledged Marie's presence. Van Zandt nodded abruptly, turning away, and led his wife toward the theater. She darted a furtive glance back at Marie, as though examining some exotic zoological specimen. They disappeared into the crowd.

Short was stung by the slight. His features colored and his mouth set in a tight line. Marie seemed embarrassed. "Talk about rude," she said in a small voice. "Did you see the look she gave me?"

"How could I miss it?" Short said. "Guess it's not their night for *noblesse oblige.*"

"What does that mean?"

" 'Be kind to the peasants.' "

Short had purchased the best seats in the house. An usher escorted them to the fifth-row center, in the orchestra. On the way down the aisle he saw Anson Tolbert and Frank Wilcox and other businessmen who regularly frequented the White Elephant. The men were with their wives, and they either offered him a curt nod or hastily averted their gaze. He felt like a leper without an invitation to the party.

Marie was taken by the splendor of the theater. A vaulted ceiling rose majestically overhead, with intricately carved woodwork bordering a spacious mural of robed figures and fleeting nymphs. The proscenium stage was crowned by an elaborate arch, bounded on the front by an orchestra pit that seated thirty musicians. She was still looking around as the house lights dimmed and the conductor raised his baton. The audience quieted.

The presentation tonight was Beethoven's *Fidelio*. The Grand Italian Opera Company, which was touring the United States, consisted of a troupe of twenty singers and a chorus drawn from local talent. The curtain rose with great fanfare on what seemed an enigma wrapped in a riddle. Set in a prison, the opera opened to reveal the jailor, Pizarro, and his handsome new assistant, Fidelio. Quickly enough, the jailor's daughter, Marceline, fell in love with Fidelio, and the plot thickened. The audience soon learned of a mysterious prisoner being held in the dungeon.

By the second act, Short and Marie were hard-pressed to follow the twists and turns. With operatic elaboration, it was unveiled that the prisoner, Florestan, had been secretly entombed for two years. Then, in a stunning turnabout, came the revelation that Fidelio, disguised as a man, was actually a woman, and the wife of the prisoner. Fidelio, deftly maintaining her disguise and playing on the delusions of Marceline, ultimately breached the dungeon and rescued her husband. Pizarro, the jailor, was left in ignominy, and his daughter collapsed of a broken heart. Love conquered all with the escape of Florestan and Fidelio—a soprano no longer in disguise.

As the curtain fell, the audience rose for a standing

ovation. The opera troupe took four curtain calls, with
Fidelio, a buxom dark-eyed brunette, clearly the hit of
the night. Short and Marie, their ears ringing with the
great mystery of arias rendered in Italian, joined in the
applause. Their enthusiasm was abetted by the fact that
they'd figured it all out.

The enigma of *Fidelio* was, in the end, a delightful
surprise.

The Lafayette Restaurant was one of the finer dining
establishments in Fort Worth. Located at the corner of
First and Main, it looked out onto the Courthouse
Square. With impeccable service and an atmosphere of
decorum, it was where wealthy men took their wives for
a night out. The restaurant was particularly popular for
a late supper following a social event.

Short had reserved a table. The food was just as good
at the White Elephant, but he wanted it to be a special
evening for Marie. As the maitre d' led them to their
table, he noted Van Zandt and Wilcox already seated
around the room. The men studiously avoided his gaze,
and his chipper mood following the opera abruptly
dropped off. A dark look came over his features.

After they were seated, Marie tried to restore the gai-
ety of the evening. "What a marvelous idea," she said
breezily. "A woman masquerading as a man! I can't get
over it."

Short studied the menu. "She had me fooled for a
while."

"I wish I could change places with her, just for a
day. Imagine what great fun that would be!"

"I doubt you'd enjoy it as much as Fidelio."

Her bright chatter was going nowhere. He was brooding and she expected to see steam spout from his ears
at any moment. She decided to try another tack.

"Aren't you Mr. Glum and Gloomy?"

Short glanced up from the menu. "Does it show that
much?"

"Of course it does," she scolded. "You really shouldn't take it so personally. Why upset yourself?"

"I'm not accustomed to being chopped off at the knees."

"Oh, lover, come on! You're a gambler and Van Zandt's an uptown swell. Did you really expect him to introduce you to his wife?"

"Why not?" Short bridled. "When he comes to the club, I treat him with courtesy. And I give his bank all my business. What's with the stuffed shirt routine?"

"Welcome to Fort Worth," she said with a little sigh. "Van Zandt will gamble with you and accept your hospitality. But that's as far as it goes, no matter what. He'll never invite you to his home."

"You're saying I'm still one of the sporting crowd."

"I'm afraid so, at least in his eyes. Uptown or downtown, to him a gambler is a gambler."

"We're legitimate," Short said angrily. "The White Elephant's not some clip joint in the Acre. Van Zandt knows that."

She kept her voice calm. "I'm sure he respects you as a gambler. But like it or not, you're not one of his crowd. You never will be."

"A rose by any other name."

"Pardon me?"

"Something out of Shakespeare," Short said dryly. "Whatever the name, it smells the same. I guess it applies to gamblers, too."

"How do you mean?"

"Tinhorn or high roller, we're all the same. If one stinks, we all stink."

"That's not true!" She protested. "No one would ever lump you in with the tinhorns. Not even Van Zandt."

Short thought of himself as a professional businessman, albeit a gambler. He felt he'd been insulted, his integrity somehow questioned, by the incident at the opera house. Still, he knew Marie was right when she said he shouldn't take it personally. Fort Worth's wealthier crowd might frequent his club, might even enjoy his company at a poker table. But he would never be invited into their homes. Nor would he be introduced to their wives. He was, in the end, a sporting man. A gambler.

The waiter came to take their orders. Short realized he was sulking, and decided to put a better face on things. Tonight was not a night to be spoiled by a display of bullheaded temper. He hoped, instead, it was a night for celebration, and he wanted Marie in a receptive mood. After ordering duck a l'orange for them both, he ordered a bottle of fine champagne. Marie looked at him as the waiter turned away.

"Champagne," she said, surprised by the sudden change in his mood. "Are we celebrating something?"

Short smiled. "I think that depends on you."

"What depends on me?"

"Whether or not our feelings are mutual."

Their affair was now into its second week. They spent their nights together, either at Short's hotel, or at her lodgings, the Commercial Hotel on Rusk Street. The liaison was common knowledge among their friends, and neither of them evidenced any interest in seeing anyone else. They were content with one another's company.

"I know how I feel," she said, after a slight pause. "I thought you felt the same way."

"All day, every day," Short said without hesitation. "But we spend a lot of time running back and forth between hotels. So I was thinking . . ."

"Yes?"

"Well, I thought maybe—if you're of the same mind . . . you might consider the notion of moving in with me."

Her eyes opened wide. "Permanently?"

"So far as I'm concerned," Short said, holding her gaze. "Of course, you're always free to change your mind. There's no strings attached."

Marie considered herself a practical woman. She had escaped the poverty of a Missouri farm, and a tyrannical father, at the age of seventeen. To survive, she had worked as a waitress and a saloongirl, following the railroads westward. In all those years, she'd had only three lovers, and none of them for any great length of time. The last one, a gambling man, had taught her the nuances of dealing faro. She had an innate sense for cards, and that, parlayed with her good looks, quickly got her a job as a dealer. Her new profession had ultimately brought her to Fort Worth.

But now, as though the earth had shifted beneath her, she felt her practical side slipping away. She had never been any man's mistress, no matter how desperate her circumstances. Still, without the slightest reservation, she knew she'd never felt about another man what she felt for the one seated across from her now. Whether it was love, or mere physical attraction, was something only time would tell. Whether he loved her seemed even more a roll of the dice. Yet she was willing to take the risk.

"All right," she said, her voice husky with emotion. "When do I move in?"

Short gave her a loopy smile. "Would tonight be too soon?"

"Not for me," she said with a coy look. "My clothes might have to wait until tomorrow."

"You won't need any clothes until tomorrow."

"Ooo, I like the sound of that."

Their waiter materialized with a bottle of champagne. He popped the cork and poured, then set the bottle in an ice bucket. As he bowed, moving away with a smile, Short and Marie stared into each other's eyes a moment. Short finally leaned across the table, his glass extended.

"A toast," he said warmly. "To our first night together."

She nodded, her eyes moist. "And all those to come."

The bubbles tickled her nose as she raised her glass.

Chapter 8

A crowd of spectators surrounded the pit. Overhead, suspended from beams, gas lamps lighted the room through a haze of smoke. The smell of sweat and tobacco blended with a sharp, pungent odor from the pit. The earthen floor reeked of fresh blood and recent death.

The pit itself was roughly twenty feet in diameter. A hard-packed arena, perhaps three feet below floor level, the dirt was stained chocolate-brown with blood. Already that evening there had been five mains, traditional fights in which two gamecocks were pitted to the death. But the event of the night, about to commence, brought on a flurry of betting. The *gallo negro* was to defend his title.

The Emerald Saloon was located on Main, off the corner of Tenth Street. Henry Burns, the owner, was a stocky man with a droopy mustache and a minor genius for the blood sports. In a room at the rear of the saloon, he conducted cockfights and dogfights, a carryover from the frontier era and still widely popular in Fort Worth. A larger room, between the pit area and the saloon itself, was reserved for prizefights, bare-knuckle brawls that drew even bigger crowds. Tonight, Henry Burns was staging two championship matches.

The *gallo negro* was unbeaten in the pit. Victor in eighteen fights to the death, the black cock was held in his owner's arms, staring calmly at nothing. His eyes were fierce bright buttons of malevolence, yet his look was one of hauteur, withdrawn and solitary. He seemed oblivious to the men crowding the pit, and no less disdainful of his adversary for the night, as though he couldn't be bothered while his wings were still pinioncd. Across the pit, restrained by his owner, was a red *gallo*, twisting its head at every sound, eyes glaring at the boisterous spectators. The betting was three to one on the *gallo negro*.

The rivalry among local cockmasters was intense. The cocks were subjected to a rigid training program in the week prior to a fight. Daily sparring sessions were held, in which the natural spurs wcre covered with leather to avoid injury, and a special diet slowly brought the bird to fighting trim. On the day of the event, the *gallos* were allowed no food, only water, and an hour before the actual pitting, they were dosed with stimulants to increase their ferocity. Then, at pitside, each cock had fastened to its natural spurs specially crafted steel spurs two inches in length. A tiny feathered warrior, shanked with steel, the *gallo* was at last ready for battle.

Henry Burns moved to the edge of the pit. He nodded to the two cockmasters, who had a side bet of a thousand dollars on the outcome. As he raised his arm, Short and Jake Johnson came through the door of the adjoining room. Neither of them were followers of the cockfights; something about birds spurring one another to death seemed lacking in dignity. But they were avid enthusiasts of the prize ring, and the fight scheduled for tonight promised to be a memorable contest. A championship bout merited a few hours away from the White Elephant, so the floor manager had been left in charge of the club. They halted at the rear of the crowd.

Burns dropped his arm and the cocks were pitted. The red *gallo* ruffled his wings, swaggering about in a menacing stance, ferocious though clearly wary. But there was nothing hesitant or indecisive about the *gallo negro*, for he'd come to fight rather than posture. When his handler released him, the little cock's toes barely touched the ground before he stalked forward to engage his adversary. The birds met in the center of the pit, and amidst squawks and beating wings, spurs flashed under the cider glow of the lamps. The pit filled with dust and an explosion of feathers, and then the *negro* leaped high in the air. The assault was fast and savage, and the *negro* drove a steel spur through the head of the red *gallo*. Over the roar of the crowd, the red cock went down, killed instantly, thrashing a moment in a welter of blood. The *gallo negro*, eyes fierce with the kill, strutted around the pit.

The *negro*'s owner jumped into the pit and scooped him up with a shout of victory. Short looked on, watching the *gallo negro*, vaguely reminded of something that eluded memory. He turned to Johnson as men around them began paying off bets. He shook his head with a bemused expression.

"Little devil does neat work, doesn't he?"

Johnson shrugged. "Sort of a one-sided match-up. The red one never had a chance."

"Funny thing," Short said, his brow wrinkled. "Watching that reminded me of something I can't put my finger on. Drew a blank."

"Something about cockfighting?"

"No, it wasn't that. Something else."

"Well, don't think about it for a while. Maybe it'll come to you."

"Maybe so."

Short turned toward the door. He and Johnson entered the adjoining room as the crowd finished settling their wagers. The room was spacious, perhaps thirty by forty, with benches aligned to form a boxlike square in the center. Lighted by overhead lamps, the square was covered with a thick carpet of sawdust and looked to be about ten feet across. They took seats in the front row of benches.

The sawdust square served as a prizefight ring. The

manly art of pugilism was one of the more popular sporting attractions across the West. Every mining camp and
boomtown, as well as major cities, was rabidly proud of
its local champion. There was considerable enterprise,
and energetic boosterism, to arranging bouts between the
various champions. Apart from the large sums of money
wagered, the bragging rights were a source of status for
the entire community. Nowhere was the esteem more
coveted than in the Acre.

Tonight's match was more about pride than money.
There was intense rivalry between Dallas and Fort
Worth, each claiming to be the hub of commerce and
finance in northern Texas. The Fort Worth champion
was Jock Mulligan, a flat-nosed scrapper who had dispatched the previous Dallas champion with embarrassing
ease. The new paladin of Dallas, a former railroad la-
borer named Boomer Doyle, was reportedly made of
sterner stuff. Dallas was determined to reclaim lost
glory.

With the cockfights ended, the room began filling
with men. Half the crowd had come over on the evening
train from Dallas, and they congregated on the benches
along the south wall. The other half, the Fort Worth
contingent, rushed to claim seats on the opposite side of
the room. The benches fronting the ring to the east,
nearer the saloon, and to the west, close by the cockfighting room, were reserved for dive owners and gamblers from the Acre. Prizefighting was considered too
brutal for the fair sex, even whores, and women were
not allowed. By eight o'clock, the house was packed.

Short was in a jaunty mood. Three nights ago, Marie
had moved into his suite at the Mansion Hotel. The following day, they had her belongings brought over from
her room at the Commercial, and the suite quickly took
on feminine airs. The lingering scent of her perfume
permeated every room, and within a day, it was as
though she had been there forever. They slept late each
morning, and made love often, and Short was amazed

at how easily she slipped into the routine of his life. He wondered why he hadn't asked her to move in sooner.

By nature, Short was not a monogamous man. He prized his freedom, and studiously avoided entanglements that might turn serious. Over the years, whether in a Kansas cowtown or a Colorado mining camp, he'd had liaisons with many different women. Some were briefer than others, and though he might have married any number of times, he exited before the wedding bells could ring. A gambler's life was in many ways a solitary life, and he'd never found a woman who could abide the erratic demands of his profession. He thought Marie might prove to be the exception.

Short's woolgathering was abruptly brought to a halt. Across the way, he saw Joe Lowe and Jim Courtright come through the door from the saloon. Almost two weeks had passed since Courtright's attempt to extort protection money from the White Elephant. He hadn't heard anything further of the incident, and he'd generally dismissed it from mind. But he was surprised to see the self-styled detective in company with Fort Worth's shadowy vice lord. He idly speculated whether Lowe had a piece of Courtright's protection racket.

The two men took seats on the opposite side of the ring. Courtright looked across at Short with a hooded stare, and their eyes locked for a moment. Then, averting his gaze, Courtright said something out of the corner of his mouth to Lowe. The remark apparently struck Lowe as humorous, for he chuckled out loud, puffing a stream of smoke from his cigar. He stood, motioning Courtright to remain seated, and made his way around the ring. His manner was that of Caesar triumphant, nodding imperiously to men who greeted him with nervous smiles. He halted before Johnson and Short.

"Jake," he said affably, nodding to Johnson. "All set for the big fight?"

"Looks to be a good one," Johnson replied. "From

what I hear on the grapevine, Doyle's no pushover. They say he's a rough customer.''

"How would you bet it?''

"Are you trying to euchre me, Joe?''

"Take your pick,'' Lowe said agreeably. "Either way, I'll take the other man. Even money.''

Johnson grunted. "I get the feeling you've seen Doyle in action.''

"Matter of fact, I saw his last fight over in Dallas. Whipped Johnny Kilrane, from Austin. Helluva brawl.''

"I heard it was a quick knockout. Ninth or tenth round.''

Some bare-knuckle fights were marathon affairs, lasting forty or fifty rounds. Lowe grinned, puffing his cigar. "Ninth round,'' he affirmed. "Doyle's as tough as they say.''

"Sounds that way,'' Johnson observed. "All the same, I'd have to take Mulligan. He's the hometown boy.''

"So we'll have ourselves a friendly wager. How's a thousand suit you?''

"Suits me just fine, Joe. Thousand it is.''

Throughout the conversation, Lowe had pointedly ignored Short. His words were addressed to Johnson, and he never once acknowledged Short's presence. The men seated nearby were aware an insult had been passed, and kept their attention focused elsewhere. Lowe leaned closer, lowering his voice.

"Glad we could make a little bet. But I really stopped by to talk about something else. I thought Jim Courtright was a friend of yours.''

Johnson's expression was guarded. "I still consider him a friend.''

"Fine way to treat a friend,'' Lowe said gruffly. "You've made him look bad all over town.''

"That wasn't the intent, Joe. It's just business.''

"How come you turned him down, anyway?''

"Well—''

"You're talking to the wrong man," Short interrupted. "I'm the one that put the damper on Courtright."

Lowe sighed heavily. "Nobody asked for your sayso, Short."

"Who asked you to butt in on White Elephant business?"

"I just don't like to see friends on the outs. Jake and Jim go back a long ways."

Short looked skeptical. "You must have changed your spots, Joe. I never took you for a do-gooder."

"What's that supposed to mean?"

"Maybe it means you've got a piece of Courtright's protection racket."

The men seated closest to them edged farther away. Lowe gestured angrily with his cigar. "You ought to watch your mouth, Mr. Fancy Dan. You'll get yourself in trouble."

Short laughed. "Trot back over there and give Courtright the message. The answer's still no."

Before Lowe could respond, the fighters and their handlers entered the ring. A ripple of excitement swept through the crowd, and Lowe stalked away, the cigar clamped in his mouth. Henry Burns, the saloon owner, walked to the center of the ring, acting now in his capacity as referee. He motioned for silence.

"Your attention, pleeze!" he announced loudly. "A night of scientific fisticuffs for your edification. Jock Mulligan, the undefeated cham-peen of Fort Worth against Boomer Doyle, the undisputed cham-peen of Dallas. Give the boys a big hand!"

Amidst boos and catcalls from the rival factions, Burns hastily moved aside. Mulligan was a brute of a man, dressed in fighting tights and a bright-green sash, his arms corded with muscle. Doyle was flat-nosed and heavily scarred, flexing his massive shoulders, clearly the survivor of countless rough-and-tumble brawls. A

stillness settled over the crowd as the fighters advanced
to the middle of the ring.

Doyle lumbered into action like a windmill in a stiff
breeze. He threw haymakers and roundhouse punches in
a blurred flurry of motion. Any one of the blows would
have felled an ox, or Jock Mulligan, but none found the
mark. Mulligan bobbed and weaved, slipping punches
or blocking them with his arms. The men came together,
wrestling in a clinch, until Mulligan broke loose. Doyle
again leaped to the attack.

Mulligan evaded the rush, setting himself. He lashed
out with a splintering left-right combination that rocked
Doyle, his eyes cocked askew. Crouching, Mulligan
flicked a punishing jab, followed by a searing left hook.
The Dallas champion retreated, wobbily stepping out of
the sawdust arena, and the crowd bodily hurled him back
into the ring. Mulligan feinted with a left, then drove a
clubbing blow flush on the other man's jaw. Doyle went
down as though struck with an axe, out cold.

The spectators were stunned by the suddeness of the
fight, less than a minute from start to finish. Then Burns
jumped into the ring, raising Jock Mulligan's arm in
victory, and the crowd erupted in pandemonium. Over
the roaring chant, Short's gaze went from the fallen man
to the arrogant, prideful grin stretched across Mulligan's
features. The look was strangely familiar, and he was
abruptly reminded of the cockfight he'd witnessed earlier. The disdainful strut of the *gallo negro* after the kill.

Short was deaf to the crowd. Something jarred his
memory and he grabbed hold of the thought that had
eluded him earlier. A thought prompted by the *gallo
negro* and the image of a black man. A prizefighter who
had never been beaten.

His name was Peter Jackson.

Chapter 9

A week later Short emerged from a hotel in St. Louis. After supper in the hotel dining room, he had some time to kill and he felt like a walk. He turned east on Olive Street.

Three days earlier Short had boarded a train in Fort Worth. The trip was the result of several telegraph messages to Boston, requesting information on John L. Sullivan. He'd finally learned that the heavyweight champion was on tour, and would appear in St. Louis the night of December 10. The next morning he had caught the first train north.

St. Louis was the largest city Short had ever visited. The population exceeded the half-million mark, and the downtown district was a hub of culture and commerce. Theaters and fashionable hotels, office buildings and banks and business establishments occupied several square blocks between Market Street and Delmar Boulevard. A sprawling industrial section lay stretched along the levee.

Steamboats were rapidly losing ground to railroads. In recent years, the city had developed into a manufacturing complex for clothing, shoes, and various types of machinery. Still, for all its advancement, St. Louis remained a major market for hides and wool, horses and mules, and a wide assortment of farm produce. However cosmopolitan, it had not yet outdistanced its origins as a trade center.

On the waterfront, Short stood for a long while staring out across the Mississippi. The Eads Bridge, completed only ten years before, spanned the great river like a steel monolith. A blustery wind whipped off the water, and he pulled the collar of his topcoat tighter. Far in the distance, he saw the lights of towns ranged along the Illinois shoreline. Not easily impressed, he was nonetheless taken with the sight.

Short had traveled the West from the Gulf of Mexico to the Black Hills of the Dakotas. But he'd never had occasion to look upon the Mississippi, the central artery of a nation. The breadth of the river, with girded steel linking one bank to another, seemed to him a marvel almost beyond comprehension. He thought back to his days on the Chisholm Trail, hazing cattle across the Red River, and slowly shook his head. Age and experience altered a man's perception of things.

Five years ago, perhaps less, he would have been content with a cowtown gaming parlor. But his return to Fort Worth seemed to have expanded his vision, put a keener edge on ambition. He was wryly reminded of the old adage that a man who reached for the sun often came away with blisters. All the same, he was gripped by the need to make his mark, undaunted by the scale of his own dreams. The White Elephant was to him a springboard, the impetus for a still grander scheme. He planned to bring John L. Sullivan to Fort Worth.

The heavyweight champion of the world was the most admired man in America. The pride of the Irish, he was known in the early days as "the Boston Strong Boy," reputed to have lifted a runaway streetcar back onto its tracks. His pugilistic career began in 1879, and three years later, in a ten-minute slugfest, he knocked out Paddy Ryan to win the championship. He was unbeaten in twenty-seven bare-fisted brawls, twenty-three of which he'd won by knockout. He was larger than life, the hero of old and young, more popular than the President. Today, he was known simply as "the Great John L."

So great was he, in fact, that he'd eliminated every worthy challenger. By early 1883, there was no one willing to test his mettle in the boxing ring. A man who lived high, with singularly large appetites for liquor and women, he looked for new ways to supplant his income. Idolized everywhere he went, he decided on a tour of America, with stops in major cities. Exhibitions were staged at each stop, with John L. offering a thousand dollars to any man who could last four rounds. Crowds eagerly paid admission to watch the slaughter, and the champion flourished on ticket sales. So far, no one had collected on the thousand.

All of which brought Sullivan to St. Louis. A local fight promoter arranged the exhibition, and found three plug-uglies willing to take their chances against the champion. The bookmakers set the odds at a hundred to one, and even on the off-chance of a lucky punch, there were few takers. The promoter got ten percent of the gate for staging the affair, and John L. tucked the balance into his wallet. None of those involved, least of all the promoter, begrudged the champion his hefty slice of the proceeds. St. Louis was honored by the mere presence of John L. Sullivan.

Short flagged a hansom cab not long after dark. A few minutes later, he was let off at a large warehouse on Biddle Street, a block from the waterfront. The exhibition was scheduled for seven o'clock, and there were already masses of people jamming through the doors. General admission was two dollars, with ringside seats priced at five, and Short quickly gauged the crowd at two thousand or more. By rough estimate, he calculated Sullivan would pull down something less than five thousand for the night. He intended to make the purse far sweeter in Fort Worth.

The inside of the warehouse was cavernous. Long

rows of tiered bleachers had been erected along all four walls of the interior. The spectators were packed shoulder to shoulder, and more were pushing through the doors by the moment. Short made his way down an aisle to ringside and found a seat beside a man who looked as though he might own half of St. Louis. Other men at ringside were equally well-dressed, and it was clear that the wealthy as well as the hoi polloi were drawn to watch America's icon of pugilism in action. He thought most of Texas would turn out to see the Great John L.

The ring was a crude affair. Four posts were anchored to the floor, with three strands of heavy rope strung between the posts. The boxlike square was some twelve feet across, and the floor of the ring was liberally blanketed with sawdust. Short inspected the ring and soon surmised that it had been built to the champion's specifications. A local challenger might try to run and backpedal for four rounds, and walk away a thousand dollars richer. The tight confines of the arena made flight difficult, if not impossible. John L. apparently liked his work close at hand.

"Splendid night," the man beside him said in an orotund voice. "I never imagined I'd see John L. Sullivan in person. Quite an exciting affair, don't you agree?"

"I do indeed," Short said. "We're lucky the great man decided to tour the country."

"I detect an accent in your voice. Texas?"

"You have a good ear. I'm from Fort Worth."

"And you came all the way from Texas to see tonight's exhibition?"

"I would have gladly traveled twice the distance."

The man was somewhere in his late forties. His hair was salt-and-pepper and his eyes were darkly inquisitive. "John Holmsby," he said, extending his hand. "I'm in the mercantile business. You may have noticed our store uptown."

"Luke Short." Short shook his hand. "I'm a merchant of sorts myself. I own a gambling emporium."

"Do you?" Holmsby said effusively. "I regret to say gambling was banned some years ago in St. Louis. Damnable do-gooders got on their bandwagon!"

"Well, we're still operating down in Texas. No do-gooders on the horizon, as yet."

"Since you're a gambling man, let me ask you a professional question. Do you think Mr. Sullivan will win all three matches?"

Short smiled. "I seriously doubt John L. will work up a sweat."

A barrage of catcalls interrupted their conversation. They turned as the evening's first challenger crawled through the ropes. He was burly, arms and shoulders quilted with muscle, wearing black boxer's tights. The boos from the bleachers indicated he was not the favorite tonight.

"Tom Kennedy," Holmsby said over the commotion. "One of our home-grown thugs. Fancies himself a pugilist."

"Looks tough enough," Short observed. "Maybe he'll make a fight of it."

A sudden roar erupted from the crowd. John L. Sullivan strode down one of the aisles with his handlers close behind. He was a bull of a man, five eleven and two hundred pounds, with a square jaw and a lush handlebar mustache. His body was corded, a solid mass of muscle, with a thick neck and rock-crusher hands. He was attired in green-and-white striped tights and a white sash knotted at his side. He waved to the crowd with a nutcracker grin.

The spectators thundered their approval. The referee motioned Sullivan and Kennedy to the center of the ring, and spoke to them over the buzz of excitement. They were to fight bare-knuckle, governed by the long-standing London Prize Ring Rules. The rules, established in the seventeenth century, dictated that a fighter could not kick, gouge, or butt with his head. A round ended when either man was knocked down, and there was a thirty-second break before the next round began.

Under the rules, it was not uncommon for bouts to last a hundred rounds. A man could not be hit when he was down, but the match went on until a knockout, or until one of the men could no longer continue. At the end of a thirty-second break, the fighters were required to "toe the line," an imaginary line drawn in the center of the ring. If a man was unable to toe the line, he lost the bout by default. Or in the worst case, he was "counted out" while on his back—more popularly known now as a knockout.

The referee signaled the crowd as the fighters walked back to their corners. He spread his arms for quiet. "I direct your attention," he bellowed grandly, "to John L. Sullivan, the heavyweight cham-peen of the world! His first opponent tonight will be a local up-and-comer, Tom Kennedy. Give them a big St. Louis welcome!"

The spectators dutifully responded with applause. Someone in the bleachers shouted, "Say your prayers, Tommy!" and the crowd broke out in nervous laughter. Then, as the fighters moved forward to toe the line, the house went still. Short saw the jovial expression disappear on Sullivan's face, to be replaced by the stolid look of an executioner inspecting the condemned. He thought Tom Kennedy was in for a drubbing.

Sullivan raised his arms in an upright fighting stance. The muscles rippled from his forearms through his knotted biceps and upward into his shoulders. He flicked a playful jab that lightly tapped Kennedy on the bridge of his nose. Kennedy flinched, dodging aside, amazed that his nose was suddenly leaking blood from such an effortless punch. He crouched, bobbing his head, and flung a sharp left jab of his own. Sullivan easily warded it off with his arm.

Kennedy lobbed an overhand right, which missed, and fell into a clinch. He was a strong man, and the fighters grappled a moment, like wrestlers seeking a hold. Sullivan finally shoved him away, and after duck-

ing a punch, Kennedy again grabbed the champion in a
tight bear hug. His strategy for lasting four rounds was
apparently to cling to Sullivan whenever possible, and
avoid being struck a damaging blow. They shuffled
around the ring, locked in an odd dance, until Sullivan
was able to free himself. He hammered Kennedy to the
floor with a sizzling right.

The referee stepped in to signal the end of the first
round. Kennedy's handlers dragged him back to his corner, and sloshed him with a pail of water. The shock
brought him around, and he ambled forward, toeing the
line, when the referee motioned the end of thirty seconds. His strategy still intact, Kennedy launched a haymaker, lurching in behind it, and grabbed for a clinch.
Sullivan nimbly stepped aside, planting himself, and
drove a crushing left hook to the ribs. Kennedy's mouth
ovaled like a goldfish, and he folded at the waist, his
features contorted. Sullivan clouted him between the
eyes with a straight right. He went down and out.

Sullivan raised his hands, clamped in victory, teeth
flashing in a broad grin. The crowd stood and cheered,
rocking the warehouse as they treated him to a wild ovation. Kennedy's handlers revived him with another
bucket of water, finally got him to his feet, and led him
from the ring at a wobbly gait. The referee scuffed
bloody sawdust with the toe of his shoe, and Sullivan
strutted around playing to the spectators. They responded with chanting praise.

"What a man!" Holmsby shouted gleefully. "There
will never be another fighter like him!"

"Probably not," Short agreed. "Not in bare-knuckle,
anyway."

"Do you think he'll ever fight under the Queensberry
rules?"

"I would tend to doubt it, Mr. Holmsby. He has
hands of steel."

"Yes, of course, you're right. Why fight with
gloves?"

Sullivan had yet to fight with gloves. Some seventeen years ago, John Douglas, the Eighth Marquis of Queensberry and an influential figure in London sports circles, had devised revolutionary new rules for boxing. He declared that the rounds would be of three minutes' duration, with a one-minute break between rounds, effectively eliminating the rule that a round ended only when a fighter was knocked down. Another change was that a fighter knocked down must toe the line, unassisted, within ten seconds or be counted out. A limit of ten seconds all but ended bouts that lasted forty or fifty rounds.

Yet the greatest innovation was the requirement of padded boxing gloves. In bare-knuckle matches, fighters were routinely maimed for life, and all too frequently killed from massive head injury. These days, the Marquis of Queensberry Rules were commonly followed in London sporting clubs operated by wealthy Englishmen. But in America, the old bare-knuckle rules still prevailed, and fighters derided the notion of pummeling one another with pillows on their hands. To them, it sissified a man's sport.

The last two fighters on tonight's card were trotted out with no great ceremony. Having seen Tom Kennedy battered unconscious, they climbed into the ring as though being led to a hangman's gallows. Sullivan apparently decided there was no need to prolong the exhibition, or his opponents' fate. He dispatched each man within one round, mercifully swift. The crowd shook the rafters with their cheers.

Short watched the mayhem with a wry, satisfied smile. The exhibition further confirmed the scheme he'd hatched a week past in Fort Worth. There was no longer any question in his mind.

The Great John L. would be a sellout in Texas.

Chapter 10

The hansom cab turned onto O'Fallon Street. Riley's Saloon was located near the waterfront, a few blocks from the U.S. Arsenal and Lyon Park. Short stepped out of the cab into a light fog drifting off the river. He handed the driver a five.

"Keep the change."

"Thanks, mister," the driver said, ducking his head at the saloon. "I'd be glad to take you somewhere else."

"Isn't this Riley's?"

"Yeah, but it's a rough joint. You've got the looks of a gentleman."

"I'll watch my step."

"You'd better, 'lessen you're an Irisher. That's a hangout for Micks."

"I appreciate the warning."

"Good luck to you, mister."

The driver popped his reins and clattered off down the street. Short turned to the saloon, which was ablaze with light in the silty fog. From inside, the sound of raucous laughter floated out into the night. He pushed through the door.

Riley's was festooned with bunting. The colors were traditional Irish, green and white, and the streamers were criss-crossed from wall to wall. A long bar was jammed with men decked out in their Sunday suits and Derby hats. Others, some accompanied by women in bright dresses, sat at tables along the opposite wall. A celebration was clearly in progress.

Short found an empty table toward the rear of the room. He doffed his hat and coat, dropping them on a chair, and took a seat. The men at nearby tables studied the fashionable cut of his suit and his pearl stickpin with cool stares. The women, their laughter momentarily stilled, looked at him as though an African had barged into their celebration. A waiter appeared at his elbow.

"You'll hafta stand at the bar," he said testily. "Tables are for ladies and gents."

Short glanced up with a slow smile. "I'm expecting company."

"A lady's joinin' you here?"

"No, not a lady."

"Who's your company, then?"

"John L. Sullivan."

The waiter blinked. "Are you serious, now?"

"Am I in the right place?" Short asked innocently. "This is Riley's Saloon, isn't it?"

"What else might it be?"

"Then Mr. Sullivan will be along shortly."

"Says you." The waiter peered at him with an owlish frown. "What's your business with the Great John L.?"

Short drilled him with a look. "That's a private matter between myself and Mr. Sullivan. Bring me a bourbon, water on the side."

"We don't serve such stuff. Irish whiskey or nothin'."

"That will do just fine."

The waiter stalked off. Short watched as he walked to the bar and whispered something to a man standing at the end of the counter. The man turned, inspected Short at length, and nodded to the waiter. After a moment, he pushed away from the bar and crossed the room. He wore a serge suit, his tie snugged tight in a celluloid collar, and a shamrock pin fixed on his lapel. He stopped at Short's table.

"Patrick Riley," he said, thumbs hooked in his vest. "I own the place."

"A pleasure to meet you, Mr. Riley. I'm Luke Short."

"I've not seen you here before."

"First time," Short said. "I came up from Texas for John L.'s exhibition."

"A far journey, Mr. Short. You know the Great Man, do you?"

"Not personally."

"Yet you've business with him?"

"Yes," Short replied. "As I told your man—private business."

Riley cocked one eye. "How'd you know he'd be here tonight?"

"I spoke with his manager, Billy Madden. Just after the exhibition."

"Did you?" Riley beamed. "Well, why didn't you say so? That makes all the difference."

"I'm curious," Short said. "Why so many questions?"

"The Irish are a clannish race, Mr. Short. We don't take much to outsiders."

"What does that have to do with John L.?"

"Well, don't you see," Riley said, spreading his hands. "We're holding a celebration for the Great Man hisself here tonight. I invited him myself, weeks ago, by telegraph. And damn me if he didn't accept!"

"So strangers aren't welcome, is that it?"

"We'll make an exception in your case. If you're okay with Billy Madden, you're okay with me."

"I appreciate the courtesy."

"Think nothing of it, Mr. Short. Drinks are on the house!"

Riley turned away. He signaled the waiter, who bustled across the room with a shot glass balanced on a tray. Short felt as though he'd passed a test of some sort, and only then by stretching the truth. He had, in fact, spoken with Sullivan's manager following the exhibition. But the conversation was brief, a quick promise by Short of riches to be found in Texas. Billy Madden had grudgingly surrendered the name of Riley's Saloon.

Short would have preferred to meet in more private circumstances. When he'd suggested Sullivan's hotel, Madden had dismissed the idea out of hand. The champion was apparently besieged at every turn by opportunists with wild, and sometimes preposterous, propositions. In the flurry of excitement after the exhibition, Madden had paused at ringside long enough to determine that Short was neither a charlatan nor a lunatic. Then he'd hurried on to the champion's makeshift dressing room at the rear of the warehouse.

The door burst open with such ferocity that Short almost pulled his pistol. John L. Sullivan strode into the saloon and stopped, fists planted on his hips. Everyone in the room froze, staring at him in a moment of awed silence. His voice boomed like a cannon shot.

"I can lick any sonofabitch in the house!"

The boast was by now world famous. Sullivan was notorious for issuing the challenge in saloons and fine restaurants and the ballrooms of wealthy admirers. The brag was meant partially in jest, but there was nothing frivolous about it. He would happily take on any man foolish enough to step forward.

A stunned moment passed before the crowd recovered their wits. With a spontaneous roar, they surged forward, their shouted cheers a babble as they ganged around him. Sullivan flashed his nutcracker grin, accepting their adulation as though it were his due, bulling through their ranks toward the bar. Patrick Riley rushed forward, his face a moon of jubilation. He clasped Sullivan's hand.

"The Great John L.!" he cackled. "Saints preserve us, I never thought I'd see the day!"

Sullivan retrieved his hand. "Who might you be, boyo?"

"Patrick Riley, the proprietor. An honor it is to have you in my establishment, Mr. Sullivan."

"Would you have anything alcoholic here, Paddy?"

"Only the finest Irish whiskey this side of Dublin."

Riley cleared a path through the onlookers. He led Sullivan and Billy Madden to the bar, his face flushed with pride. A bartender scurried forward with a bottle and glasses, and poured to the brim. Sullivan hoisted his glass to the rapt crowd.

"God bless all here." He tossed off the whiskey and slammed his glass on the bar. "A drink for the house on John L. Sullivan!"

A stampede developed as men and woman jostled for position at the bar. The three bartenders rushed back and forth, pouring drinks as fast as glasses were emptied. Patrick Riley, dubbed "Paddy" by his guest of honor, struggled against the crush to hold his place beside Sullivan. The hubbub increased in direct proportion to the liquor consumed, with Sullivan leading the way. In between drinks, he began to regale his audience with highlights of the night's pugilistic exhibition. The crowd shuddered and cheered as he acted out the fights blow by blow.

Short watched from his table with an amused smile. He thought Sullivan gloried in the limelight, a brash exhibitionist in or out of the boxing ring. But then, searching his memory, he remembered that Sullivan was only twenty-five, and already the most idolized figure in America. His gaze strayed to Billy Madden, who stood at Sullivan's shoulder, eyes vacant, as though he'd heard it all before. Madden was thin as a stick, a horsy-looking Irishman with tombstone teeth and a patch of hair the color of a pumpkin. He appeared content to stand in the Great Man's shadow.

An hour or so into the celebration, Madden seemingly grew bored. He stepped out of the crowd ganged around Sullivan and briskly rubbed his face with his hands. His gaze roved around the saloon and came to rest on Short, a solitary figure seated at the rear of the room. For a moment his eyes clouded, as though he were trying to put a name to the man. Then he nodded, more to himself than to Short. He walked back to the table.

"Short, wasn't it?" he asked. "I never forget a face, not often, anyway. But I'm a bad one for names."

"Luke Short." Short motioned to a chair. "Join me."

Madden slumped into the chair. "You're a patient man, Luke Short. Have you been waiting here all this time?"

"I don't mind the wait. I traveled a long way to see Mr. Sullivan. Could I offer you a drink?"

"Another and I'd be on my arse. I haven't John L.'s tolerance for the stuff."

Short smiled. "He certainly appreciates his public. Not many men in his position would go to the trouble."

"There's none like him, and that's a fact." Madden crossed his gangly legs. "So what's this about a fight in Texas? I'll need the particulars."

"The particulars are fairly straightforward. A winner-take-all match and I'll post the stakes. Twenty thousand dollars."

"Twenty thousand."

"That's the figure."

Madden eyed him skeptically. "How do we know you have the money? You wouldn't be trying to hood-wink John L., would you?"

"I'm on the square," Short assured him. "We'll wire my banker in Fort Worth tomorrow morning. He will confirm the offer's legitimate."

"Billy!" Sullivan approached the table, whiskey glass in hand. "Thought I'd lost you somehows. Who's your friend?"

"John L. Sullivan"—Madden waved his hand— "meet Luke Short. He wants to promote a fight in Texas."

Short stood, extending his hand. "A great honor to

meet you, Mr. Sullivan. I've been an admirer of yours for years."

"Everybody calls me John L." Sullivan wrung his hand. "Are you of the Irish persuasion, Luke?"

"Just a tad," Short said with a humorous shrug. "I'm Scotch-Irish."

"Better than none at all, and there's a mortal truth. Whereabouts would this fight take place?"

"Fort Worth," Madden interjected. "A purse of twenty thousand and he'd post the stakes. Winner-take-all."

"Twenty thousand!" Sullivan bellowed. "By the Christ, I like the stakes. Who's the challenger?"

"Peter Jackson." Short told him. "Some say he's the best in the world."

"And what do you say?"

"I'd put my money on you, John L. All day, any day."

Peter Jackson was the British Empire Heavyweight Champion. A West Indian, reportedly blacker than midnight, he fought out of Great Britain. Apart from Sullivan, he had fought every heavyweight of merit throughout the world. He'd never been beaten.

"I don't fight coloreds," Sullivan said, almost sadly. "That's just the way it is."

Short was aware that Sullivan had drawn the color line. Yet he had come to St. Louis confident that he could change the champion's mind. Newspapers in London, and some in New York, speculated that Sullivan was fearful of losing his crown. They questioned whether he could beat Jackson in the ring.

"Why not put the rumors to rest?" Short said now. "John L. Sullivan and Peter Jackson would be the greatest fight of the century. I'm willing to stake twenty thousand that says you'll whip him."

"You're right on that," Sullivan said with conviction. "But this is a white man's sport, and I mean to keep it that way. I'll not fight a colored."

"Think about it from a business standpoint, John L. Twenty thousand would be the biggest payday of your career."

"Damn me, you're a bulldog, aren't you? I like a man who doesn't quit, but it changes nothing. My mind's made up."

Short saw it slipping away. He pulled a cheroot from his inside pocket, and struck a match. As he lit up, he tried to formulate a more persuasive argument. Sullivan pointed to the cheroot.

"Have you another of those fine cigars?"

"Certainly," Short said, reaching inside his jacket. "I have to admit I'm curious. Doesn't smoking affect your wind?"

"Not at all." Sullivan lighted the cheroot with a flourish. "I follow a strict training routine. A shot of whiskey and a cold bath before every fight." He paused, puffing smoke. "Hasn't failed me yet."

"And the cigars?"

"All part of my training, Luke. Keeps me in trim."

"Apparently it works," Short conceded. "You're still the champion."

Sullivan snorted laughter. "A cold bath and good, clean living. That's the ticket."

Short forced himself to smile. He realized they were at an impasse, the fight of the century little more than a pipe dream. Sullivan saw his deflated look and glanced around at Madden. "Billy."

"Yes, John L.?"

"When are we to fight in Los Angeles?"

Madden considered a moment. "We're set there for January twenty-fifth."

"So we'll leave a day early," Sullivan said, casually flicking an ash off his cheroot. "Find a way to route our train schedule through Fort Worth. We'll stop there for a night and give Luke his show."

Short was flabbergasted. He suddenly realized that he'd misjudged the Great John L. For all his rigidness about the color line, Sullivan could be thoughtful, not to mention generous, toward those he liked. Even total strangers.

"I don't know what to say," Short finally got out. "Gratitude's hardly the proper word."

"Understand now," Sullivan said, gesturing with his cheroot. "I've no intention of doing an exhibition for the fun of it. I expect to put something in my pocket."

"John L., I will personally guarantee you five thousand. We might be able to double that."

"Your word's good enough for me. Now, there's one other thing I must ask."

"What's that?"

Sullivan grinned. "Do you have anybody worth fighting in Fort Worth?"

"Jock Mulligan," Short said. "A good Irish boy and our local champion. He's a bruiser."

"Is he indeed?" Sullivan laughed, his eyes merry. "I'll show him a thing or two he's not seen before. I eat bruisers for breakfast."

"John L., I have no doubt of it. No doubt whatever."

Short felt like clicking his heels. A moment ago, he'd thought all was lost. But now, like a roll of the dice, he had pulled it off. A coup with his name on it.

John L. Sullivan was coming to Fort Worth.

Chapter 11

A crackling fire blazed in the fireplace. Short sat in an easy chair, a brandy snifter in one hand. He took a sip, staring into the flames, his gaze faraway. His look was pensive.

Try as he might, he couldn't remember what he was doing last Christmas Eve. He thought it quite probable that it had somehow involved a poker game. Like most gamblers, he'd always tended to treat holidays with no great ceremony. On Christmas Eve, like any other night of the year, there was no scarcity of men looking for a game. Nor was there a scarcity of gaming parlors eager to accommodate them.

Lost in a moment of introspection, he tried to remember a time when it was different. He searched back through his memory, touching on Dodge City, Leadville, and Deadwood. He felt sure he'd toasted the season with Masterson or Earp, probably any number of friends. Yet he couldn't summon an image of celebration, a festive occasion. All he recalled were the card games.

Nor were there any women who came to mind. He vaguely remembered faces, a few names, but none who were able to distract him from the tables. None until Marie, and tonight, the first Christmas Eve in recollection he hadn't spent playing poker. His gaze went to the fireplace mantel, where she'd hung Christmas stockings, one with his name and one with hers. The stockings were the only decorations in the suite, and yet there was no scarcity of cheer. She somehow enlivened the spirit of the season.

From the bedroom, he heard her humming a Christmas carol. She had a nice voice, and by her bustling cheeriness, he knew he'd made her happy. Earlier that day, much to her surprise, he had told her they were taking the night off. The club would be slower than usual tonight, and he rationalized that as the excuse. But the truth was, he was in a mood to celebrate the Christmas season, and he was taking her out on the town. He'd made reservations at the Theater Comique.

Short finished his brandy. He pulled the pocket watch from his vest and checked the time. "Hurry up in there," he called out, rising from his chair. "We'll miss the show."

"Have a little patience, lover."

"They won't hold the curtain, you know."

"We still have plenty of time."

Marie moved through the bedroom doorway. She stopped and posed, her features radiant. She wore an exquisite gown of royal blue, and a gold necklace with a sapphire pendant. The bodice of the gown was cut low and cinched at the waist, displaying her figure to full advantage. Her hair was upswept and drawn back, with a soft cluster of curls fluffed high on her forehead. She looked at once regal and sensual.

Short thought he'd never seen anything so beautiful. She tilted her head in a minxish expression. "Well?"

"I have to say . . ." he took her in at a glance. "You are most definitely worth the wait."

She laughed. "Flattery will get you everywhere."

"Is that a promise?"

"Oh, my, yes! Especially on Christmas Eve."

In the foyer, Short helped her on with her wrap and shrugged into his topcoat. They took the elevator downstairs and a moment later emerged from the hotel. The night was blustery and overcast, with a crisp, damp smell in the air. At the corner, they turned north onto Main Street, which was festively decorated with fir wreaths sprouting bright red bows from every lamppost. She hugged his arm with excitement.

Everyone they met on the street exchanged season's greetings. The stores were closed, but the restaurants and theaters and clubs were ablaze with light. Short noted that the White Elephant was fairly crowded, and felt a tug of guilt that he'd put it all on Jake Johnson tonight. Yet the feeling was quickly come and quickly gone, for he had delivered on their bargain ten times over. His partner thought he'd hung the moon.

The Theater Comique was mobbed with revelers. The main room was gaily decorated with green-and-red bunting, and a full-size replica of Saint Nicholas was suspended over the archway to the theater. A throng of people, men and women attired in their finest, were filing through the archway, their voices filled with laughter. The bar was lined with men who had nowhere better to go on Christmas Eve. One of the solitary drinkers was Jim Courtright.

Short started to move on past. He wondered why Courtright, a married man with family, wasn't home with his wife and children on Christmas Eve. But then, imbued with the spirit of the season, he decided on a gesture of good will rather than let the hard feelings persist. He detached himself from Marie, asking her to wait, and walked to the bar. He stopped beside Courtright.

"Good evening."

Courtright turned from the bar. His eyes were bloodshot and his breath reeked of liquor. "Well looky who's here."

"Merry Christmas." Short offered his hand. "I thought we might let bygones be bygones. Start fresh."

"Did you?" Courtright ignored the handshake, his words slurred. "Peace on earth and good will to men. That the idea?"

"More or less," Short said, lowering his hand.

"Christmas seems a good time to put hard feelings behind."

"Well, ho, ho, ho! You gonna stuff some money in my stocking?"

"No, I don't think so, Courtright."

"Then keep your goddamn good will."

"Don't say I didn't try."

Short turned away. Courtright lurched after him and lost his balance, arms flailing drunkenly. He staggered forward, then backward, and finally got his feet untangled. The men around him broke out laughing as he slammed into the bar and clutched at the counter for support. His features flushed and his eyes went wild with anger. He waved off the men with a dopey leer.

"Mind you own goddamn business. Barkeep, gimme another drink!"

Short ignored the commotion. He took Marie's arm and walked her toward the theater entrance. She gave him a concerned look. "I think he wanted to fight you."

"Not much chance of that," Short said. "He's barely able to navigate."

"I'm afraid your Christmas spirit was wasted."

"Then that's his loss, not mine."

George Holland, the owner of the Comique, met them outside the theater archway. He shook Short's hand and nodded apologetically toward the bar. "Sorry for the inconvenience, Luke. He's a troublesome drunk."

"Don't worry about it," Short said genially. "We won't let it spoil our evening."

"I should say not!" Marie added zestfully. "Christmas only comes once a year."

"Maybe twice this year," Holland amended. "Everybody in town's talking about John L. Sullivan. How'd you pull it off, Luke?"

Short grinned. "I told him I'd kissed the Blarney Stone. The Great John L. has a weak spot for the Irish."

"Yeah, sure," Holland said with a chuckle. "I'll just bet there was more to it than that."

"Well, now that you mention it, there was some discussion of money. You wouldn't mind donating to the kitty, would you, George?"

"To see John L. Sullivan fight? Put me first on your list."

"I like a man with civic spirit."

"Let me tell you, you've made a name for yourself in Fort Worth. You're the man of the hour."

"All for a good cause, George."

"We'll talk about it another time. C'mon now, I don't want you folks to miss the show. I saved you the best seats in the house."

Holland led them through the archway. The theater was a large room with tables and chairs neatly aligned in geometric rows. A proscenium stage occupied the far wall, with an orchestra pit for the musicians. Waiters scurried back and forth taking drink orders from a crowd of some three hundred people. The first show of the evening was sold out.

The house lights dimmed as Holland got Short and Marie seated. Their table was in the front row, directly opposite center stage, with the most commanding view in the theater. A waiter appeared with a bottle of champagne, courtesy of the house, nestled in a standing ice bucket. As he poured, the footlights came up and the orchestra broke out in a rousing dance number. The curtain swished open.

A line of chorus girls burst out of the wings and went high-stepping across the stage. The star of the show, Lily Germain, raised her skirts, revealing a shapely leg, and joined them in a prancing cakewalk. The girls squealed and Lily flashed her bloomers as the tempo of the music quickened. The crowd roared with delight and Marie clapped her hands in time to the music. Short thought he'd never seen her so happy.

The number went on for several minutes. The girls swirled around the stage, kicking high in the air, their underdrawers bright in the footlights. Then the orchestra thumped into the finale with a blare of trumpets and a clash of cymbals. The chorus line, in a twirl of raised skirts and jiggling breasts, went cavorting into the wings. Lily Germain blew the crowd a kiss, dazzling them with a smile, and followed the girls offstage. The audience went wild with cheers.

"Weren't they wonderful!" Marie bubbled. "I wish they would do it all over again!"

Her excitement was infectious, and Short laughed. "I think they might need a breather. That was quite a routine."

The chorus line was followed by a team of jugglers, who were entertaining if not sensational. The next act was a comic with a song-and-dance patter, and then a midget who performed death-defying stunts on roller skates. Finally, the orchestra segued into a slower tempo and Lily Germain walked to center stage. She stood bathed in the cider glow of a spotlight, demurely dressed in a white gown, her eyes woeful. Her clear alto voice, pitched low and intimate, filled the hall.

Short watched her with a look of warm approval. She sang a heartrending ballad of unrequited love, her performance flawless. She acted out the song with poignant emotion, and her sultry voice somehow gave the lyrics a haunting quality. The audience was captivated, caught up in a melancholy tale that was all the more sorrowful because of her striking good looks. There was hardly a dry eye in the house, and she played it for all it was worth. She held the crowd enthralled to the very last note.

The theater vibrated to thunderous applause. Lily Germain took a bow, then another and another, and still the audience cheered. The spotlight followed her across the stage, and she bowed a final time before disappearing into the wings. Marie wiped her eyes with a hanky as the orchestra faded and the footlights dimmed. The curtain swished closed, and as the houselights came up.

Short poured the last of the champagne. He lifted his glass to Marie.

"I take it you enjoyed the show."

"God, what a tear-jerker," she said, still dabbing her eyes. "I haven't cried so much in years."

"I felt a tug or two myself."

"I always knew you were a softy."

Short chuckled. "One of my best-kept secrets."

On their way out, they saw Jim Courtright still draped over the bar. Marie felt Short tense, but they were mixed in with the crowd and carried along to the doors. A light snow was falling as they emerged onto the street, and she hugged his arm to her breast. She could almost hear him thinking.

"Penny for your thoughts," she said. "And don't give me any guff about Lily Germain and the show."

Short patted her hand. "You've become a mind-reader."

"What are you going to do about Courtright?"

"Nothing."

"Nothing?" she echoed blankly. "You don't think that was whiskey talking tonight, do you? He means you harm."

"That's entirely possible," Short allowed. "We'll see how it works out."

"You're awfully calm about it, lover. Aren't you worried?"

"I try not to borrow trouble. Whatever happens, happens."

"Aren't you the fatalist," she said anxiously. "Everyone says he's a dangerous man. Doesn't that concern you?"

Short shrugged it off. "For all we know, Courtright's all wind and no whistle. He might forget the whole thing."

"And if he doesn't?"

"I'll worry about it then."

Marie decided not to press him on the matter. She

sensed he would handle it in his own way, in his own time, and she had no wish to spoil their evening. They walked on in the gusting snowfall and a few minutes later entered the hotel. Upstairs, he moved in front of her, unlocking the door, then stepped aside. She stopped just inside the door, her mouth ovaled in surprise. Her eyes went misty.

The suite had been transformed in their absence. A tall Christmas tree stood in the corner, festooned with brightly-colored ornaments and crowned with a replica of a winged angel. The mantel over the fireplace was decorated with silver and gold garlands, and their stockings were stuffed full. Underneath the tree were gaily wrapped packages with fluffy bows.

"Luke," she said on an indrawn breath. "Where did it all come from?"

Short grinned. "I put the elves to work while we were gone."

"You mean the hotel staff?"

"Them, too."

"Who are all those presents for?"

"Open them and find out."

"Omigosh!"

She hurried into the bedroom. A moment later she returned with a wrapped box bound by an elaborate bow. "Here!" she said, kissing him full on the mouth. "I had it hidden beneath the bed."

Short nudged her toward the tree. "Aren't you curious what's under there?"

She tore into the packages like a small girl awakening to her first Christmas. She yelped when she found a diamond bracelet with an intricate gold clasp. The next package, a five-strand pearl choker, brought a louder squeal of delight. By then, Short stood in his velvet smoking jacket, imported from England, waiting for her to reach the last and largest package. She came out from under the tree with a full-length Russian sable coat. Her eyes were round.

"Oh, Luke! Oh my God, Luke! I love it!"

Short slowly wagged his head. "Wait till they see you at the White Elephant."

Chapter 12

Jim."

"Ummm."

"Wake up."

"Lemme alone."

"Get up—right *now*!"

Courtright lay buried in the covers. He rolled over on his back and gradually pried open his eyes. His head pulsated with pain and his mouth tasted like rotten cow dung. He finally managed to focus on his wife.

"What's wrong?"

"Oh, nothing," she snapped. "It's only Christmas morning."

"Why're you yellin'?"

"I am not yelling. Your children are waiting for their father to open their Christmas presents. I want you to get out of that bed."

A shaft of light filtered through the window, and Courtright covered his eyes. "What time is it?"

"Ten o'clock."

"In the morning?"

"Of course in the morning."

"Christ."

"No, Jim, not Christ—Christmas!"

Elizabeth stormed out of the bedroom. Courtright lay as though wrapped in a muzzy fog. After several moments, he struggled out of the covers and swung his legs over the edge of the bed. His head pounded like the steady beat of a drum, and his ears rang with a shrill, piercing sound. He gingerly levered himself erect.

The room swayed. Courtright steadied himself on the bedpost, waiting for a rolling wave of dizziness to subside. He finally got himself oriented, and wobbled down the hall to the washroom. He looked in the mirror and saw the ravaged face of a stranger, bloated cheeks and smudged circles under his eyes. His stomach heaved in a foul, gassy belch.

A quick splash of cold water brought him awake. He rinsed the fetid taste from his mouth and tried to remember what time he'd gotten home last night. Somewhat vaguely, he recalled ending up at the Comique and staggering home in what seemed a blizzard of snow. Yet try as he might, he couldn't fix a time. He just remembered it was dark and cold.

Some while later, Courtright walked into the parlor. He was dressed and shaved, and carrying a steaming mug of coffee. His head still throbbed, and he was suffering from a hangover that jangled his nerves. But he was on his third cup of coffee, and his mind was clear, if not altogether focused. He nodded vacantly to Elizabeth, aware of the children watching him with hidden glances. He wearily lowered himself into a chair.

"Merry Christmas," he said, trying for a jolly tone. "How long you kids been up?"

Sarah, his eldest girl, gave him a kiss on the cheek. "Not all that long, Poppa. We didn't mind waiting."

"Says you!" Timothy, filled with nervous energy, shifted from foot to foot. "C'mon, Pa, we've been waitin' forever. Can't we open our presents?"

Ellen, the youngest of the three, danced around the room. "I wanna see what Saint Nick brought me. Please! Please!"

"Hop to it." Courtright motioned with his mug. "Let's see what you got."

The Christmas tree was decorated with shiny ornaments and strands of popcorn on white thread. The children raced across the parlor and feverishly began sorting through the packages. Ellen shrieked with joy when she unwrapped a baby doll with rosy cheeks and hair the color of straw. Tim jumped up and down with a wooden rifle that fired corks, and Sarah pressed her face to the softness of a pale blue sweater. They rummaged through the litter for more presents.

Elizabeth walked to the tree. She collected two packages and moved back across the room. "Merry Christmas," she said, handing one package to Courtright and holding the other out. "I assume this is for me."

" 'Course it is, Betty," Courtright said with an awkward grin. "You think I'd forget you on Christmas?"

"No, I knew you wouldn't forget."

Courtright set his mug on the floor and untied the ribbon on the package. He pulled out a plaid woolen scarf and made a show of draping it around his neck. Elizabeth opened her present and removed a delicate cameo brooch. She held it to the light, and her eyes shone with a hint of tears. She smiled at her husband.

"Thank you," she said in a small voice. "It's really quite beautiful."

"Thought you'd like it," Courtright said, pleased. "Pretty girl deserves something pretty."

"That's the first time you've said that in a long time."

"Well, maybe so, but I think it all the time."

She merely nodded, affixing the brooch over the breast of her dress. They fell silent, watching the children pillage the Christmas tree. The girls looked like their mother, and the boy was a miniature version of his father. There were two presents for each of them, bought with money Elizabeth had hoarded from house funds over the year. They showed off their gifts, happy and animated, chattering among themselves. All three agreed that Saint Nick had heard their prayers.

Courtright reclaimed his coffee mug. He took a long

sip, oddly saddened by the happiness of his own children. Their presents seemed to him a Christmas born of poverty, and for that he blamed himself. He knew he drank too much, and the thousand or so dollars he collected from the dives every month was largely squandered at the gaming tables. His family deserved better at Christmas, and for that matter, all through the year. Yet he seemed caught in a spiral of his own dissolution, unable to right himself. He led a life of beggarly means, brought low by cards and drink. A waste.

A vivid image suddenly flitted through his mind. He recalled the run-in with Short last night, and how the men at the Comique bar had laughed at him. There was a bitter aftertaste to the incident, tinged with a sour dose of spite, and even worse, envy. Short was the talk of the town, the man responsible for bringing John L. Sullivan to Fort Worth. The man who had turned the White Elephant around, earned the respect of the high rollers and the uptown crowd. A man with the golden touch.

Courtright despised himself for petty jealousy. But he was unable to suppress a dark sense of loathing and anger toward Short. All over town, he was being held up to ridicule—not to his face, but he'd heard the talk—all because Short refused to pay for protection. The injustice of it seemed to him incomprehensible, particularly since Short could afford the payoffs, probably burned up a hundred a month on cigars. The thought of it set his head to throbbing, and the hangover struck him with renewed force. He desperately needed a drink.

Which conjured yet another problem. Elizabeth adamantly refused to allow liquor in the house, and he'd lost that battle long ago. She was protective of the children, like a lioness with cubs, determined that they would not be exposed to the evils of alcohol in her home. Yet today was one of those days when he needed a drink simply to pull himself together, to clear his head. He sat brooding on it, his mouth dry and pasty, hesitant to start a fight in front of the children. But when she went into the kitchen to start preparing Christmas dinner, he decided there was no way around it. He couldn't get through the day without a drink.

Elizabeth glanced up as he came through the kitchen door. She was standing at a counter, loading her bread stuffing into a large, plump turkey. A pot was boiling on the stove, and the pungent smell of onions almost made him gag. He placed his mug on the drainboard, aware that there was no easy way to slide into the subject. He nodded at the turkey.

"What time you planning dinner?"

"Oh, somewhere around three."

"Well, that's fine," he said casually. "Thought I'd take a walk uptown. Get myself a breath of fresh air."

She stopped, her hands smeared with stuffing. "I won't have it, Jim Courtright. You hear me? Not on Christmas day."

"What the devil you talking about?"

"You know very well what I'm talking about. You'll get off with your cronies and we won't see you until who knows when. Probably tomorrow."

"C'mon now, Betty, don't get like that. I'll be back in plenty of time for dinner."

"You'd better," she said sharply. "If you spoil Christmas for the kids I'll . . . I don't know what I'll do, but you won't like it! Do you hear me?"

"I just reckon half the town can hear you."

Courtright walked out of the kitchen. She stood perfectly still, listening as he collected his gun belt and coat and slammed out the door. Her eyes welled over with tears and she tried to get control of herself. She was thirty-six years old and sometimes she felt a hundred. Or older.

She told herself not to expect him for dinner.

Courtright caught the streetcar downtown.

There was a dusting of snow on the ground, melting under a hazy sun. Something about it bothered him, and when the streetcar stopped for a passenger at Ninth Street, he realized what it was. Last night, staggering home at some ungodly hour, he would have sworn he was trudging through a blizzard. He decided he had been drunker than he'd thought.

The Acre was swarming with activity. Laborers and cowhands, for the most part single men, had nowhere else to go on Christmas. They celebrated the birth of Christ as though it were the Fourth of July, just another holiday. Saloons and gaming dives were swamped, and for some reason, bawdy houses did a flourishing business. Lonely men took comfort in the arms of a whore.

The sporting crowd looked upon Christmas as a windfall. Working men everywhere had the day off, and those without family naturally gravitated to the Acre. A festive atmosphere prevailed, for all the dives had decorated their haunts in the traditional red and green colors. Some even had Christmas trees, and with men celebrating the occasion in a sea of alcohol, cardsharps raked in a small fortune. Whorehouses, tongue in cheek, hung mistletoe over every door.

Downtown, at the corner of Fourteenth and Main, Courtright stepped off the streetcar. He made straight for the Buckhorn, which was packed with cowhands, and wedged himself a spot at the bar. His first drink settled his stomach, and the second routed his headache as though he'd downed an elixir. Cal Pierce, the proprietor, was in a holiday mood and wouldn't hear of him paying for the drinks. His Christmas treat was whiskey on the house.

By the time he left the saloon, Courtright was feeling his old self. There was a swagger in his stride, and the warmth of the liquor gave him renewed vitality. He fully intended to keep his promise and return home to spend Christmas with the children. But across the street, he saw the Maverick Saloon, and in the spirit of the season, he dropped in to pay his respects. From there, spreading glad tidings as he went, he moved on to the Tivoli in the next block, and the Empress a block farther on. All of the owners insisted that he be a guest of the house.

Even with the liquor he'd consumed, Courtright's intentions were still good. He was working his way uptown, pausing here and there to exchange greetings with saloonkeepers and madams, all of them clients of the Commercial Detective Agency. His mood soaring, he convinced himself that these courtesy calls were smart business, imparting holiday cheer to those who contributed to his livelihood. He nonetheless meant to be home in time for dinner, and redeem himself with Elizabeth and the children. Yet there was always one more stop, another valued client.

On toward three o'clock Courtright wandered into the Centennial. A special matinee show was under way in the theater, and the bar was lined with men who took their holiday cheer in liquid form. For all he'd had to drink, Courtright was still clear headed, and something struck him as odd the moment he came through the door. Then, on second glance, he realized the Centennial, unlike other places in town, was devoid of Christmas decoration. He spotted Lowe standing with Kate at the front of the bar.

"Joe. Kate." He greeted them with a jack-o'-lantern grin. "Merry Christmas to you."

Lowe pulled a face. "Kate and me don't hold with Christmas."

"Why not?"

"Christ wasn't nothing but a con man. Not taking anything away from him, you understand. Greatest goddamn grifter in history."

"I'll be switched." Courtright seemed genuinely perplexed by the thought. "Guess you don't believe in Saint Nick, neither?"

"You're drunk," Kate said severely. "I hope you're not expecting a handout just because it's Christmas."

"Let him be," Lowe ordered, signaling the bartender.

"Least we can do is offer him a drink. How about it, Jim?"

"I don't suppose I'd refuse."

The bartender poured and Courtright downed it neat. Lowe exchanged a look with Kate, and happened to glance out the front window. Across the street, he saw Short and the Blair girl walking toward the White Elephant. He nudged Courtright.

"Have you wished Mr. Hotshot a Merry Christmas?"

Courtright's good mood evaporated on the instant. "Sorry bastard," he muttered, staring out the window. "Only thing I'd wish him is bad luck. Lots of it."

They watched in silence as Short and Marie entered the White Elephant. "Heard about last night," Lowe said in a sly voice. "Your little dustup with Short at the Comique. Everybody's saying he made a fool of you."

"Good thing for him I was drunk."

"Maybe you ought to try him when you're sober."

"Maybe I will."

"Just let me know," Lowe goaded him. "I'd pay admission to see it."

Courtright suddenly appeared uncomfortable. He glanced up at the clock on the wall and pushed off the bar. "Where the devil'd the time go? Betty's expectin' me home for Christmas dinner. I gotta get a move on."

"Have another drink," Lowe offered. "One for the road."

"No, thanks all the same, Joe. Another time."

Courtright hurried out the door. Lowe stared after him, a slight smile at the corner of his mouth. Kate studied her husband a moment.

"All right, slick," she said, her eyes narrowed. "What was that all about?"

"Friend Jim's a martyr in search of a cross. I mean to help him find it."

Lowe was tired of hearing about Luke Short and John L. Sullivan, and what a great thing it was for Fort Worth. Even more, he was tired of losing business to the White

Elephant, another of Short's swift and tricky moves. Lately, he'd begun to feel he was playing second-fiddle in his own town.

Kate intruded on his thoughts. "Try running that past me again. You plan to nail Courtright to a cross?"

"No," Lowe said, shaking his head. "Not Courtright."

"Then who?"

"Take a guess."

"Oh." Kate looked across the street. "Him."

Lowe nodded sullenly. "You just won the nickel cigar."

Chapter 13

The overhead lamp bathed the players in an amber glow. Seated around the table were three businessmen, a couple of ranchers, and a man Short took to be a drummer stranded in Fort Worth over the holiday. All of them were bachelors, and their interest tonight was in cards rather than women. They preferred to party at a poker table.

New Year's Eve was one of the better nights at the White Elephant. Everyone was in a celebratory mood, and men who fancied themselves gamblers were convinced Lady Luck would favor them as the clock ticked toward midnight. The club was packed, men ganged two and three deep around every table, revelers chasing fortune as the old year wound down. Tonight they were ushering in 1884.

Short was ahead almost eight hundred dollars. He'd been the steady winner, drawing unbeatable cards for the past three hours. The drummer was dealing now, and Short considered the board as the fifth card was dealt. He calculated that the best hand on the table was two pair, jacks and treys, one trey in the hole. He had two aces showing and a third hidden, his hole card. He checked the bet.

The rules were dealer's choice, restricted to five-card stud and five-card draw. Ante was twenty dollars, with a hundred-dollar limit and three raises. Check and raise was permitted, which made it a game perfectly suited to Short's style of play. Long ago, in cowtowns and mining camps across the West, he had developed his own technique for wining at cutthroat poker. The secret was to keep them guessing.

Other men found it difficult to fathom Short. He had an uncanny knack for reading his opponents, and he won on what appeared to be weak hands. There was no pattern to his betting and raising; his erratic play made him unpredictable and somewhat intimidating. He would bluff on a bad hand as often as he folded, and he seldom folded. More often than not his bluff went undetected.

On good hands, he would sometimes raise the limit, allowing the money to speak for itself. At other times, when he held good cards, he would lay back and sucker his opponents into heedless raises. On occasion, merely calling all bets and raises, he let the other players build the pot, only to turn up the winning hand. No one was ever sure of what he held.

Carl Richter, one of the ranchers, stared at his aces. On the board, the aces beat the cattleman's jacks. But Richter had a trey hidden, which paired with the three of hearts exposed on the table. The question he considered now was Short's fifth card, the one in the hole. And why a man with the high hand showing would check.

"I dunno, Luke," he said, drumming his fingers on the table. "Wouldn't be trying to sandbag me, would you?"

Short lit a cheroot. He snuffed the match, puffing smoke around a wide smile. "Your first hunch was right, Carl. Time to fold."

Richter studied him a moment. "You know, a little bird tells me I ought to bet. Hate to think you'd scared me out."

"Perish the thought," Short said affably. "Especially if you have something to go with those jacks."

"Hundred's the bet," Richter said, tossing a chip into the pot. "Guess that ought to tell you something."

The drummer, two of the businessmen, and the other rancher folded. Orville Wallach, who owned the town's largest livery stable, chuffed a crafty grin. "Your hundred," he said without the slightest hesitation, "and a hundred more."

Short gave his cards another inspection. On the board were a ten, a seven, and a pair of nines. His original calculation had pegged Wallach for two pair, probably tens and nines. But the raise indicated now that the liveryman had a third nine in the hole. Even more, the raise announced that Wallach correctly figured Richter for two pair, and didn't believe Short held three of a kind. All of which presented Short with an interesting problem. How to keep them in the game?

"You know what?" he said, looking from one to the other. "I think you're both trying to buy it."

Wallach was a man of some girth, with heavy jowls and a rosy nose. His mouth dimpled in a wet chuckle. "One way to find out, Luke."

"Never try to bluff a bluffer," Short said, feigning open amusement. "That's the first rule of poker, Orville." He tossed chips into the pot. "Carl's hundred, your hundred, and to keep you honest—raise a hundred."

"Whoa now, Nellie!" Richter said confidently. "You boys just don't know when you're beat. I'll take the last raise."

Wallach called, and Short sailed a purple chip onto the table. Richter laughed and turned over two pair, jacks and treys. Wallach laughed louder, and flipped his bottom card to reveal three nines. A low groan erupted from Richter and they both looked around at Short. He turned his hole card.

"How about that?" he said with a straight face. "Three of a kind, all aces."

"I'll be go to hell!" Richter blurted. "You sandbagged right from the start."

Wallach shook his jowls. "I'll have to remember that,

Luke. What was it again—never bluff a bluffer?''

Elmer Pryor, one of the other businessmen, let go a whooping laugh. ''You gents fell into it like blind men. Anybody could've seen he had the third ace.''

''That a fact?'' Richter countered. ''When's the last time you won a pot?''

The other players broke out in laughter. Short glanced up from dragging in the pot and saw Marie watching him from her faro table. On any number of occasions, she had commented on his gift for trimming high rollers and sending them away with their humor intact. Short dipped his head in an imperceptible nod, careful that no one else caught their amused byplay. She batted one eyelash in a sly wink.

Marie was herself a student of human nature. She recognized that male pride was perhaps the most fragile element in all the universe. The men who frequented her faro table were convinced they could outfox a delicate little lady with innocent eyes. Yet she invariably won, soothing their pride with a smile and a word, and vanity rarely ever allowed them to admit defeat. She was the only woman dealer in Fort Worth, and men routinely waited in line to try their luck. Her looks, and her joking manner, made losing almost a pleasure.

''Cards coming out,'' she said to the crowd gathered around her table. ''Place your bets, gentlemen.''

The men quickly checked the casekeeper. After every deal, Marie operated this abacus-like device to display the cards already played. In theory, knowing the cards left in the deck gave a player some slight advantage in placing his bets. In practice, any man who played long enough was ultimately ground down by the house odds. Yet faro remained one of the more popular games in Western towns, the name derived from the image of an Egyptian pharaoh on the back of the cards. A favorite of European royalty, the game had originated a century earlier in France.

Cards were dealt from a specially adapted box, and

the players bet against the house. Every card from ace to deuce was embossed on the cloth layout that covered the table. A player placed his chips on the card of his choice, and two cards were then drawn face-up from the box. The first card drawn lost on all bets and the second card was a winner. The player could "copper" his play by betting a card to lose instead of win. There were twenty-five turns, since the first and last cards in the deck paid nothing. When the box was empty, the dealer shuffled and the game began anew.

Marie was unusually adept, fast and skillful with the cards. She was vivacious as well, charming the players with lively chatter as she dealt, collecting losers and paying out winners. She was quick to congratulate a winner, and just as quick to express genuine, almost heartfelt sympathy for a loser. Her gift was that she could disarm men with her sensual looks, and encourage them in the same breath to lose still more. She magically gave them hope that they could always recoup their losses.

One of the players, a well-dressed man with wire-rimmed glasses, sat back in his chair after an hour at the table. All of his chips were on her side of the layout, and he shook his head with a rueful smile. "You have whittled me down in record time, good lady. I usually manage to hold my own."

"The night's still young," she said lightly. "Your luck's bound to change. You have that look about you."

"What look is that?"

"Oh, you know what I mean—a winner."

"And you have a charming way of deadening the pain."

"Well, like they say, luck be a lady tonight. You just have to give her a chance."

She smiled approvingly when he pulled out a roll of bills. As she was exchanging chips for cash, she saw Jake Johnson appear at the head of the staircase. Johnson's features were flushed, and she was struck by his agitated manner. Shuffling the cards, she watched as he caught Short's eye and gestured with a rapid motion. She knew then that there was a serious problem of some sort downstairs. He *never* pulled Short from a game with high rollers.

Short excused himself from the table. The other players protested, for he was the big winner for the night. He passed it off with a humorous remark, assuring them he wouldn't be gone long. He crossed the room and Johnson took his arm, leading him down the staircase. Johnson appeared flustered, and worried.

"We've got problems," he said. "Jim Courtright's in my office. He's set on making trouble."

"What sort of trouble?"

"I haven't got that out of him yet. He barged in on me a few minutes ago and demanded to see you."

"All right," Short said as they descended to the ground floor. "Mr. Courtright's about to get his wish. Is he drunk?"

"Not that I could tell," Johnson said nervously. "But he's hot under the collar. Threatened to close us down."

"How could he manage that?"

"I asked him the same thing. That's when he demanded to see you."

Short grunted. "He's liable to see me once too often."

"Luke, don't push him," Johnson insisted. "He's nobody to mess with."

"Neither am I."

A moment later, they walked into the office. Courtright was seated in a chair, one foot braced on the edge of the desk. He appeared stone-cold sober, hat tilted at a rakish angle on the back of his head. His expression was one of arrogant confidence.

"Well, well," he said, looking Short up and down. "The little big man himself. How's tricks?"

"Let's get to it," Short said without ceremony. "What's this about closing us down?"

"Time you and me came to an understanding. Start the New Year off right."

"Go ahead, spell it out."

Courtright spread his hands. "Way I figure it, you owe me for two months. Hundred a month."

"No dice," Short said curtly. "We've covered that ground before."

"Yeah, but I forgot to tell you something. I've still got friends on the police force."

"So?"

"So all it'd take is a word from me. Guaran-damn-tee you, they'll raid your joint tonight. Padlock the doors."

"Why would the police raid us?"

"Oh, that's the easy part," Courtright said with an offhand gesture. "You're running crooked games upstairs."

"Are we?" Short said, watching him closely. "How do you intend to prove it?"

"You checked your ladyfriend's faro table lately?"

"I'm not in the mood for riddles. Get to it."

"You might've noticed one of the players. Nifty dresser, wears glasses, real upstanding type. He'll swear your sweetheart's dealing seconds."

The practice was common in clip joints. A crooked dealer, employing sleight-of-hand, held back a card until it could be dealt as a loser. Short realized the man with glasses was a plant, a stooge of Courtright's. His features went hard.

"Bring on the police," he said in a cold voice. "When you do, I'll charge you with extortion. That's a criminal offense."

"Bullshit," Courtright said derisively. "You'd never make it stick."

"Wouldn't I?" Short said. "I'm told that's how you lost the job of marshal. Extorting money from dives in the Acre. Isn't that right, Jake?"

"That's what they said," Johnson sputtered. "Nobody ever brought charges, though."

"I will," Short said, staring at Courtright. "And with Jake as a witness, we'll make it stick. You might end up on the rock pile."

Courtright slammed out of his chair. "You sawed-off little sonovabitch. I oughta stop your ticker."

"Try it."

Johnson's face paled. He backed against the wall, certain Courtright would pull a gun. A long moment elapsed, with Short and Courtright locked in a staring contest. Then, as though unwilling to carry it further, Courtright moved toward the door. He brushed past Short.

"We're not done yet, Fancypants. I'll see you around."

Short nodded. "You know where to find me."

When the door closed, Johnson let out a gusty sigh. "Christ, that was close. Why'd he back off?"

"I just imagine he had to check with Joe Lowe."

"What's Lowe got to do with it?"

"Courtright's not clever enough to work out this sort of set-up. Lowe arranged to put a plant at Marie's table."

"How can you be sure?"

"Jake, I'd bet the bank on it."

Upstairs again, Short collared the man in the wire-rimmed glasses and hustled him out of the club room. Marie turned her table over to another dealer and rushed after them. She caught up just as Short waltzed the man to the front door and roughly shoved him onto the street. Her eyes were wide with alarm.

"Luke, what's going on? Why did you throw him out?"

"Courtright was here," Short said. "The fellow I just gave the boot was his plant. You were about to be charged with dealing crooked."

"Why the dirty—"

The clock behind the bar began to toll twelve. They stopped, looking first at the clock, and then at one another. All throughout the White Elephant, the crowd raised their voices in celebration as the old year slipped away. Marie put her arms around Short's neck, their troubles abruptly forgotten. She kissed him full on the mouth.

"Happy New Year, lover."

Short held her close. "The happiest of them all."

"Do you mean that—really?"

"You tell me. Do I?"

She laughed. "You know you're stuck with me, don't you?"

"I knew that a long time ago."

"How long ago?"

"The first time I saw you."

She kissed him long after the clock stopped tolling.

`Chapter 14

Short awoke earlier than usual. A bright morning sun spilled through the window, and he saw that it was a fair day. He lay for a moment listening to the even rise and fall of Marie's breathing. Then, careful not to disturb her, he eased out of bed.

A clock on the dresser marked the time at half past nine. He slipped into a bathrobe and paused, his gaze drawn again to the bed. Marie's hair was fanned out over the pillow, and he was struck by how she slept the peaceful sleep of a child. Even in repose, the look of her stirred something within him.

In the bathroom, he closed the door and went about his morning ritual. After brushing his teeth, he filled the tub and luxuriated in a hot bath. Then he shaved, trimming his mustache with a small pair of scissors, and splashed tonic on his face. He gave himself a cursory inspection in the mirror, his hair combed neatly back on the sides. He thought he would pass muster.

Steam billowed from the door when he moved back into the bedroom. Marie was still asleep, and it occurred to him that she might not wake before noon. Yesterday, with the club closed for New Year's Day, he had rented a buggy and they'd gone for a ride in the country. Last night, after supper at the Lafayette, they had attended a blackface minstrel show at one of the variety theaters. Upon returning to the suite, they ended their holiday by making love far into the night. He wondered that he had the energy to get on with the day's business.

Still in his bathrobe, he padded softly to the armoire. He selected a somber navy blue suit, with a starchy white shirt and a dark, muted tie. He moved about the room quietly, hoping to slip out of the suite without waking her. But as he shrugged into his jacket, her eyes fluttered open and she lay bathed in sunlight. She stretched, stifling a small yawn, and saw him standing by the door. A look of sleepy surprise came over her face.

"What time is it?"

"Almost ten," Short said. "I tried not to wake you."

"Ummm," she said dreamily. "Why are you dressed?"

"I have to go out."

"So early?"

Short moved to the side of the bed. She held out her arms, and he sat down, lifting her into an embrace. The sweet, musky smell of her filled his head, and he stroked her hair. "Did you sleep well?"

"Oh, yes," she murmured, hugging him around the neck. "You gave me the best sleeping potion of all last night."

Her breasts, full and round in her nightgown, pressed softly against his chest. "Careful now," he said with mock seriousness. "I'm liable to climb back in bed."

She hugged him tighter. "I think that would be a splendid idea."

"You're shameless."

"You've made a wanton hussy of me."

"Have I?" Short said jestfully. "Maybe we could arrange something this afternoon."

She nuzzled closer. "Why not now?"

"Well, like I said, I have to go out."

"Where are you going?"

"City Hall."

"What on earth for?"

"I'll explain later. You go back to sleep. Try to dream of me."

"I won't have to try. That's easy."

Short kissed her on the cheek. She smiled, her eyes drooping closed, and snuggled back into her pillow. He walked from the bedroom, collecting his topcoat and hat as he went through the sitting room. Downstairs, he took breakfast in the hotel dining room, lingering over a second cup of coffee. When he was finished, he felt eager to get on with the day's business. He thought it a good way to start the New Year.

Outside the hotel, Short turned east on Fourth. The crisp air was invigorating, and a few minutes later, he crossed the intersection of Second and Rusk. A two-story building occupied the northeast corner, housing City Hall and the fire department. The fire department, as well as the city jail, was located on the ground floor. The upper floor was a warren of offices for city officials and the police force. He turned into a door that led to the second-story stairwell.

Upstairs, he found the mayor's office at the end of the corridor. After a brief wait in the anteroom, he was ushered into the private office of Mayor John P. Smith. The room was handsomely decorated in dark woods, overlooking Rusk Street and a view beyond to the courthouse dome. Smith was a portly man, with a walrus mustache and thinning hair, and the ever-ready smile of a politician. He greeted Short with an effusive handshake.

"Have a chair," he said, seating himself behind his ornate walnut desk. "Let me congratulate you on bringing John L. Sullivan to our fair city. You've done Fort Worth a great service, Mr. Short."

Short waved it off with an idle gesture. "I just happened to catch John L. in a good mood. Another day and he might have turned me down."

"You're far too modest, Mr. Short. I always say give credit where credit is due."

Smith was a crafty politician beneath his affable veneer. The city government consisted of the mayor and six aldermen, elected to office for a one-year term in municipal elections held each spring. By its charter, Fort Worth was divided into three wards, with two aldermen elected from each district. The First Ward encompassed all of uptown, and the Second Ward spilled over from uptown into Hell's Half Acre. The Third Ward, comprised solely of the Acre, and allied by the vice trade with part of the Second Ward, carried the swing vote in any election. Smith walked the line between uptown and downtown with the agility of a trapeze artist.

Short was no great admirer of politicians. He knew the mayor was aligned with Joe Lowe, who controlled the Acre, and he strongly suspected Smith would somehow claim a lion's share of the credit for John L. Sullivan. But the purpose of his call dealt with another matter entirely, and he planned to use the machinations of Fort Worth's politics to his own advantage. He took his time lighting a cheroot.

"Mr. Mayor, I find myself in something of a fix." He paused, puffing a thick cloud of smoke. "I've come seeking your assistance in a personal matter."

"Delighted to oblige," Smith said, looking interested. "How can I be of service?"

"You're familiar with a man by the name of Jim Courtright?"

"Well, only by reputation. Why do you ask?"

"Courtright is an extortionist." Short allowed the words to hang in the air a moment. "On New Year's Eve, he threatened to close down the White Elephant."

Smith appeared confused. "How could he close down a business establishment?"

"I'm quoting, you understand, not lodging an allegation. Courtright said he could arrange a raid by the Fort Worth police department."

"What?"

"In his own words, he threatened to use his influence

with the police department and have our doors pad-
locked. Unless, of course, I agreed to pay him off.''

"That's preposterous!'' Smith said indignantly. ''Our
police department would never be involved in such a
thing.''

Short blew smoke at him. ''Then how do you explain
Courtright's threat?''

"I can't,'' Smith said. ''But we'll get to the bottom
of this right now.''

The mayor rose, moved to the door, and spoke to his
secretary. Five minutes later, City Marshal Bill Rea
walked into the office, clearly surprised to find Short
seated before the desk. Smith quickly explained the allegations, and the lawman's reaction was one of stunned
anger. He looked at Short.

"Not a word of truth to it,'' he said brusquely.
"Courtright's the biggest liar ever to come down the
pike. He was trying to run a bunco game on you.''

Short shrugged. ''I have to say he was pretty confident of himself. Why wouldn't he think I'd report the
incident to you?''

"Because Jim Courtright's thick as a brick. Do you
want to prefer charges?''

"No, nothing like that.''

Rea exchanged a glance with the mayor. ''Unless you
press charges, what's your point? Why are you here?''

"I want it stopped,'' Short said earnestly. ''Courtright has a reputation for violence, and I take the threat
seriously. I demand protection from the police department.''

"And you'll have it,'' Smith assured him. ''Marshal
Rea will personally see to it. Won't you, Marshal?''

"Yessir, Mr. Mayor,'' Rea said promptly. ''I know
just how to handle Jim Courtright. It's as good as done.''

Short departed after a round of handshakes. On the
street, he mentally gave himself a pat on the back. The
irony of it amused him, for all of City Hall shared in
the payoffs from the Acre. But Bill Rea was known to

be the bagman, and that provided a direct pipeline to Rowdy Joe Lowe. He was confident the message would be delivered.

All in all, he felt he'd manipulated events to his advantage. Fort Worth's vice lord wanted nothing to upset the applecart, least of all a petty grifter involved in nickel-and-dime extortion. There was a certainty to the whole affair.

Rowdy Joe would put the quietus on Jim Courtright.

Late that evening, Bill Rea slipped into the alley behind the Centennial. He walked directly to a door at the rear of the theater and entered a dimly lit hallway. He sent one of the stagehands to fetch Lowe.

A short time later, Lowe came through the door of his office. The room was off the hallway that led from the rear of the theater below stage level. His desk was littered with paperwork, and the walls were covered with old showbills. He found Rea seated in a chair.

"What's up?" he said, slumping into his chair behind the desk. "You're not due till the end of the week."

Rea nodded agreement. "Everybody's real happy with what you kicked in at Christmas. I'm not here about money."

"So what brings you around?"

"We've got a problem with Courtright."

"Yeah?" Lowe said with no great interest. "What's ol' Jim done now?"

"Too damn much." Rea ticked off the points on his fingers. "Tried to extort a payoff out of the White Elephant. Claimed he could have the police shut them down. Threatened Luke Short's life." He paused, ticked off a final point. "Generally made an ass of himself."

"How'd you find all this out?"

"Short paid a call on the mayor this morning. Smith got his bowels in an uproar and put me on the spot. Ordered me to come down hard on Courtright."

Lowe considered a moment. "Why didn't Short press charges?"

"Beats the hell out of me," Rea said. "I asked him and he just sort of sloughed it off. Got the idea he's halfway scared of Courtright."

"Sure, and bird dogs fly, too."

"What d'you mean?"

"I mean Short's a tough cookie. Just because he's a runt, don't let that fool you. Hell, he's killed four men I know of—maybe more."

Rea appeared unconvinced. "Courtright's killed his share, and then some. I wouldn't want to try him with a gun."

"Neither would I."

Lowe fell silent. Some visceral instinct warned him that things were not as they appeared. A game was being played out, and he got the feeling it was layered like an onion. A man could peel off one strip, and then another, and another, and another. When he got to the heart of the onion, what he found was seldom what he'd expected, maybe nothing at all. Things were rarely what they appeared to be beneath the surface.

What bothered him most was that Short had filed a complaint. From the old days, back in the Kansas cowtowns, he knew that Short held politicians, and most law officers, in low regard. He knew as well that Short, despite his bantam size, feared no man, Jim Courtright or any other. All of which raised the question of why Short would lodge a protest with the authorities, and ask the law to solve his problem. He told himself there was more to this onion than met the eye.

"So?" he said at length. "Why come to me?"

Rea held his gaze. "All this started when Short took over the White Elephant. It's no secret he told Courtright to stuff it, where payoffs are concerned."

"That's the story on the street."

"Not any secret, either, that you let Courtright run

his protection racket. Everybody in the Acre knows he couldn't operate without your say-so.''

Lowe dismissed it with a wave. ''What's your point?''

''Way it looks . . .'' Rea hesitated, choosing his words with care. ''Courtright's bound and determined to cause trouble with Short. So I've got to ask you, Joe. Are you backing his play?''

''What's the difference one way or another?''

''Well, you might say it's my tit in the wringer. I've been ordered to get tough with Courtright. Let's suppose I don't, and the damn fool kills Short. You think the mayor will support me come election time?''

''You worry too much,'' Lowe said evenly. ''Courtright's like a school-yard bully. Gets his fun pushing people around.''

''No argument there,'' Rea agreed. ''But that still don't answer my question. What if he kills Short?''

''How about I take you off the hook?''

''I don't follow you.''

''Courtright's harmless,'' Lowe said with a breezy chuckle. ''A regular dimdot, not too sharp in the brains department. I'll have a talk with him.''

''I wouldn't mind,'' Rea said quickly. ''You think he'll listen?''

''Ol' Jimbo does whatever I tell him to do.''

''That would take a load off my shoulders. I'd be obliged, Joe.''

''Always happy to help a friend.''

Rea was still grinning when he went out the door. Lowe leaned back in his chair, steepling his fingers, and stared off into the middle distance. He fully intended to have a talk with Courtright, but along a different vein. Get down to the heart of things.

Time to peel the onion.

Chapter 15

A week later Short brought Richard Clark to town. The gambling fraternity was astounded by what represented a coup of major proportions. All of Fort Worth was talking about the White Elephant.

Clark was a legend in gambling circles. A man of impeccable dress and courtly manners, he was among the elite of Western high rollers. He headquartered out of Tombstone, Arizona, where Short had met him in 1881. Tombstone was still the site of the richest silver strike in history, and Clark was known as "King of the Gamblers." He refused to play in a game with stakes of less than ten thousand.

On the night of January 10, Short and Clark emerged from the hotel and walked toward Main Street. Clark was in town for a week, and the first big game of his stay had been arranged for tonight. The game was by invitation only, and Fort Worth's high rollers were clamoring for a seat at the table. For many, the chance to play against a man of Clark's stature was considered a once-in-a-lifetime opportunity. The week was booked solid, with a long waiting list.

Short looked on it as one more step in his overall plan. Just as he had with Bat Masterson, he'd widely publicized Clark's arrival in Fort Worth. The trip from Tombstone was long and arduous, and it spoke volumes for Short's influence that a man of Clark's distinction would travel all that way. There was no longer any question that Short was preeminent among the city's gamblers, an impresario of high-stakes games as well as a civic booster. The White Elephant was regarded as the hottest club in town.

Richard Clark was lean and angular, not quite six feet tall, almost foxlike in appearance. His hair was prematurely gray and his eyes were friendly but alert, a touch of cunning beneath the warmth. "How did Masterson do?" he asked as they turned onto Main Street. "Quite well, I would assume."

Short chuckled softly. "Bat won about three thousand for the week. He was happy with himself."

"Good for him," Clark remarked. "Does he stay in touch with Earp and Holliday?"

Like many sporting men, Clark had been drawn to Tombstone in the early days of the silver strike. With ore assaying at twenty thousand dollars a ton, millions were extracted from the mines each year. Clark had witnessed the passage of the Earp Brothers and Holliday and any number of frontier notables who came to claim their share of the bonanza. He still made the dusty helldorado his home.

"Wyatt's in Idaho," Short said in answer to his question. "Bat told me he's operating a gaming parlor in Coeur d'Alene. Doc's still traveling the circuit."

"I often wonder he's lived so long."

"To hear Bat tell it, that might not be so long. He said Doc's pretty much on his last legs."

"One of the great mysteries," Clark said thoughtfully. "I never understood the friendship between Earp and Holliday. They seemed to me two very dissimilar men."

Short nodded. "I always felt the same way. Wyatt's a hard man, but he'll try to steer clear of trouble. Doc goes looking for a fight."

"A classic case of the fatalist. I suspect he'd sooner die from a gunshot than consumption."

"There's no question it would be an easier death."

"You should know," Clark said in a jocular tone. "I remember well the night you sent Charley Storms to the great beyond. God, what a fool the man was!"

The incident had taken place in the Oriental Saloon, one of Tombstone's better gaming establishments. Short had accused Storms of cheating at cards, and gunplay appeared imminent. Clark intervened, arguing for a peaceful settlement; but Storms belligerently refused to shake hands, and walked out of the saloon. A few minutes later, Storms returned, demanding satisfaction, and went for his gun. Short beat him to the draw and shot him three times, all fatal wounds. A coroner's jury ruled it justifiable homicide.

"I was never so impressed," Clark went on. "Three shots not a handspan apart, all in the chest. And Storms never got off a shot!"

"Guess it was my lucky night," Short said, shrugging it off. "Sometimes you just can't lose."

"Luke, that sums it up perfectly. You've led a charmed life, my friend. Perhaps you have a guardian angel."

"God loves saints and sinners alike."

"And how would you classify yourself?"

"Somewhere south of sainthood."

Clark laughed. "I have to say, I've missed your droll humor. Tombstone was never the same without you."

"Then it's just like old times," Short said. "You're in for a barrel of laughs."

"I presume you're talking about pigeons waiting to be plucked."

"Richard, I'll thank you to remember they are my select clientele. Do your plucking with a gentle hand."

"I will leave them elated to have lost their feathers."

"Not to mention their bankrolls."

"Yes, that too."

In high spirits, they walked into the White Elephant. Jake Johnson waved them to the bar, where he was serving champagne in honor of the occasion. Waiting to be introduced were the club's more prominent high rollers, Karl Van Zandt, Frank Wilcox, and Anson Tolbert. The men shook Clark's hand as though welcoming royalty, eager to test themselves against a gambler of his reputation. All around the restaurant, the evening's diners looked on with titillated curiosity.

After a round of toasts, the men adjourned to the club room upstairs. A special table, once again roped off and centered in the room, waited in a blaze of light. Throughout the club customers interrupted play and craned for a better view of the renowned gambling man from Tombstone. Short nodded to Marie as he led them to the table, and she gave him a lighthearted wink. The last two players, perhaps fearful of losing their place, were already seated at the table.

Short quickly reviewed the rules of the game. The buy-in for a seat was ten thousand dollars, and a player could replenish his stake at any time. The deal would pass after every hand, with the dealer's choice limited to draw or stud. Though a gentleman's game, it was nonetheless serious poker, and a player was allowed to check his bet and then raise any bet made. Three raises were permitted, with a hundred-dollar ante and a betting limit of one thousand dollars. A player was entitled to replenish his stake only with the funds on his person. No borrowing allowed.

None of the men were surprised that Short took a seat in the game. His reputation was unimpeachable, and his presence ensured that every card dealt would be dealt on the square. Nor were the men concerned that they would be pitted against two of the elite among the ranks of professional gamblers. If anything, going head-to-head with Richard Clark *and* Luke Short made the game all the more tantalizing. A man who won in such company would have won far more than money. He would have claimed bragging rights for life.

A half hour into the game the deal passed to Frank

Wilcox, the liquor wholesaler. He dealt five-card stud, the first card down and four exposed one at a time. On the opening round, Van Zandt was high with a king showing, and he bet two hundred. Clark, who had a nine up, raised three hundred and the other players folded. Van Zandt deliberated a moment, studying the nine, then called the raise. As the hand played out, Van Zandt caught a queen on the fifth card, pairing one already on the board. He bet five hundred.

Clark, with a pair of fours showing, raised the limit. "Your five, Mr. Van Zandt, and a thousand more."

Van Zandt stared at the fours. He looked up, assessing Clark's features, and found nothing there but a pleasant smile. He folded his cards with a heavy sigh.

"I know it's not good poker," he said with an apologetic shrug. "But perhaps you'll look on it as an act of charity, Mr. Clark. I'm undone by my own curiosity. Two pair or three of a kind?"

"I understand," Clark said amiably. "As one sporting man to another, I'm happy to make an exception to the rules." He turned his hole card, a jack. "It appears I have a pair—both fours."

"I'll be damned!" Van Zandt said, clearly astonished. "You raised into my queens with a pair of fours? *A pair of fours.*"

"I plead guilty to an unmitigated bluff. But, of course, that's poker, Mr. Van Zandt."

Van Zandt was forced to smile. "Sir, I compliment your bold and unorthodox play. The lesson was worth every nickel of my five hundred."

Clark raked in the pot. "Perhaps you'll catch me out next time, Mr. Van Zandt. Who knows?"

Short kept a straight face. He was amused by Clark's clever tactics, performed with guileless skill. In responding to Van Zandt's curiosity, Clark had actually seized on opportunity and planted a seed of doubt. From now on, the other players might suspect he was bluffing on a weak hand. But then, never certain, they would wonder if he held a strong hand and was simply trying to sucker them into a raise. Their confusion worked to Clark's advantage, which was smart poker. He now held a slight edge.

A commotion toward the rear of the room attracted Short's attention. He saw a customer arguing with the dealer at the twenty-one table. Another customer suddenly joined in the argument and they both began berating the dealer. The sound of the dispute abruptly grew louder, and considerably more heated. He rose from his chair.

"Deal me out," he said, nodding to the other players. "I won't be long."

Short walked toward the commotion. There were rarely any problems in the club, and he'd never experienced difficulty at the twenty-one table. The game had originated in France, and *vingt-et-un* was reputed to have been Napoleon's favorite. Imported to New Orleans, it had spread westward, and eventually became a staple in most gaming parlors. The simplicity of it made it popular.

The game was fast, decided on the turn of a few cards. Whether there was one bettor or more, every player was on his own and went directly against the house. The closest hand to a count of twenty-one, whether the dealer or a player, was declared the winner. Sam Moore, the dealer, was one of the most capable men in the club. There had never been a complaint at his table.

The shouting match suddenly got louder. Short pushed through the crowd as the two customers directed their anger at Moore. One of the men was stoutly built, with a gold tooth and broad features. The other was lean and muscular, with muddy eyes and close-cropped hair. The one with the gold tooth slammed his hand on the table.

"You're a goddamn tinhorn!" he bellowed. "You've been cheatin' the whole night!"

Short eased alongside the men. "What's the problem here?"

"You're Luke Short, aren't you? Don't you run this place?"

"You have the advantage of me."

"I'm Earl Porter and this here's my friend Will Rutledge."

"I'll ask you again, Mr. Porter. What's the problem?"

"We've been cheated," Porter said hotly. "Your dealer's an out-and-out cardsharp."

Short glanced across the table. "How'd this get started, Sam?"

"Search me, Mr. Short." Moore nodded at the two men. "Between them, they haven't lost a hundred dollars. All of a sudden, this one"—he indicated Porter—"claimed I was using a marked deck."

"Marked how?"

"See for yourself," Porter chimed in. "He pricked all the high cards. I just caught on a minute ago."

The practice was common in rigged games. A pinprick on the undersurface raised an almost undetectable nub on the top of the card. Dealers with sensitive fingers could "read" the cards by touch, and deal seconds with only slight risk of detection. By holding back high cards, or dealing them to put a player over twenty-one, the house gained an insurmountable edge. There was no chance at all for a player to win.

Short took the deck off the table. He riffled through the cards and felt the telltale nubs on the top surface. When he fanned the deck, he saw that every card, ten through ace, was marked. Never for a moment did he suspect Sam Moore of crooked dealing; but someone had skillfully marked the entire deck. His attention turned to Porter and Rutledge.

"Are you gentlemen from Fort Worth?"

" 'Course we are," Porter said. "What's that got to do with anything?"

"Maybe nothing," Short said levelly. "Where are you employed?"

"Listen, mister, we're the ones that got cheated! Where we work's none of your goddamn business."

The reaction was an octave too strident, and oddly evasive. Short inspected the men closer, and his eye was drawn to a ring on Porter's right hand. A sudden sixth sense gave him the answer. "Would you mind if I have a look at that ring?"

"Yeah, I'd mind," Porter bridled. "We come to the White Elephant and get gypped, and you start with the questions. You got a helluva nerve!"

Short fixed him with a stare. "Let me see the ring."

"Kiss my ass."

Porter launched a whistling haymaker. Short side-stepped the punch, whipping his coattail aside in the same motion, and drew his pistol. His arm lashed out and he laid the barrel of the Colt across Porter's skull with a solid *thunk*. Porter dropped to his knees, then fell to the floor. He was down and out.

Short wagged the snout of his pistol at Rutledge. "Hands in the air."

Rutledge hastily thrust his arms overhead. Short knelt down and twisted Porter's right hand palm-side up. On the inside band of the ring was a short, sharp spike, so small that it was all but unnoticeable. In the trade, it was known as a needle ring, and its sole purpose was to mark cards. The tiny pinpricks on the twenty-one deck were a mystery no longer.

A cold sensation rippled along Short's backbone. He stood, scowling at Rutledge. "Who put you up to this?"

Rutledge avoided his gaze. "I don't know what you're talkin' about. We just come in to play cards."

For a moment, Short considered having them arrested. But then, just as quickly, he discarded the notion. He ordered Rutledge to lift his friend off the floor, and with Moore's help, they got the unconscious man draped over Rutledge's shoulder. The crowd parted to let them through, a murmured buzz trailing in their wake. He escorted Rutledge out of the club.

Jake Johnson, all but dumbstruck, rushed forward as they came down the stairs. "Good God, Luke, what happened?"

"Somebody tried a set-up," Short said. "These boys were the stooges."

"What kind of set-up?"

"A fix to get us charged with crooked games."

Rutledge staggered out the front door under his load. Short gave him a boot in the rump, and he fell, spilling Porter onto the sidewalk. Several passersby stopped, their mouths agape, and stood gawking at the sight. Porter lay limp as a dead dog, and Rutledge slowly pushed himself to his feet. He darted a look across the street.

Short followed his gaze. He saw Joe and Kate Lowe, with Courtright at their side, staring out the window of the Centennial. Johnson saw them at the same time, and he grunted something under his breath. He glanced at Short.

"You think they're behind this?"

"Jake, I'd say it's the safest bet in town."

Short flipped a mocking salute in the direction of the Centennial. Then, holstering his pistol, he left Johnson on the sidewalk and turned back through the door. Upstairs, he traded a dark look with Marie, and collected himself as he approached the roped-off poker table. He took his chair.

"Sorry for the disturbance," he said with easy nonchalance. "Did I miss anything worth the telling?"

The men stared at him in dumbfounded silence. Finally, with a chortling laugh, Richard Clark shook his head. "Luke, I see you haven't lost your touch."

Short smiled. "Gentlemen, let's play poker. Ante a hundred."

Chapter 16

A fiery sun went down in a splash of orange and gold beyond the river. All along Main Street the lamplights winked to life as a cold, wintry dusk settled over the town. The Acre cranked into gear for another night of sin for sale.

Off the corner of Twelfth Street, lights flickered through the plate-glass windows of the Empress Saloon. Like most dives in the Acre, the Empress was devoted to games of chance and cheap liquor, a hangout for workingmen. A long bar occupied one wall, with a gaudy clutch of whiskey bottles reflected in a dulled mirror of ancient origins. On either side of the mirror hung paintings of frolicking women in various states of undress.

Opposite the bar were faro and twenty-one layouts, anchored by a dice table near the door and a roulette wheel at the other end. Toward the rear of the room were four tables for those who preferred poker in their pursuit of fortune. The hour was early, with suppertime still claiming the evening crowd, and three of the tables were empty. A lamp, suspended from the ceiling, cast a halo of light across the fourth table. Five men sat slouched over their cards.

Dave Miller, owner of the Empress, was dealing. On his left were three Missouri Pacific men, employed at the railyards, who worked the graveyard shift. Directly opposite him was Harry Leigh, known to friends and associates as a cardsharp of passing skill. Leigh operated in many guises, frequently changing his appearance, and drifted from dive to dive throughout the Acre. His guise tonight was that of a farmer, with filthy bib overalls and the odoriferous fragrance of hog dung. He was working in league with Miller.

"Tell you, boys," Miller said as Leigh won yet another pot. "For a pig farmer, he's hell on wheels. He ought to be playing up at the White Elephant."

"Wish't to Christ he was." Fred Hoyt, one of the railroad men, took the deck and began shuffling. "With his luck, he'd likely take Clark over the hurdles."

Leigh feigned modesty. "I ain't in their class, no siree. Ten thousand just to get yerself a chair." He mugged slackjawed amazement. "Jehoshaphat!"

Richard Clark and his run at the White Elephant was the talk of the town. In three days, he was rumored to have won four thousand dollars, some said closer to five. For workingmen, whose wages seldom exceeded fifty dollars a month, the sum was staggering. Their brand of poker was two-bit ante and a dollar limit.

Some played merely as a pastime, and others chased the end of the rainbow. Yet their universal attitude was that every game was rigged in some manner. The Acre served as a magnet to tinhorns and confidence men, ever on the lookout for an easy mark. A few worked alone, but the majority operated in league with one or more confederates. The game of choice was poker, and the wiles they employed were seemingly endless. Their craft, the ability to cheat, was brazen by any standard.

A favorite dodge of cardsharps was to introduce a marked deck into a game. The practice was so common that "readers," cards with secret marks on the backs of the deck, were widely advertised by manufacturers. Another trick was shaved cards, trimmed along the sides, employed by those with the dexterity to stack a deck, or deal from the bottom. Mastery of the various tricks required a deft touch, and no small amount of time devoted to practice. A cardsharp, no less than a magician, relied on sleight-of-hand.

Hoyt, the railroad man, finished shuffling. The game was into its second hour, and he was down almost fifteen dollars, a week's pay. Something about it smelled fishy, and his suspicion centered on the proprietor, Dave Miller. All too often, when Miller dealt, the hog farmer ended up with the winning hand. Stranger still, the farmer frequently dealt Miller a winner. He suspected they were in cahoots.

After Miller cut, Hoyt prepared to deal. He called five-card draw, waiting for the men to ante, and idly ran his finger along the side of the deck. His expression changed, and he suddenly felt like a dunce, for he hadn't caught it in all the times he'd dealt. With his fingertip, he detected that they were playing with a "stripper" deck, one in which the high cards had been trimmed ever so slightly on the edges. He was no tyro at poker, and that made him feel all the more foolish. He placed the deck on the table.

"Them cards are crooked," he said sourly. "Somebody put a shaved deck into the game."

Miller gave him a dirty look. "You've got a helluva nerve. Those are house cards."

Hoyt collected the deck. With a careful touch, he dealt two stacks of cards, one small and one large. He turned over the smaller stack, revealing mostly aces and face cards. The other two railroad men exchanged a glance, aware that the situation had suddenly turned dangerous. Dave Miller was known to have a violent streak.

"I don't want no trouble," Hoyt said in a tight voice. "Give us our money back and we'll call it quits."

"Mister, you'd better haul ass," Miller said roughly. "I don't let no man call me a card cheat."

"I ain't leavin' here without my money."

"Like hell!"

Miller kicked back his chair. He pulled a pistol from

a shoulder holster inside his coat, and covered the three
men. The house bouncer, a bullet-headed gorilla with
mean eyes, hurried from his post by the roulette table.
At Miller's command, he grabbed Hoyt by the collar and
manhandled him toward the door. The other railroad
workers were prodded along by Miller, his pistol at their
backs. The bouncer bodily tossed Hoyt into the street.

"Don't come back!" Miller yelled. "You're not welcome here no more."

The door slammed shut. Hoyt got himself untangled,
and scrambled to his feet. A dark look of rage settled
over his face, his eyes cold as a stone adder. His hand
dipped inside his coat and came out with a stubby bulldog revolver. One of the workmen tried to restrain him.

"C'mon, Fred, don't make it worse."

"Nobody puts a hand on me."

"You're gonna get yourself killed."

"Lemme be, goddamnit!"

The railroad men hastily retreated across the street.
On the sidewalk, passersby scurried for cover as Hoyt
raised his revolver. He took deliberate aim on one of the
plate-glass windows fronting the Empress, and fired. The
window imploded, shattered by the slug, and shards of
glass rained down in a splintering shower. His next shot
blew out the other window.

Miller stepped into the gaping hole of the first window. As his pistol came level, the mule-drawn streetcar
approached the intersection. He fired three quick shots,
the reports echoing off nearby buildings. The first
plucked at the sleeve of Hoyt's coat just as the streetcar
trundled into the line of fire. The second struck the
driver and the third dusted a passenger who sat facing
the saloon. The mule took off at a lumbering gallop.

Hoyt abruptly decided to quit the fight. He winged a
final shot, which whistled harmlessly through the maw
of the window frame. As he turned to run, Miller drew
a fine bead, tracking him, and fired. The slug drilled
Hoyt below the left shoulder and exited in a spray of

blood through his breastbone. His legs kept pumping a moment, jerking him forward in a nerveless dance, then stopped. He fell facedown in the middle of the intersection.

The mule dragged the streetcar all the way to the end of the line. The driver stumbled off, clutching at his side, blood seeping through his fingers. He collapsed at the edge of the tracks.

The passenger sat dead in his seat.

The meeting was hastily organized. On the east side of Courthouse Square, the lights burned brightly in the First National Bank. The men began arriving shortly before eight o'clock.

Karl Van Zandt was the nominal leader of the conclave. On his own initiative, he had invited prominent spokesmen from diverse fields within the community. The men represented business and industry, church and state, and county law enforcement. They took seats arranged in an orderly row outside the bank vault.

"Gentlemen," Van Zandt opened the meeting, standing before them. "I asked you here to discuss a perilous situation. Earlier tonight there was a shootout in the Acre." He paused, his expression solemn. "You may already have heard that two men were killed and one was wounded."

"God have mercy on their souls," intoned Reverend Francis Grant, pastor of the First Baptist Church. "Do I have it correct? The two unfortunates were a railroad worker and a passenger on the streetcar?"

Van Zandt nodded soberly. "I gather a saloonkeeper and one of his customers, the railroad man, became involved in a dispute. A gunfight developed and the customer was killed."

"And the streetcar conductor?" Grant asked. "Have you heard anything on his condition?"

"The latest reports are that he will live."

"What about the saloonkeeper?" interrupted Thomas

Anderson, the largest industrialist in town. "Has he been taken into custody?"

"So I understand," Van Zandt replied. "He was arrested shortly after the incident. He's being held in the city jail."

"Why wasn't I informed?" barked Ned Bowlin, chief prosecutor of Tarrant County. "Murder falls under my jurisdiction. It's a capital offense!"

"Don't feel bad," Sheriff Walter Maddox said indignantly. "I only heard about it an hour ago."

The group erupted in a harsh murmur of agreement. In addition to the sheriff and the county prosecutor, Judge Edward Hovenkamp, who presided over the district court, was present. The clergy, apart from Francis Grant, was represented by Reverend Thomas Jefferson Mayweather, pastor of the Methodist Evangelical Church, and Father John O'Malley, pastor of St. Patrick's Catholic Church. Thomas Anderson, the wealthiest man in Fort Worth, and Van Zandt were the acknowledged leaders of the town's business interests.

"Gentlemen, gentlemen!" Van Zandt quieted them with upraised palms. "I've asked you here in an effort to mobilize our efforts in a common cause. Let's get to the heart of the matter."

Father O'Malley looked at him. "What is it you have in mind?"

"A coalition to rid our community of Hell's Half Acre."

The statement was met with stunned surprise. "Glory hallelujah!" Reverend Mayweather exclaimed. "Do you believe in miracles, Karl?"

"I do indeed," Van Zandt said firmly. "To the extent that I've asked the *Democrat* and the *Gazette* to hold the presses on their morning editions. I told them we would have an announcement by ten tonight."

Under other circumstances, Van Zandt would have made a brilliant military tactician. His strategy was to bring together diverse factions, each with their own axe to grind, and unite them in a common goal. The court-house crowd, until now consigned to a secondary role in Tarrant County, would jump at any chance to wrest control of the political machinery from City Hall. The clergy, ever eager to rail against sin and depravity, would rally their parishioners under the banner of deliverance and march forth to battle Satan. The battleground, appropriately, would be Hell's Half Acre.

The business community would readily climb aboard the bandwagon. Among the uptown crowd there was already strong sentiment to wipe out the image of Fort Worth as a crass and backward cowtown. All the more, there was underlying support to propel the city toward a new century, with an image of progressive sophistication and industrial might. There were even now two foundries, three planing mills, and plants manufacturing carriages, boilers and windmills. Civic leaders would gladly raze Hell's Half Acre to the ground to create further room for expansion.

Until tonight, the one element lacking was an offense so onerous that it would bond the various factions together into a cohesive force. A bloody shootout with innocent men dead and wounded seemed to Van Zandt the glue necessary to form a coalition. He faced the assembled leaders.

"We must somehow arouse the public," he said forcefully. "Enlist their support in an all-out campaign against the sporting crowd. Not to put too strong a word on it—a crusade."

"Yes, indeed, a *crusade!*" Reverend Grant echoed, his eyes afire. "I will deliver a sermon to my congregation along those very lines. Smite the Philistines in our midst!"

The other clergymen nodded approval. Anderson motioned for the group's attention. "Newspaper articles and sermons are all well and good. But what we desperately need is an organization, and a man with the zeal to lead the fight. I believe that man is the one who summoned us here tonight—Karl Van Zandt.''

There was a moment of strained silence. At length, when no one spoke out, Judge Hovencamp turned to Van Zandt. ''Karl, you are one of the most respected men in Fort Worth. At the same time, your penchant for gambling is widely known. That might well create opposition in some quarters.''

Van Zandt appeared bemused. ''Judge, the White Elephant is a gentleman's club. Some of the finest men in town frequent the place.''

''Yes, that's true. But it is still a gambling den operated by the sporting crowd. Like it or not, the onus is there.''

Reverend Mayweather pursed his mouth. ''You could hardly lead a crusade if you continue to associate with gamblers. People just wouldn't understand that, not at all.''

''I didn't ask for the job,'' Van Zandt said. ''Anyone here is qualified to lead the fight. Appoint someone else.''

''No,'' Anderson said flatly. ''We have to rally the public to our cause. A banker will be seen as representing the community as a whole. You are the *only* man for the job.''

''Excellent point,'' Judge Hovencamp agreed. ''A politician, even a clergyman, wouldn't be seen in the same light. Of course, the gambling is a problem. Any way around that, Karl?''

Van Zandt deliberated on it, aware of their scrutiny. ''All right,'' he said finally. ''From now on, you may consider me an ex-gambler. I'll make a statement to the newspapers tonight.''

''A man of conscience!'' Father O'Malley declared. ''Renouncing vice in all its forms. That will make a fine headline.''

The group voted Van Zandt the president of their fledgling organization. They then considered the matter of a proper name for their reform movement. A unanimous stamp of approval went to the one suggested by Judge Hovencamp.

The Citizens' Law and Order Association.

Chapter 17

A knock sounded at the door. Short, attired in trousers and a silk dressing robe, crossed the sitting room. He unlocked the door and swung it open.

"Good morning, Mr. Short."

"Good morning, Amos."

The waiter rolled a serving cart into the room. Sometimes, when they slept late, Short ordered breakfast brought to the suite. Marie was a picky eater in the morning, usually toast and a soft-boiled egg. Short awoke famished every morning, and today was no exception. Apart from a pot of coffee, his order included bacon and eggs with a generous portion of fried potatoes. He waited while the waiter extended wings on the cart to form a linen-covered table.

"There we are, sir," the waiter said, motioning to the china and silver tableware. "I'll just leave the warmer covers on till you're ready."

"Thank you, Amos," Short said, slipping him three dollars. "We'll serve ourselves."

"Yessir, and thank you, Mr. Short. Always a pleasure serving you. Left you the morning paper on the table."

"You think of everything, Amos."

"I surely do try, Mr. Short. Surely do."

Short escorted him to the door. Once it was closed and locked, he turned back into the sitting room and crossed to the bedroom. The bedcovers were still mussed, and the room smelled vaguely of spent ardor. He oftentimes awoke randy, refreshed by sleep and full of ginger. Today was one of those days.

Outside the bathroom he rapped lightly on the door. "Time to face the world, lazybones. Breakfast is served."

"Hold your horses." Marie's disembodied voice floated through the door. "I'll be out in a minute."

"I've heard that story before. Your food's getting cold."

"You're the one who ravaged me before I got my eyes open. Give a girl a break!"

"Don't make yourself too beautiful. We might have to skip breakfast."

"Aren't you the dreamer."

Short chuckled, walking back to the sitting room. He moved to the table and poured himself a cup of coffee. He unfolded the *Democrat*, glancing at the headline, and the cup stopped halfway to his mouth. His face drained of color.

TOWN LEADERS DEMAND VICE CRACKDOWN

The banner headline leaped off the front page. Quickly, fearing the worst, he scanned the lengthy article. The muscles in his jaw tightened, and he set his coffee cup aside. He read the article through again, more slowly this time, absorbing details. The gist of it was that the most prominent men in Fort Worth had formed a coalition to bring about reform. Karl Van Zandt, newly elected president of the coalition, called on all public-minded citizens to join in the movement. The goal was nothing less than complete and total eradication of Hell's Half Acre.

Like everyone else in town, Short had heard of the shootout early yesterday evening. But the owner of the saloon had been arrested, and he'd thought that was the end of an unfortunate incident. Clearly, from what the newspaper reported, that was just the beginning, an excuse for the reformers to mobilize. Worse yet, influential business leaders had joined forces with the churches and the key politicos in the courthouse. He was shocked even more that Van Zandt, a confirmed high roller, would foreswear gambling. The implications were staggering.

"How do I look?"

Marie struck a pose in the bedroom doorway. She wore a filmy pink peignoir over a sheer nightgown, and the combination left little to the imagination. Her cheeks were lightly rouged, her lips bee-stung red, and her eyes sparkled with devilry. She looked like innocence lost.

Short barely glanced at her. His features were still leeched of color and he appeared somehow stricken. She hurried across the room, frightened by his expression, and even more, his unresponsive silence. Only a moment ago he'd been joking with her.

"Luke." She touched his arm. "What's the matter, sugar?"

Short handed her the newspaper. "See for yourself."

The headline stopped her for an instant. Then her brow furrowed in tiny lines as she read the article. The full import of it struck her only when she came across Van Zandt's name. She lowered the paper, her face a question mark.

"Why would Van Zandt get involved with reformers? He's one of our biggest high rollers."

"Change that to the past tense," Short said. "He *was* one of our biggest high rollers. I seriously doubt we'll see him at Clark's table tonight."

Richard Clark was still the main attraction at the White Elephant. Over the past four days, his game had seesawed back and forth; but he was nonetheless reported to be ahead by several thousand dollars. A growing list of men were anxious to try his game before he left town. He was scheduled to depart for Tombstone in three days.

"I'm a little lost here," Marie said. "Is it Van Zandt that has you looking like a ghost?"

"Yes and no," Short said, reclaiming the newspaper and staring at the headline. "Any number of men will grab Van Zandt's seat tonight. But his involvement with reformers is another matter entirely."

"Why do you say that?"

"A reformed gambler is like a reformed drunk. People tend to put them on a pedestal and treat their pronouncements like Moses offering up the Burning Tablets. Van Zandt's the perfect man to lead a crusade."

"But the article talks about reform in the Acre. What does that have to do with us?"

"Don't believe what you read in the papers. Once the do-gooders get started, they never quit. The Acre's just the opening gun."

She seemed unconvinced. "How could they ever touch the White Elephant? Some of the most important men in town play at our tables."

"Did you see the list of names here?" Short said, waving the newspaper. "A judge and ministers, not to mention Thomas Anderson. I hear he doesn't drink, smoke, or gamble. And he's got more money than God."

"You're saying he'll finance the reformers?"

"I'm saying it's like a snowball. The farther it rolls, the bigger it gets. Things like this take on momentum all their own."

"A snowball," she said, considering the thought. "So it could spread to the uptown clubs."

"In the blink of an eye," Short affirmed. "Uptown or downtown, it's all the same to reformers. They lump one with another."

"Well, you can't do anything about it right this minute. Let's have breakfast before it gets cold."

"I've lost my appetite."

Short tossed the newspaper on the table. He stared off into space, chasing the phantoms of his past. He re-

called all too vividly the reformers of Dodge City, and
the futility of one man taking on the entrenched powers.
With the success of the White Elephant, he thought he'd
outdistanced those older hazards. Yet he saw now that
it wasn't so. A man had to adapt to survive.

"You look so far away." Her voice broke into his
ruminations. "What are you thinking?"

"I'm thinking that the sporting crowd doesn't have a
chance against reformers. And like it or not, we're part
of the sporting crowd."

"So where does that leave us?"

"If you can't beat 'em, join them," Short said, toying
with the germ of an idea. "There's only one way to save
the uptown clubs. We have to clean up the Acre."

"You're not serious!" she said. "How on earth
would you do that?"

"Joe Lowe."

"What?"

"Rowdy Joe," Short said, nodding to himself. "In
the Acre, he's King of the Hill. I'll have a talk with
him."

"Good luck, lover." Her eyes were skeptical.
"You're not exactly Lowe's bosom buddy. Why would
he listen?"

"The root of all evil—money."

"You mean to appeal to his greed?"

"I'll try to be more tactful. But, yes, that's the general idea."

Short's appetite was suddenly restored. While Marie
picked at her food, he tore into his breakfast with renewed vitality. Lowe was a gambler, and among the fraternity, there was a common language. The language of
survivors.

He thought Rowdy Joe would listen to reason.

The Centennial was in the midst of the afternoon lull.
The noon-hour rush had come and gone, and the bar-
room was practically empty. Lights were dimmed in the

theater, and the upstairs club was all but deserted. The nighttime crowd, like vampire bats, awaited the coming of dark.

Lowe sat alone in his office. His feet were propped on the desk, hands locked behind his head, and a soggy, unlit cigar jutted from the corner of his mouth. His gaze was fixed somewhere between infinity and eternity, and his mind was centered on what might or might not be a problem. He was thinking of the morning headlines.

There was an irritating familiarity to the whole mess. Years ago, when he was hopscotching about the Kansas cowtowns, he'd come across reformers in every guise. The toughest of them all, and he chortled at the memory, was the Ladies Temperance League. He recalled that they hated whiskey worse than the devil hated Holy Water. And for a bunch of old biddies in whalebone corsets, they were rough customers. He had never quite gotten the hang of fighting women.

The men do-gooders were horses of a different color. For the most part preachers, sometimes aligned with sanctimonious businessmen, they were considerably less formidable than the women, and rarely as well organized. Lowe employed a combination of threats and bribes, and an occasional back-alley beating, to persuade them that righteousness was a misguided notion. In every instance, he had either outlasted them or outfought them, and he had never lost the battle. Do-gooders, to his way of thinking, were all cream puffs.

Today, munching his cigar, he contemplated the latest development in Fort Worth. The highfalutin moniker "Citizens' Law and Order Association" gave him a laugh. He was singularly unimpressed by the roster of charter members in what smacked of county politicians squaring off against City Hall. Van Zandt and Anderson were the only businessmen involved, and the clergymen were a matter of no great consequence. He'd decided long ago that preachers were as worthless as tits on a boar hog. The underpinning for the whole thing, he told himself, was a grab for political power. The Bible-thumpers were just along for the headlines.

The thing that bothered him most was the arrest of Dave Miller. From all he'd heard, and what he read in the newspapers, Miller was almost certain to be convicted of manslaughter. One of the killings was provoked, and the other accidental, and it seemed unlikely the saloonkeeper would ever face a hangman's noose. All of which infuriated Lowe, and left him with a sense of justice undone. Had the police been less efficient, he would have made an object lesson of Miller for all the Acre to see. Anybody that stupid, he mused, deserved to be shot down and dumped in the gutter. Only a dim-dot got caught dealing crooked by a railyard grease-monkey!

"Afternoon, Joe." Short stepped through the doorway. "Looks like you're taking your leisure."

Lowe swung his feet to the floor. "Who let you in here?"

"I asked up front for directions. One of the barmen told me how to find your office."

"I'll tend to him later. What d'you want?"

"We need to talk." Short invited himself to take a chair. "I assume you've read the morning papers."

"I read 'em," Lowe said gruffly. "So what?"

"So we've got ourselves a problem. By 'we,' I mean the uptown club owners."

"How's it got anything to do with the uptown clubs?"

Short lit a cheroot. "Think of it as a cholera epidemic," he said, the words ringed in smoke. "Once it starts in the Acre, it will spread uptown. None of us are immune."

"You scare easy, don't you?" Lowe leaned back in his chair. "Who says it'll get started in the Acre?"

"Joe, there's an old Chinese proverb. Something along the lines of never underestimate your enemy. Van

Zandt and his crowd will mobilize the whole town. They're already calling it a crusade.''

"Quit dancin' around and get to it. What are you after?''

"You call the shots in the Acre,'' Short said. "Order a cleanup of your own—put a lid on the violence before the reformers get themselves organized. Take the play away from them.''

Lowe grunted a corrosive laugh. "The chumps that go there like the Acre just the way it is. Hell, we'd lose half our business.''

"How would you like to lose the Centennial?''

"Well, don't you see, that'll never happen. All this bullshit about reform will fizzle out before it gets started. Nothing's gonna change in the Acre—or uptown.''

Short exhaled smoke. "What makes you so sure?''

"Simplest thing there is,'' Lowe informed him. "I control the vote in the Acre. Those jaybirds in City Hall will do whatever I tell 'em. Nobody's fixin' to support these do-gooders.''

"Nobody except the churches, and the courthouse crowd, and the business community. You're underestimating the opposition.''

"C'mon, Short, get your head screwed on straight. How's anybody gonna have reform without City Hall? Just won't happen.''

"You're wrong, Joe,'' Short said pointedly. "The old days are long gone, dead as a doornail. We're living in a whole new world.''

"Yeah?'' Lowe said, amused. "What's your crystal ball tell you?''

"Van Zandt's not some half-baked preacher. He'll rally public support and turn this town upside down. You're in for the fight of your life.''

"Let's just suppose you're right. Where do you stand?''

"Not with you.''

"Where, then?''

"I'll look after my own. I always have."

"That sounds a little bit like a threat."

"Take it any way you like it."

Short got to his feet. Lowe watched him out the door, his eyes dark with anger. He lit his soggy cigar and took a long, thoughtful puff. His mouth razored into a thin smile.

He told himself to get on with skinning the cat.

Chapter 18

Sunday was like any other day in the Acre. Working-men had the day off and few of them observed the Sabbath. Their interests centered instead on women, whiskey and cards, usually in that order. Lust forever rode roughshod over the Seventh Commandment.

Dolly Love came downstairs shortly before nine o'clock. A splitting headache had awakened her almost an hour earlier, and she'd finally given up hope of getting back to sleep. Last night, like any Saturday night, hadn't ended until around three, when she ran the last customer out. She felt doped with only four hours' sleep.

The house was located on Rusk, between Fourteenth and Fifteenth. Dolly owned the property, and she prided herself on running an orderly establishment. Her girls were comely and wholesome, selected as much for their deportment as their looks. Her cardinal rule, rigidly enforced, was that they conduct themselves as ladies. She liked to think of them as courtesans rather than whores.

A buxom woman in her late thirties, she operated one of the classier parlor houses in the Acre. Her real name was Erma Latsky, but she had long ago adopted a sobriquet more in keeping with her profession. She was a good manager, stern but understanding with her girls, and she never allowed riffraff to frequent her house. Some of the wealthiest men in town were regular patrons, and their secrets were safe with her. She catered to their tastes, no matter how bizarre, with discretion.

The rear of the house faced east, and bright sunshine flooded the kitchen windows. Dolly uttered a moan, shielding her eyes with her arm, as she came through the door. The light lanced her head like a knife, and her temples throbbed with blinding pain. She walked to a cabinet, pulling down a bottle of Dr. Hostetter's Celebrated Bitters. The nostrum purported to cure everything from bilious fever to old age. She took a long slug of the foul-tasting liquid.

The potion, like most patent medicines, was heavily laced with alcohol. The effect was immediate and pleasant, and the pounding in her head diminished as the dose rippled through her system. She took another shot for good measure and returned the bottle to the cabinet. Then she turned on the tap, splashed her face with cold water, and drew a deep, slow breath. She felt almost human.

No one else was about so early in the morning. The cook generally arrived around ten o'clock, and the house opened for business at two on Sundays. Dolly debated making a pot of coffee, and quickly discarded the idea. The wood stove was cold and she was in no mood to kindle a fire. She dried her face with a dish towel, idly wondering where all her energy had gone. There was a time, she remembered, when she could go all day and all night without a wink of sleep. She thought there was everything to be said for youth.

A flash of color outside caught her attention. She peered through the window, trying to block the sun with her arm, but the light was too strong. Some twenty yards behind the house, the woodshed stood silhouetted against the flare of the early morning sun. On the front of the woodshed, something fluttered in the breeze, and she sensed that it was cloth of some sort. Her curiosity was piqued, for she couldn't imagine why cloth of any nature would be attached to the woodshed. Yet she was unable to make it out against the light. She decided to have a look.

The wind was sharp. Dolly pulled her housecoat tighter as she moved through the door into the backyard. She advanced a few steps, still shielding her eyes, until the roof of the shed obscured the glint of the sunlight. She suddenly stopped, her mouth ovaled in a gasp, unable to credit what she thought she saw. At first she told herself it was a scarecrow, someone's idea of a crude joke. But then, forcing herself a few steps closer, a rush of bile scalded her throat. She recognized Velma.

The girl was nailed to the wall of the woodshed. Her skirt fluttered in the wind, a glimmer of cerulean blue in the bright sunlight. Her throat was scarlet, cut from ear to ear, open like a gaping mouth in a hideous grin. The front of her dress was splotched with caked blood, dark reddish-brown from the cold night air. Her arms were spread wide, hands spiked to the wall with ten-penny nails, still another driven through her crossed feet. She hung limp, her eyes white with terror, crucified on the wall of a whorehouse woodshed. A bloodied hammer lay at her feet on the ground.

Dolly Love ran screaming toward the street.

Officer Gabe Rowan was the first policeman on the scene. Summoned by the screams, he sprinted over from Main Street and found the hysterical madam pointing at the rear of her house. In the backyard he stopped, his gorge brackish, stupefied by the sight. He vomited his breakfast on the ground.

Some thirty minutes later, Marshal Bill Rea rounded the corner of the house. A crowd was gathered on the street, and girls from neighboring bordellos stood watching from their windows. By now there were three policemen in the backyard, their eyes hollow, their features dazed. Rea walked past them, halting a few paces from the woodshed. His stomach turned upside down.

"Who . . ." He swallowed hard. "Who was the first man here?"

Officer Rowan moved forward. "I'd just come on duty. Heard Dolly Love screamin' all the way over on Main."

"Who's the girl?"

"Her name's Velma Banks. She works for Dolly."

"Not anymore," Rea observed quietly. "Was this how you found her?"

"Just like that," Rowan said, trying not to look at the girl. "Goddamn, what a way to die."

"Have you questioned Dolly?"

"Figured I'd wait for you, Marshal. She's half crazy."

"Wouldn't wonder."

Rea slowly inspected the girl. The dried blood told him she had been killed hours ago, sometime during the night. A gout of blood on the ground indicated she'd been cut, her throat ripped open, and bled to death where she had fallen. All the signs led to the conclusion that she had been killed before being crucified. Her killer had then taken his time nailing her to the wall.

"Somebody went off his rocker," Rea said in a deliberate tone. "That's the work of a man gone mad-dog wild."

Rowan kept his gaze averted. "Sonovabitch must've hated her awful bad."

"Any idea where he got the nails and hammer?"

"I looked in the woodshed. There's a bag of nails in there just like that. He didn't have to go far."

"I'll have a word with Dolly. Send one of the boys to fetch the coroner."

"You want her moved?"

"The quicker the better."

Rea walked to the house. He found Dolly Love in the parlor, a sodden handkerchief knotted in her hands. Four girls, still dressed in their nightclothes, were seated around her. Their faces were damp with tears, their eyes wide with shock. He took a chair across from the sofa.

"Dolly," he said gently. "I need to ask you some questions."

She sniffled, dabbing at her eyes. "Oh, God, Bill, she was such a sweet little thing. You've got to hang the bastard."

"You know who did it?"

"I'd bet anything it was Fred Hurst."

"Who's Fred Hurst?"

"A bartender at the Bismark Saloon."

"Why would he kill her?"

"Jealous, that's why!" She took a deep shuddering breath. "He wanted her to quit the business and marry him. She wouldn't do it."

Rea saw the other girls nodding their heads. "Did he ever threaten her?"

"Just last night, after he got off at the Bismark. He was drunk out of his mind, carrying on something awful. They had a terrible row."

"What happened?"

"I had my bouncer throw him out. He almost wrecked the place."

Rea considered a moment. "Any chance she met him later?"

"She must have," Dolly said. "Why else would she have been out there in the middle of the night?"

"How do we know for sure it was Hurst? She could have met anybody."

One of the girls scooted forward on the sofa. "It was Hurst, all right," she said. "Velma told me."

Rea looked at her. "Who are you?"

"Ida May Terrell," the girl said. "Velma and me were best friends."

"What was it Velma told you?"

"Just before Mac—Mac's the bouncer—just before he threw Hurst out, Velma got a word with him. She promised to meet him after we closed."

"Promises are one thing," Rea said. "How do you know she met him?"

Ida May darted a sheepish glance at the madam. "You're not gonna hold it against me, are you?"

"Don't you worry, honey." Dolly patted her on the knee. "You tell the Marshal everything."

"Well, you know . . ." Ida May hesitated, finally nodded to Rea with a little shrug. "We're not supposed to meet men after hours. Velma stopped by my room just before she snuck out."

"Go on," Rea coaxed. "What did she say?"

"Told me she was gonna have it out with Fred Hurst once and for all. She'd had enough of his nonsense."

"And you saw her leave?"

"Yes," Ida May said in a small voice. "She went down the back stairs."

"There you are!" Dolly exclaimed, staring at Rea. "You've got to get him, Bill. Get him and hang him!"

"Don't worry, we'll get him."

Rea left Dolly Love and her girls in the parlor. As he went out the back door, he saw his men lowering Velma Banks to the ground. Doc Phelps, the coroner, watched with a grave expression. Rea's gaze was drawn again to the girl.

He thought the least they could do was hang Fred Hurst.

Early that afternoon, Joe Lowe sat staring at the wall. The door to his office was closed, and he puffed thoughtfully on a cigar. He was considering the matter of dead whores and outraged reformers. One seemed unavoidably linked to the other.

By late that morning word of the girl's murder had spread throughout town. The sensational nature of the killing—a whore crucified—shocked even the most hardened members of the sporting crowd. For Lowe, who viewed the Acre as his personal domain, the timing could not have been worse. He saw it as fodder for the reformers' mill.

A week had passed since the formation of the Law and Order Association. Karl Van Zandt had made several public statements, all duly reported by the newspapers, calling for an end to Hell's Half Acre. Every church in town was solidly behind the movement, and there was widespread support within the business community. But as yet, it was all talk and no action, a furor of words. Nothing to ignite the spark.

Lowe knew that it was all about to change. A crucified whore was far worse than two men shot to death. The reformers would pounce on the brutal nature of the crime and wave it like a battle flag before the public. By tomorrow, the whore would have been transformed into a pathetic victim, a symbol of all that was corrupt and evil in the Acre. The crusade would then have the needed spark, the tinder to inflame action. Unless . . .

The door swung open. Kate moved into the office, followed by a man. "Roy's here."

Roy Tutt was the manager of the Tivoli Saloon, one of the dives owned by Lowe. He was a ferret of a man, lean and quick, with beady eyes and hard features. An overseer of sorts, he led the gang of hooligans Lowe employed in the Acre. He stopped before the desk.

"You sent for me, boss?"

"Have a seat." Lowe motioned him to a chair. "Guess you heard about the girl at Dolly Love's."

"The word's out," Tutt said impassively. "Tough way to go."

Kate laughed. "You're a corker, Roy. Have a little pity, for chrissakes!"

Tutt stared straight ahead. Lowe shot Kate a warning look, then leaned back in his chair. "They're saying some bartender killed her, Fred Hurst. You know him?"

"I've seen him around."

"The law's looking for him. Seems like he disappeared."

Tutt evidenced no surprise. He felt reasonably certain that Lowe's information came from the law itself. He shrugged. "Thing like that, he's smart to run."

"I want him found," Lowe said flatly. "Use your contacts in the Acre and get a lead. Think you can handle that?"

"Don't see why not," Tutt said. "More'n likely, he's hiding out over in Dallas. Somebody'll cough him up."

"Wherever he went, I want him back here by tonight."

"Tonight's a tall order, boss. I dunno about that."

"Get your ears unplugged," Lowe grated. "I said tonight and that's the end of it. You with me?"

Tutt nodded. "I'll get on it."

"Turn out every man on the payroll and start beating the bushes. Don't let me down, Roy."

"What d'you want done with Hurst when we find him?"

"Hold him in the back room at the Tivoli. I'll explain what's to be done once you've got him."

"Whatever you say, boss."

"Do it right and there's a thousand bonus. Don't even think about doing it wrong."

"I'll have him for you tonight."

Tutt rose, bobbing his head, and walked out the door. As his footsteps faded in the hallway, Kate closed the door and took a chair. She gave her husband a strange look.

"A thousand?" she said skeptically. "For some jackass that killed a whore?"

"There's more to it than that, Kate."

"I'd hope so, for a thousand bounty. What've you got up your sleeve, slick?"

"You wouldn't believe me if I told you."

"Try me."

Lowe told her, and he was right. She didn't believe him.

Chapter 19

The White Elephant was almost empty. Monday nights were routinely slow, and the club usually operated on half-staff. Gamblers took their day of rest after the hectic pace of a weekend.

Downstairs, the restaurant business was off as well. Fully a third of the tables were empty at the height of the supper hour. Waiters stood about conversing in low tones, and there was only one bartender on duty. Four solitary drinkers lined the bar.

Short and Marie sat with Jake Johnson at one of the rear tables. They were dining on fresh oysters, freighted by railroad from the Gulf in barrels of ice. The chef prepared what were widely regarded as the finest fried oysters in Fort Worth. His delicate blend of herbs was a closely guarded secret.

"What a genius," Johnson said, savoring a bite of oyster. "Of course, I'm talking about myself, not Antone. The genius was in hiring him."

"Aren't we proud of ourselves," Marie said with a wicked smile. "Antone told me you practically abducted him away from the Lafayette."

Johnson chuckled. "I abducted him by doubling his salary. He's a pirate who passes himself off as a chef."

"Pirate or not . . ." Short speared a chunk of oyster on his fork. "You made the right play, Jake. He's worth every penny."

On Monday evenings Short and Marie generally attended one of the theater shows around town. With the club half empty, and high rollers recuperating from the weekend, they could justify a night just for themselves. Yet they had no plans tonight for catching the latest vaudeville act, or one of the stage shows. For all their jestful banter, their mood was somber.

The morning newspapers carried banner headlines about the death of Velma Banks. Her profession was alluded to with tactful subtlety, noting that she was a resident of a "ladies' boardinghouse" on Rusk Street. Readers of the *Democrat* and the *Gazette* easily translated this polite and somewhat quaint euphemism for a brothel. Her manner of death was treated in a considerably more sensational fashion. The articles spoke of murder by a "severed throat" and went on to recount details of the "beastly crucifixion." No one doubted that a whore had been spiked to the wall of Dolly Love's woodshed.

City Marshal William Rea was quoted as well in the articles. He identified the chief suspect in the case as one Frederick Hurst, a bartender at the Bismark Saloon. His theory as to motive, based on interviews of the dead woman's closest friends, was a lovers' quarrel gone terribly wrong. He went on to state that the Fort Worth Police Department was conducting a citywide manhunt for the suspected murderer. He predicted the imminent arrest of Frederick Hurst.

Short, upon reading the newspapers that morning, felt a quickening sense of dread. The gruesome nature of the murder, he told Marie, would generate added support for the reform movement. The woman's death merely confirmed what everyone already believed: the Acre was a breeding ground for violence. Not an hour later, word began circulating that the predication of Marshal Rea had proved to be only half right. The murder suspect had been found, but not arrested.

The janitor at the courthouse regularly arrived for

work before anyone else. That morning, shortly after seven o'clock, he had discovered the body of a man outside the entrance to the county jail. Within a matter of hours, the sheriff's office identified the dead man as the murder suspect, Frederick Hurst. In a bizarre twist of justice, Hurst's throat was slashed, and his hands and feet were staked to the lawn with tenpenny nails. The parties responsible apparently believed that symbolism delivered its own message. Here was the man who had killed Velma Banks.

By the noon hour, the whole town was talking of nothing else. A rumor took wing that the Citizens' Law and Order Association had been called into emergency session. Not long afterward, printed circulars, signed by Karl Van Zandt, were being handed out on the streets. Van Zandt, as president of the Association, called on all public-spirited citizens to assemble on the courthouse lawn at seven o'clock that evening. There a town forum would be held to decide the future of Fort Worth and Hell's Half Acre. Every man and woman of conscience was urged to attend.

"Aren't we something," Marie said now, finishing the last oyster on her plate. "Stuffing ourselves when there is absolutely nothing to celebrate. It's hardly the night for it."

"Eat, drink and be merry," Short commented wryly, toasting them with his wineglass. "For tomorrow we shall die."

Johnson frowned. "C'mon, Luke, it's not that bad."

"You think not?" Short said, his tone abruptly solemn. "Maybe you shouldn't attend the meeting tonight. You won't like what you hear."

"This whole mess revolves around the Acre. That's what everybody's concerned about."

"Jake, you've never dealt with reformers before. I guarantee you they're not satisfied with half a loaf."

"Luke's right," Marie noted. "The Acre today, the uptown clubs tomorrow. That will be their motto."

"I just can't believe it," Johnson said. "We're legitimate businessmen, just like a mercantile or a pharmacy. We don't get involved in violence."

"Don't we?" Short countered. "Who do you think had Fred Hurst killed?"

Marie gave him an odd look. All day, he'd been brooding on something, though he hadn't voiced his concern aloud. She saw now that he had been deliberating on who killed the killer. She waited to hear what he would say.

"I give up," Johnson conceded. "Who killed Hurst?"

Short nodded toward the street. "Throw a rock and you'll break his window. Our none-too-friendly competitor."

"Joe Lowe?"

"Who else?"

"I don't get it," Johnson said, baffled. "Why would Lowe have him killed? Dolly Love's house isn't one of his joints. Why would he even care?"

"You have to remember something," Short replied. "Rowdy Joe's never been known to play with a full deck. His brain works along curved lines."

"Are you saying he's nuts?"

"I'm saying he's a little skewed. Joe probably got some wild idea that a sacrificial lamb would appease the reformers. So he gave them one—Fred Hurst."

"That's insane!" Marie burst out. "How would another killing appease them? Especially the way it was done."

A sudden silence fell over the table. They all three experienced a chilling vision of a man, his throat cut, staked with nails to the courthouse lawn. At length, Short slowly shook his head. His features were grim.

"An eye for an eye," he said. "Not that Lowe's big on Biblical justice. But I'd guess he thought it would satisfy the uptown crowd." His mouth set in a tight line. "A woman murdered and her killer executed in the same manner. What better form of retribution?"

Marie looked sick. "You really believe he murdered that man in cold blood—don't you?"

"Yeah, I do," Short acknowledged. "I'd tend to doubt he did the dirty work himself. But I'd bet the farm he ordered it done."

"My God." She hugged herself with a shudder. "That makes him worse than the man who killed that poor girl."

"Lowe won't let anybody threaten his control of the Acre. In his own way, he was sending a message to the sporting crowd. Hold down the violence."

"Or else get killed?" she asked. "Is that the message?"

"More or less," Short said. "Odd thing is, it will likely save lives. We'll see less violence in the Acre."

"I've never heard anything so terrible. Don't kill or you'll be killed! That's almost . . . barbarian."

"When you think about it, it's not too different from the state hanging a man for committing murder. Life's full of little ironies."

"Of course it's different!" she protested. "The state has the legal right to execute a murderer. That's the law."

Short shrugged. "Rowdy Joe makes his own laws."

"The man's a damn fool," Johnson said heatedly. "All he's done is make a bad situation worse. What do you think will happen tonight?"

"I think the reformers will declare war."

A faint roar sounded from somewhere downtown. The noise grew steadily louder, voices raised in song over the thump of drums and the blare of trumpets. Short and Marie, followed by Johnson, joined the customers moving toward the front of the restaurant. The sound suddenly rattled the windows.

On the street, Karl Van Zandt appeared at the head of a torchlit parade. Directly behind him was the marching band from Texas Wesleyan College, resplendent in their brass-buttoned uniforms. Formed in ranks of four, to the rear of the band were the town's clergymen and courthouse officials, and a hundred or more men and women. The marchers carried flaming torches, lighting the street, and waved placards decrying the infamy of Hell's Half Acre. Their voices resounded in song.

> "Onward, Christian soldiers,
> Marching as to war,
> With the cross of Jesus
> Going on before."

"Good Lord!" Marie shouted over the trumpeting din. "Do you think they marched through the Acre?"

"No doubt of it," Short yelled back. "You stay here, and don't give me any argument. There's liable to be trouble."

"You were right," Johnson said. "They've declared war!"

Short led him out the door. Across the way, they saw Lowe emerge from the Centennial, his face a mask of befuddled astonishment. Theaters and clubs along the street began emptying as the band marched past. Throngs of people fell in behind the torch-bearers, trailing them as the parade proceeded north on Main. The crowds got larger every block along the way.

Farther uptown, Van Zandt and the band led the parade onto Courthouse Square. By now, Short and Johnson were mixed in with a crush of more than a thousand people. Short saw Lowe jostling for position, and ahead, he spotted a sea of men and women waiting on the courthouse lawn. He estimated the crowd to be at least three thousand, and pulled Johnson along as their ranks parted to let the band through. The music ended with a last blare of trumpets.

Van Zandt mounted the courthouse steps. Gathered around him were the clergymen and county officials and several prominent businessmen. He stared out over the throng of faces a moment, and then raised his arms for quiet. The crowd fell silent.

"Townspeople of Fort Worth," he called out. "We come here tonight to determine the future of our community. Growth and prosperity or gunfire and anarchy!"

The force of the statement claimed their attention. Van Zandt went on to cite the shootout of a week ago, the woman murdered yesterday, and the dead man left on the courthouse lawn that very morning. He abruptly stopped, holding them a moment in a frozen tableau. Then his voice rang out.

"Four people slain on our streets in a matter of eight days! Are you safe, are your children safe? *Do you want change?*"

The crowd thundered their response. Flash-pans popped, lighting the courthouse steps, as newspaper photographers caught Van Zandt with his arms outstretched. He again quieted the townspeople, and then, one by one, introduced the founding members of the Law and Order Association. Reverend Francis Grant and the other clergymen spoke of the iniquity and immorality of Hell's Half Acre, damning it as an abomination in the eyes of God. They urged the women to keep their men at home, and the men to avoid temptation, damnation. Their voices crackled with fire and brimstone.

Judge Hovenkamp lambasted the perfidy and corruption that touched every corner of the Acre. He delivered a scathing denunciation of the sporting crowd, a gallery of rogues devoted to larceny and licentious behavior. Sheriff Maddox and County Prosecutor Ned Bowlin railed against the pervasive lawlessness below Seventh Street, and charged city officials with tolerating a sinkhole in which a woman could be crucified with hammer and nails. Thomas Anderson, speaking for the business community, told the onlookers that no town could attract industry and investment when its reputation was that of a killing ground. He exhorted them to quick riddance of Hell's Half Acre.

Van Zandt once more stepped forward. His eyes were fierce in the torchlight, and he held the massed gathering by sheer force of will. "Your city government is corrupt!" he boomed. "Your mayor and your police department are on the payroll of those who control the Acre!"

A stillness came over the throng and he chopped the air with his hand. "This year, as every year, our municipal elections will be held on April tenth. I say to you tonight, stand together and act together at the ballot box. Throw the scoundrels out of office—reclaim your town!"

The crowd roared approval. A chant went up, and then, as though on cue, the Texas Wesleyan band broke out in a hymn familiar to them all. Their voices filled the night with song and seemed to unite them even more than the speeches, a song that foretold the fate of Hell's Half Acre and City Hall.

"Amazing grace, how sweet the sound

That saved a wretch like me,

I once was lost, but now am found,

Was blind, but now I see."

"Believe me now?" Short said, nudging Johnson. "Van Zandt was born to lead a crusade. He's a natural spellbinder."

"Luke, we're in deep trouble," Johnson groaned. "They'll take us down with the Acre."

Lowe appeared out of the crowd. His features were flushed beet-red and his eyes were wild. "What the hell's the matter with these idiots? That whore's killer got delivered on their goddamn doorstep! Why are they yellin' for reform?"

Short spread his hands. "Guess it's like I told you, Joe."

"Told me what?"

"The old days are gone. Long gone."

The strains of *Amazing Grace* carried all the way to the Acre.

Chapter 20

Early the next afternoon Nat Kramer emerged from the Cattle Exchange. The club was located at Houston and Second, a block west of Main Street. He paused a moment, lighting a cigar, and scanned the cloudless sky. A biting wind sliced down out of the northwest.

Kramer tugged the collar of his topcoat tighter. He was fifty-eight and he'd discovered that age colored a man's perspective of things. His plumbing no longer worked so well, and he found himself admiring attractive women more than he pursued them. Nor was he immune to the cold as he had been in his younger years. He'd come to detest winter.

These days, apart from walking from his home to the club, he rarely ventured outside. From late November to the onset of spring, he avoided exposure to the elements whenever possible. His wife, a woman of mordant humor, often remarked that he went into hibernation during the winter. Her criticism was entirely justified, and he never debated the point. Sometimes he felt like an old and grizzled bear.

Today was one of those days. As he turned south along Houston, he sensed the embers of his spirit were at a low ebb. Late last night, one of the dealers from the White Elephant had brought him a sealed note from Luke Short. The note, somewhat cryptic in nature, alluded to an emergency meeting of the uptown club owners. The place was Short's suite at the Mansion Hotel and the time was two o'clock today. Short urged him to attend.

There was no question in Kramer's mind as to the purpose of the meeting. The torchlit parade through the Acre, and the open forum at the courthouse, had been widely reported in the morning papers. Everyone in town was taking about the stemwinder of a speech delivered by Karl Van Zandt, and its effect on those who were present. The overriding consensus was that Van Zandt had rallied the public to the reformers' cause. The Acre was in for hard times.

Kramer had not attended the rally. By the very nature of his profession, he had nothing in common with reformers, who tended to adopt a holier-than-thou attitude. At the same time, he had little in common with the cardsharps and grifters who infested the Acre. The sporting crowd was fully as wanton and unscrupulous as portrayed in the newspapers. He disliked thinking of himself as an elitist, but the label, in this instance, was altogether fitting. He wanted nothing to do with sleazy tinhorns.

Overnight, restlessly tossing and turning, Kramer realized that he was ambivalent about the whole affair. Fort Worth had been his home for almost fifteen years, and he'd watched it grow from a rowdy cowtown to a cosmopolitan city. He took considerable personal pride in his adopted town, though he privately felt that the Acre was a cancer on the progressive measures advocated by business leaders. Yet he was leery of the reformers, all too aware that zealotry sometimes ended with saints and sinners alike being burned at the stake. He felt caught betwixt and between.

Still, in perilous times, a man was often forced to make a choice. He was reasonably certain he knew the purpose behind Short's hastily called meeting. Like himself, Short was a gentleman, a man of honor and integrity, with a reputation to uphold. But in the looming battle between the reformers and the sporting crowd, there was no way for a gambler, however honorable, to walk the fence. He thought Short would come down on the side of the sporting crowd, for no gaming parlor was assured of survival if the Acre lost the struggle. Expediency, in the end, sometimes overrode the dictates of honor. He wasn't sure he could go along.

For all that, he had no wish to make an enemy of Short. He admired a little man with big ideas and the brass to transform them into reality. Short's campaign to revitalize the White Elephant, by importing Bat Masterson and Richard Clark, was a masterstroke. No less impressive was Short's enterprise, conducted with flair and zest, in promoting a prizefight with John L. Sullivan. Yet, more than anything else, he respected Short for taking a stand against Jim Courtright, refusing to pay protection. The little man had sand.

None of which would affect Kramer's decision one way or another. He would listen, weigh the arguments pro and con, and act according to what he thought best for himself and his club. As he turned the corner onto Fourth Street, he was reminded that pragmatism and honor were not mutually exclusive. A wise man viewed them as kissing cousins.

He would play the cards he was dealt.

The suite had been rearranged to accommodate a meeting. Short had extra chairs brought into the sitting room and positioned them around the sofa in a rough circle. No one spot dominated the others, and there was a sense of equality about the whole. Everyone who attended would have a choice seat.

Short was wary of creating the wrong impression. The men he'd invited were the lords of the gambling fraternity in Fort Worth. Their clubs were classy operations, and collectively, they had been in business for over thirty years. He was the johnny-come-lately of the group, and he knew that lecturing them would never put across what he was trying to sell. He planned to accord them the respect they were due.

Jake Johnson nervously paced the floor. Marie busied herself with a coffee service brought in by the hotel staff. They knew what he intended, for the three of them had discussed it at length last night following the courthouse rally. Finally, after obtaining Johnson's agreement, Short had sent out the invitations to the other club owners. But Johnson was by nature a worrywart, and he continued to have second thoughts. He saw no way to hedge today's bet.

The first of the men to arrive was Albert Lynch, owner of the Pacific Saloon. He was a tall man, in his early fifties, with an alert, birdlike manner. His club was located at the corner of Main and Courthouse Square, and he'd first opened his doors when trailhands were still driving longhorns up the Chisholm Trail. Over the years, he had transformed a busthead saloon into an elegant gaming parlor for gentlemen. No longer a saloonkeeper, he had transformed himself as well. He was no less a gentleman than his clientele.

The next to arrive was Phil Rayner. A long-time veteran of the gambling circuit, he now owned the Merchant's Exchange, located a few doors downstreet from the White Elephant. His stout frame and moonlike face belied a steel-trap mind that could calculate the odds on any game of chance at lightning speed. He was in his early forties, balding and rumpled, his vest forever riding up over his rounded belly. Of all the club owners, he was known for his jolly manner and spirited wit, a chubby prankster. Yet he was a clever businessman with a nose for investments, and reportedly one of the largest landowners in Fort Worth. For all his girth, he was sharp as a tack.

Nat Kramer, ever precise, arrived on the stroke of two. His cheeks were spanked red from the cold wind, but when he removed his hat, his shock of white hair was immaculately groomed. He extended a warm handshake to Short, and made his way around the room greeting the others. Their manner toward him was at once cordial and deferential, undisguised respect for the senior member of the fraternity. His years plying the Mississippi as a riverboat gambler had left him with a dignity and graciousness than none of the others, even on their best days, could hope to possess. His bearing was that of an apostle among acolytes.

Marie served them coffee from a bone-china carafe. While she moved around the room, Short watched the byplay between Kramer and the other men. He was all too aware that to win them over, he must first convince the dean of a very select gathering, each of them singularly successful in their own right. Kramer's reaction to his plan would be closely scrutinized, and the older man had the power to sway them one way or the other. Marie finished serving coffee, then excused herself, and retreated into the bedroom, closing the door behind her. Short moved directly to open the meeting.

"Thank you all for coming," he said. "Before we're through, I believe you will agree it was worth your while."

"I'm sure we will," Rayner interrupted with a quizzical smile. "But I thought this was a meeting of the uptown club owners. Aren't we missing somebody?"

"I purposely didn't invite Joe Lowe. The reason will become apparent when we get into discussion of certain issues. I ask you to bear with me until then."

"Why not?" Rayner said with a quick grin. "I could go a month of Sundays and never miss Rowdy Joe."

Everyone laughed, clearly of the same sentiment. Short looked from one to the other. "So far as I'm concerned, this is a private meeting. Unless you told someone, then nobody knows you're here."

"Sounds fair," Lynch said. "So why are we here?"

"To discuss mutual interests," Short replied. "After last night, I don't think any of us questions the danger of a well-organized reform movement. We're all in the same boat.''

Lynch raised an eyebrow. "Which boat is that?''

"A lifeboat," Short said. "The ship's already begun to sink.''

"Aren't you being a little melodramatic? The reformers are out to close the Acre. What's that got to do with us?''

"The Acre would just be a first step. No self-respecting reformer would stop there. We'd be next on the list.''

"That's your opinion," Lynch said. "I haven't heard anybody say anything about the uptown clubs. Nothing in the newspapers, either." He turned to Kramer. "What do you think, Nat? Are we in trouble?''

Everyone waited for Kramer to speak. "I have to agree with Luke," he said. "There's a steamroller effect to a reform movement. Once it gets started, it's hard to stop.''

Lynch stubbornly shook his head. "Half the men who frequent our clubs are well-to-do businessmen. Gambling's part of their lives, gets them out of the house and away from their wives. You really think they'd let the reformers close us down?''

There was some merit to the argument. Gambling was an institution in Western towns, a part of the social fabric. For a great many men, it was their chief diversion in life, almost a form of entertainment. Affluent businessmen often looked upon gaming clubs as they would the Knights of Pythias, or any other fraternal order. A place to socialize with their own kind.

"Stop and think about it," Short said. "Karl Van Zandt and Thomas Anderson are the two most influential businessmen in Fort Worth. With them leading the reform movement, the others will fall in line. No man wants the reputation of standing in the way of progress.''

"Not to mention their wives," Rayner added. "Women support the churches and the churches support reform. That puts a lot of pressure on the men. Go along to get along.''

"So what's the solution?'' Lynch said, glancing at Short. "I take it you've got something in mind.''

Short nodded, his voice measured. "I suggest we join ranks with the reformers. Support the move to close the Acre.''

There was a beat of dead silence. "What's your play?'' Lynch finally got out. "You just said we'll be next after the Acre. Wouldn't we be cutting our own throats?''

"I don't think so,'' Short said with conviction. "To survive, we have to present ourselves as legitimate, progressive businessmen. Our best bet is to jump on the reformers' bandwagon.''

Rayner laughed. "By God, it might just work! The reformers would probably welcome us into the fold. That makes their case against the Acre all the stronger.''

"Sounds risky to me,'' Lynch said doubtfully. He looked at Kramer. "How about you, Nat?''

Kramer took a moment to reply. He reminded himself again that pragmatism and honor were often different sides of the same coin. He was impressed with Short's perceptive grasp of the situation. To survive was the only issue.

"Luke has the right idea,'' he said at length. "We take a stand for law and order, and disassociate ourselves from the Acre. The question is, how do we strike an alliance with the reformers?'' His gaze went to Short. "Any suggestions?''

"Deal them a winning hand,'' Short said evenly. "We run ads in both newspapers, throwing our support to the reformers. Their cause gets a big boost, and the newspapers will love it. Honest gamblers versus crooked gamblers.''

"I like it.'' Kramer nodded approval. "Something of a quid pro quo that defuses any move against our clubs. A very clever play, Luke.''

"Only one problem," Lynch objected. "What do we do about Joe Lowe?"

"We ignore him," Short said. "Everybody in town knows he had that bartender killed. We can't afford to be tarred with the same brush." He glanced from man to man. "We have to put distance between ourselves and Lowe."

"Easier said than done," Lynch commented dourly. "Knowing Lowe, he'll figure we betrayed him. He's liable to get on the war path."

"Everything carries risk," Kramer observed. "By doing nothing, we risk losing our clubs. The other way, we risk a fight with Lowe. Speaking personally, the choice is clear. I cast my vote with Luke."

"That goes for me, too," Rayner said quickly. "To hell with Rowdy Joe and the Acre. Let's take care of our own."

Lynch made it unanimous. "I'll go along, but remember what I said. We'll have trouble with Lowe."

The men spent some while working on the language to be used in the newspaper advertisements. Short took responsibility for placing the ads, and the meeting ended with a final round of handshakes. Kramer, who was the last to leave, paused at the door. He clapped Short on the shoulder.

"You've done us all a service," he said earnestly. "Frankly, I would never have thought of the idea. I'm in your debt."

"That works both ways," Short said. "To pull it off, we all have to stick together."

"Where do you find time to hatch all these schemes? I would think you'd be preoccupied with the prizefight."

John L. Sullivan was scheduled to arrive in Fort Worth the next day. The killings in the Acre, particularly the crucifixion of Velma Banks, had briefly overshadowed the boxing exhibition. But the morning papers had devoted more space to the prizefight than to the reformers' rally. Everyone in town was clamoring for a seat to see the Great John L.

"Nothing much left to do with the fight," Short said. "I've had the details worked out for a week or more."

"You're a whirlwind," Kramer said with a cordial smile. "I trust you've saved me a good seat."

"The best in the house."

"I appreciate the courtesy."

"Anytime, Nat."

Kramer followed the other club owners toward the elevator. When Short closed the door, he turned to find Marie standing with Johnson in the sitting room. Their expressions were sober, and Johnson, who hadn't said a word during the meeting, slowly shook his head. His mouth was downturned.

"Once that ad hits the papers, you'd better start looking over your shoulder. Joe Lowe will know you're behind it."

"What makes you think he'll know?"

"Al Lynch will tell him," Johnson said. "Al figures to play both ends against the middle. I heard it in his voice."

Short nodded. "I guess a gambler has to hedge his bet."

"How do you plan to hedge yours?"

Short tried to think of a snappy comeback. He drew a blank.

Chapter 21

A carriage waited at curbside under a bright morning sun. The driver hopped down as Lowe and Kate emerged from the house and came down the walkway. The top was up on the carriage and the driver held the door. He tipped his hat.

"Mornin', Mr. Lowe."

"Fair day, Harry."

"Yessir, a nice one. Mornin', Miz Lowe."

Kate squinched her eyes against the sun. "How're the kids, Harry?"

"Just fine, ma'am." He assisted her into the carriage. "Thank you for askin'."

Kate cared little for children. She found them noisy and bothersome, and she had taken precautions never to have any of her own. But she tried to play the grande dame with the help, and part of the role was taking an interest in their personal affairs. Lowe, who thought of children as a pesky nuisance, never asked.

Their house was at the corner of Belknap and Throckmorton. A three-story Victorian structure, it was located in the residential enclave west of Courthouse Square. Their neighbors were affluent businessmen, with a sprinkling of lawyers and doctors, all part of the social swirl of Fort Worth. None of them had ever invited the Lowes to their homes.

The house was meant to be Lowe's crown jewel. He

had purposely bought it in a respectable neighborhood, a showplace among the town's upper class. But the pretense impressed no one, for he and Kate were unable to outdistance their ties to the Acre. They slept there, though they never had guests, and they rarely took a meal at home. They were strangers in their own neighborhood.

The carriage arrived promptly at eleven o'clock every morning. Still another pretense of status, the carriage and driver were on call throughout the day and into the evening. Yet its principal function was to transport the Lowes from their home to the Centennial, a distance of six blocks, and return them at night. For the most part, driver and carriage sat idle at a livery stable.

Today, watching houses roll past, Lowe's mind was on the Acre. He still found it baffling that Van Zandt and the reformers had attracted such widespread support. But he was largely unconcerned, for city elections were over six weeks away, and even then, he controlled the swing vote. Whatever slate of candidates the reformers put forth, it would be an exercise in folly. The Acre would decide the election.

On Monday night, following the courthouse rally, he had met secretly with Mayor Smith and Marshal Rea. His purpose was to dampen their fears and deliver the gospel according to Joe Lowe. He assured them that they would be returned to office in April, but only if they followed orders and ignored the cries for reform. The Acre was to operate as usual, with token raids on the more infamous dives to satisfy the newspapers. Throw the public a bone, he told them, and the reform movement would lose steam long before April. They agreed to his patchwork plan because they had no real choice.

Lowe's thoughts turned to other matters as the carriage rounded the corner of Third Street. John L. Sullivan was due to arrive today, and the prizefight exhibition was set for that night. The local challenger, Jock Mulligan, was a hundred-to-one underdog, but it nonetheless promised to be a memorable evening. Like the other club owners, Lowe had donated to the purse, and obtained seats for himself and Jim Courtright. The one drawback to the whole affair was that it was being promoted by Luke Short, and that tempered his enthusiasm. He got a rancid taste in his mouth just thinking about Short.

The carriage deposited them in front of the Centennial. Lowe put on gentlemanly airs for anyone who might be watching, and gave Kate a hand down. Once inside, he quickly dropped the airs and got on with the morning routine. Kate felt that cooking, like children, wasn't worth the effort, and they always took breakfast at the club. A table at the rear was set and waiting, with stacks of pancakes, fried eggs, and thick slabs of bacon. They tore into the spread with relish, washing the food down with gulps of hot coffee. Neither of them spoke as they ate.

Frank Meade, the club manager, waited until they'd pushed their plates away. When Lowe lit a cigar, he warily approached the table, a newspaper in hand. He nodded to Kate, who was picking her teeth with a fingernail. He stopped beside Lowe's chair.

"Morning, boss."

"Frank." Lowe puffed smoke. "What's up?"

Meade placed a copy of the morning *Gazette* on the table. "Thought you ought to see this."

"Yeah?" Lowe scanned the headlines, noting the date was January 23. "Says the Great John L.'s coming to town. No news in that."

"Try page three."

Lowe turned the page. His eyes stopped, then darted through an advertisement that occupied the whole of page three, and snapped back to the top. He stared at the ad headline.

UPTOWN GAMING CLUBS ENDORSE REFORM

The ad itself was worded in plain language. The up-town clubs, in unequivocal terms, pledged their support to the Citizens' Law and Order Association. The text of the ad decried wanton violence in Hell's Half Acre, and took City Hall to task for its lax law enforcement. A donation of four thousand dollars was promised by the clubs to fund the fight for eradication of the Acre. Listed at the bottom of the ad were the four clubs sponsoring the reform movement, and the names of their owners. Conspicuous by its absence was any reference to the Centennial.

"The sonsabitches!" Lowe exploded in a guttural curse. "The *dirty* sonsabitches!"

Kate dropped her coffee cup. "What's the matter?"

"We've been stabbed in the back!"

"What're you talking about?"

"Here!"

Lowe shoved the paper across the table. He sat wrapped in a cone of outraged silence, furiously puffing his cigar. Abruptly, slamming back his chair, he stalked off toward the front door. Kate jumped to her feet.

"Where are you going?"

"Where the hell d'you think!"

Outside, Lowe pounded across the street. He burst through the doors of the White Elephant, pushing a customer aside, his eyes searching the room. At the rear of the restaurant, he saw Short and Marie seated at a table. A waiter finished pouring coffee and turned toward the kitchen. Lowe walked forward, his features contorted with rage.

"You rotten bastard!" he shouted. "You double-crossed me!"

Short rose from his chair. "I see you've read the newspaper."

"You're goddamned right I read it. Why the hell wasn't I asked to have my name in there?"

"You have a faulty memory, Joe. I came to you the

day the reformers announced their campaign. You threw me out of your office.''

"Don't get cute," Lowe said angrily. "That was some nonsense about me cleaning up the Acre. You didn't say nothin' about the uptown clubs getting together.''

"I hadn't thought of it then," Short said. "But you couldn't have joined us anyway, Joe. That would have made you a liar.''

"What the hell's that supposed to mean?''

"Think about it. Joe Lowe supporting the reformers? Everybody would know it's beeswax.''

Lowe took a step closer. "I'm gonna have to teach you a lesson.''

"You can try." Short brushed aside the skirt of his suit jacket. "I wouldn't advise it.''

Lowe stopped dead. He knew Short carried a gun under his jacket. He knew as well that the little gambler would use it rather than be manhandled. They stood locked in leaden silence.

"I can lick any sonovabitch in the house!"

The booming challenge echoed through the room. Short looked toward the front and saw John L. Sullivan just inside the door. The champion's fists were planted on his hips, and behind him was his manager, Billy Madden. Lowe turned, recognizing the most famous face in America, and his jaw dropped. Short hurried forward.

"John L.," he said, extending his hand. "Where'd you come from? I was going to meet your train.''

"Wouldn't you know, we were early," Sullivan said with his nutcracker grin. "I asked where to find Luke Short and they told me the White Elephant. So here I am.''

"Welcome to Fort Worth," Short said, reaching past him to exchange a handshake with Madden. "Good to see you again, Billy.''

"Tell me now," Sullivan said, still grinning. "I'm dry as a bone and in desperate need of a drink. Would you have any Irish whiskey in the house?''

Short led them to the bar. Out of the corner of his eye, he saw Lowe shuffle past, still gawking at the champion, and slip through the door. The thought occurred that his troubles with Lowe had only been postponed. But he told himself that it was a matter for another time. He slapped the bar with the palm of his hand.

"Irish whiskey for the Great John L.!"

The exhibition was held in the opera house. A boxing ring, complete with sawdust and ropes, had been assembled on the stage. Overhead, a bank of lights had been rigged to light the ring.

The opera house was the only facility in Fort Worth large enough to accommodate the event. At first, when Short proposed the idea, the theater owner had been less than enthusiastic. Patrons of the opera, he argued, might think it a desecration to hold a prizefight on a stage where the arts were performed. But Short had enlisted the aid of town leaders, and a deal was eventually struck. The opera house was his for the night.

The prize purse was simpler to arrange. Short had tapped uptown gaming clubs and variety theaters for a total of ten thousand dollars. In exchange for their contribution, the owners each got two tickets in the orchestra section, the best seats in the house. He made no overtures to the dives in the Acre, and refused to discuss the matter when he was approached. The demand for tickets was much as he'd expected, and the house quickly sold out. There was standing room only.

That afternoon, Short had handed Billy Madden ten thousand in cash. The amount was double what he'd promised Sullivan in St. Louis, and the champion celebrated by killing half a bottle of whiskey. Jock Mulligan, the challenger for the night, was to receive a thousand dollars simply for crawling in the ring. After deducting rental charges on the opera house, Short and Jake Johnson donated the balance, some six thousand dollars, to the town's churches. Their generosity made the White Elephant the big winner for the night.

To further burnish the image of the uptown clubs, Short had invited the founding members of the reform movement as guests of the house. Karl Van Zandt and Thomas Anderson, along with the clergymen and the courthouse crowd, readily accepted. Father John O'Malley, the only Catholic in the bunch, and a staunch Irishman, was particularly grateful for a chance to see the Great John L. in action. The entire contingent of the Law and Order Association was seated in the orchestra section. Their mere presence lent an added touch of respectability to the event.

The exhibition was scheduled for four rounds. The bout would be conducted under the London Prize Ring Rules for bare-knuckle boxing. Hardly anyone expected Jock Mulligan to last four rounds; but they nonetheless paid the price of admission, hopeful he would make a decent showing for Fort Worth. Billy Madden had agreed to act as referee, and Short had appointed himself as master of ceremonies. By eight o'clock, the house was packed, the crowd eager to get on with the fight. The house lights dimmed, leaving the stage in a glow of brilliance. A hush settled over the spectators.

Short walked to center stage. He made a few introductory remarks, welcoming dignitaries in the audience, and quickly got on with the show. Mulligan was brought on stage from the left wing to a round of applause and shouts of encouragement from the townspeople. Then the Great John L. was brought on from the right wing, and the crowd greeted him with a thunderous roar that rocked the hall. Short moved out of the lights, disappearing backstage as the contestants stepped into the ring. Madden took charge, briefly reviewing the rules, and signaled the fighters to toe the line. The gong rang.

Mulligan was determined not to disgrace himself or his town. He gamely waded in with a flurry of blows, none of which found the mark. Sullivan slipped punches, blocked others with his arms, easily weathering the assault. After bobbing beneath a haymaker, he flicked a left jab, followed with a right cross, and dumped Mulligan on the seat of his boxing tights. The crowd groaned, fearing it was over before it began, and urged Mulligan to his feet. He toed the line before the thirty-second time limit.

Sullivan apparently decided to give the spectators their money's worth. He allowed the challenger to whale away, occasionally rapping out with a jab, never once in danger. The crowd sensed he was carrying the fight, but they were mesmerized by the display of pugilistic artistry. As though timing it, every ten minutes or so the champion would unleash a thunderbolt and drop Mulligan to the floor. In the fourth round, still unmarked, Sullivan uncorked a whistling right and a murderous left hook. Mulligan went down and out, finished for the night.

The crowd roared, their shouts and cheers reverberating through the opera house. Sullivan paraded around the ring, hands clasped overhead, his nutcracker grin ablaze beneath the lights. As the handlers carried Mulligan to his corner, the champion stepped out of the ring and moved to stage center. He bowed from the waist, acknowledging the ovation, then threw his arms out in a bold stance of victory. The audience shook the house with a wave of applause.

From the wings, Short thought he'd never seen a greater showman. He was waiting when Sullivan finally moved out of the lights, still waving to the crowd, and walked off stage. He took the Champion's sledgehammer paw in a firm handclasp.

"John L., you're one in a million."

"You're wrong there," Sullivan said with a booming laugh. "I'm one of a kind!"

Short thought the Great John L. was right. He was an original.

Chapter 22

The raids began the next night. The police force descended on the Acre shortly after dark and systematically hit selected dives. Wagons from the city street department were pressed into service to haul away prisoners.

Marshal Bill Rea supervised the operation from the corner of Twelfth and Main. His police force was split into two squads, invading dives in a flying wedge. Their targets were predetermined, taken from a list known only to Rea and the mayor. The sporting crowd was caught completely off guard.

On Twelfth Street, a crowd gathered outside the Two Minnies. With its second-story glass floor and naked women, the establishment was the most notorious bordello in the Acre. Minnie Stover and her partner, Minnie Biddle, fought like wildcats as officers dragged them out and bodily hoisted them into a wagon. The naked whores, hastily wrapped in housecoats, screeched and wailed as they were marched from the building. Fourteen women and three bartenders were arrested.

"Bill Rea, you sonofabitch!" Minnie Stover screamed as the wagon turned onto Main Street. "You ought to be ashamed of yourself!"

The crowd of onlookers hooted at the whores. Rea ignored the commotion, standing square-shouldered and steely-eyed, trying for a military bearing. By prearrangement, reporters from the *Democrat* and the *Gazette* had been alerted to the raids. The purpose of the drill was to garner newspaper coverage, and sap strength from the reform movement. As the man in charge, Rea was to act as spokesman for the city government. One of the reporters approached with pad and pencil in hand.

"Quite a night, Marshal," he said, pointing at the wagon. "How many joints are you going to raid?"

Rea motioned aimlessly. "Depends on how things go. We'll just have to wait and see."

"Will you conduct more raids tomorrow?"

"I can't talk about that now. No need to give anybody advance warning."

"More raids imminent," the reporter said, inventing a quote as he scribbled in his notepad. "Is this in response to the demands by the Law and Order Association?"

"Mayor Smith ordered the police to take action," Rea said importantly. "The people of Fort Worth want things cleaned up down here and we intend to get that done. Doesn't matter how long it takes."

"The reform element wants the Acre cleaned out, not cleaned up. What are your thoughts on that?"

"We'll do whatever's necessary to get the job done. Tonight's just the first step."

Rea walked off as another raid got under way. He thought he'd said enough for a decent quote, promising everything and nothing. Which was essentially the strategy the mayor and the city council had decided to adopt. His orders were to make a show of force, create turmoil in the Acre. Arrest whores and gamblers and parade them through the middle of town. A sideshow to grab headlines.

Three days earlier, following the courthouse rally, the mayor had convened an emergency session of the city council. Of the six aldermen, the three elected from the uptown district demanded speedy action to close down the Acre. The three from the downtown district, answerable only to Joe Lowe, were equally adamant that business continue as normal. Mayor Smith, ever the canny politician, then hammered out a compromise that was middle-of-the-road. There would be a crackdown in the Acre, but nothing draconian. A first step toward reform.

Later, in a private meeting, Smith had laid it out for Rea. The measures taken would have the appearance of a legitimate crackdown on the sporting crowd. The uptown aldermen and the reformers would be led to believe that their demands were being met. In reality, the police would drag their feet, conducting sporadic raids, and nothing would really change. The public would soon lose interest, and just as Lowe had predicted, the reform movement would gradually blow over. Time was on the side of sin.

The raids were delayed until after the boxing exhibition. John L. Sullivan was certain to capture the headlines, and Smith wanted nothing to detract from the newsworthy nature of the crackdown. The Great John L. had departed town on the noon train, and the press was eager for fresh news. Later that night, when the raids were completed, the mayor planned to hold a meeting with reporters. He would issue a statement praising the police and roundly condemning the denizens of the Acre. All in time for the morning editions.

Rea stood by as a police squad burst through the door of the Empress Saloon. The owner was in jail, having killed two men in the now infamous shootout, and that was old news. But the dive was familiar to the public because of the killings, and would attract attention in the newspapers. The squad of officers would confiscate several decks of cards, almost certain to be marked, and arrest any number of gamblers on charges of operating a crooked enterprise. The Empress Saloon would serve as added fodder for the crackdown.

Before the night was out, Rea planned a sweep of the Acre. In all, four whorehouses, two gaming dives, and three dance halls would be raided. Those arrested would be carted off to court, where City Judge Horace Jackson would levy stiff fines. By midnight, those who paid their fines would be back in business, and in large degree, none the worse for the experience. But it would all make for titillating headlines, and the public would applaud the valiant efforts of the police. Which merely served to underscore the purpose of the drill.

Perception, in the political arena, was more persuasive than truth.

The White Elephant was crowded. Waiters scurried back and forth in the restaurant, and the upstairs club room was jammed with men in pursuit of fortune. The whirr of the roulette wheel was lost in the drone of conversation.

Short attributed the large crowd to last night's prizefight. Every man of sporting blood had turned out to witness the Great John L. pulverize the local champion. There was virtually no betting, with Jock Mulligan a hundred-to-one underdog, and tonight, men were eager to test their luck. Even more, they wanted to try the tables at the White Elephant. The club that had brought John L. Sullivan to town was again the talk of Fort Worth.

All the chairs were taken at Short's poker table. The play was fast, and he'd been winning steadily throughout the evening. But his mind was elsewhere, still spinning with the triumph of the prizefight. Late that morning, he had engaged a carriage to take Sullivan and Madden to the train station. At the depot, just before they boarded, the Great John L. had pulled him into an affectionate bearhug, almost maudlin with sentiment. They parted with mutual assurances that their paths would cross again, and soon.

Short thought it unlikely. That saddened him, for in their brief time together, he had become fast friends with the most famous man in America. But Sullivan traveled in different circles, hob-nobbing with royalty and Presidents as well as followers of the sport. Last night, holding court at the bar, Sullivan had regaled admirers with tales of his exploits in and out of the ring. Short imagined the Champion held people spellbound whether it was a crowded saloon or a host of dignitaries at the White House. He would miss the Great John L.

A sudden commotion distracted the players at the poker table. From the street, they heard a chorus of jeers and catcalls that carried all the way to the second floor. Drawn by the noise, men deserted gaming tables to crowd around the front windows. Short signaled the club manager to watch his spot in the poker game, and hurried across the room. He traded a puzzled glance with Marie as he rushed past the faro layout and went down the stairs. The uproar got louder when he reached the ground floor.

Half the people in the restaurant had moved out onto the sidewalk. The others were ganged around the windows, laughing and pointing to something on the street. Short worked his way through the crowd and saw Johnson standing in the doorway. He joined his partner just as a wagon filled with disheveled women, their voices raised in a strident hullabaloo, rolled past the White Elephant. The crowd on the sidewalk mocked them with hoots of laughter.

"What the deuce?" Short said, staring at the women. "Who are they, Jake?"

"Ladies of the evening," Johnson replied. "The two older ones are Minnie Stover and Minnie Biddle. They operate the raunchiest cathouse in the Acre."

Short noticed a policeman riding beside the wagon driver. "Have they been arrested?"

"Word's spreading along the street," Johnson said. "The police are out raiding the dives downtown. Sounds like a real shake-up."

"Why would Lowe turn the police loose on the sporting crowd? That's his power base."

"Maybe he's lost his influence at City Hall. The reformers might have put the fear of God into Smith and that bunch."

"No," Short said, slowly shaking his head. "I smell a rat."

Johnson looked startled. "You think it's a phony play? Just to throw off the reformers?"

"I think Joe Lowe never made a straight play in his life. What you see isn't what you get."

"So what's his angle?"

"I don't know," Short said, thoughtful a moment. "Maybe to buy time, let the dust settle. Fool people into believing the police have put a lid on the Acre."

"No skin off our nose," Johnson said. "We've made our peace with the reformers, and then some. John L. Sullivan was the icing on the cake."

"Jake, they could turn on us overnight. Especially if they were made to look like dunces in the public eye. No club in town would be safe."

"Well, hell's bells, we're on record as supporting their cause. We even donated money to their war chest. What more could they want?"

"Hard to say." Short was silent awhile, considering options. "I think we better buy ourselves some extra insurance."

"What sort of insurance?"

"Show everybody we're big boosters of law and order. How would you like to have Bat Masterson *and* Wyatt Earp at the White Elephant?"

Johnson blinked a couple of times. "You could pull that off?"

Short watched as the wagon with the whores turned the corner. Something told him that it was all smoke and mirrors, designed to steal the show from the reformers. Something told him as well that the White Elephant was not yet out of jeopardy.

He thought they could use all the insurance they could get.

* * *

Not long after midnight Bill Rea entered the Centennial by the alley door. He sent a stagehand to find Lowe, and made himself comfortable in the office. He was pleased with the night's work.

Lowe came through the door a few minutes later. A cigar was wedged in the corner of his mouth, and he seemed almost jolly. "How goes the good fight, Marshal?"

"We won," Rea said wryly. "I think I deserve a medal."

"Do you?" Lowe dropped into the chair behind his desk. "What's the count?"

"Forty-four whores, eleven cardsharps, and a whole slew of shady characters. Took fifteen wagon loads to get 'em all to jail."

"Have they had their day in court?"

"What a circus," Rea said with a chuckle. "Judge Jackson fined them the limit and they squawled like banshees. We could've charged admission."

"How about the newspapers?" Lowe asked. "Did they stick around till the end?"

"We'll get the front page of both papers. They even took pictures of the Two Minnies. I couldn't hardly keep a straight face."

"Did the mayor give them an interview?"

"Talked them blue in the face," Rea said. "The reporters took it all down like it was scripture. You'd think he was chairman of the Law and Order Association."

"Smith's a windbag," Lowe observed. "But he knows how to give a speech. You think the press bought the story?"

"Swallowed it hook, line and sinker. So far as they're concerned, we've declared war on the Acre."

"I'd like to be a fly on the wall when Van Zandt and his holy rollers get the news. We flat stole their thunder."

"Yeah, me, too," Rea said. "You reckon it's enough to piss on their parade?"

Lowe puffed smoke. "They'll have no choice but to shut their traps. After tonight, only a damn fool would criticize City Hall."

"The mayor's got the nervous fidgets. Him and me had a little talk after his interview. He's worried it won't last."

"What won't last?"

"The reformers holding their peace," Rea said, gesturing off into space. "I mean, all them whores and tinhorns are already back in business and it's barely midnight. Somebody's bound to call it a crock."

"Let 'em," Lowe said sharply. "You tell hizzoner I'll do the thinking around here. Nobody got the jump on me yet."

"So what happens when the reformers start yellin' again?"

"Well, first off, they'll sit on their thumbs and wait to see how things play out. When they finally get wise and start squawkin', we'll just raid some more whorehouses. Simple as that."

"They yell, and we pull another raid. We just keep stealin' their thunder. That the idea?"

"Folks lose interest real quick when somebody yells wolf too often. We'll win this fight in the newspapers—guarantee it."

Rea grinned. "Way it sounds, it won't be much of a fight."

Lowe munched his cigar. His mind abruptly strayed to another fight, one not yet fought. A fight no less important to him than the one with the reformers, maybe more so. For it was a personal matter.

A dirty little bastard named Short.

Chapter 23

The train ground to a halt. A blast of steam from the engine drifted back over the people waiting outside Union Depot. Some were there to board, and others, like Short, were there to meet friends or family. He walked forward on the station house platform.

Wyatt Earp stepped off the lead passenger coach. He waved to Short, then turned and assisted his wife onto the platform. Directly behind her was Bat Masterson, dapper in a chesterfield topcoat and Derby hat. Earp cleared a path through the crowd ganged around the train.

"Good to see you, Wyatt." Short shook his hand with genuine warmth. "I appreciate you coming all this way."

Earp pumped his arm. "We left the day after we got your wire. You remember Josie."

Josephine Earp was a svelte woman with a trim figure and lustrous dark hair. She kissed Short on the check. "It's been too long, Luke. What is it now, three years?"

"Just about," Short said. "You're looking beautiful as ever, Josie."

"Oh, my, I do love a flatterer!"

Short had first met her during his stay in Tombstone. At the time, she was a member of a stage troupe touring the Western mining camps. She was courted by Earp and his chief rival for political power, the local sheriff. Earp eventually won her hand.

"Well, Luke, old sport," Masterson said, slapping him across the back. "I thought you outran the reformers when you left Dodge City. What happened?"

"Times change," Short said simply. "I'll tell you about it on the way uptown."

Earp signaled a porter to collect their luggage. He gave Short a wry look. "You ought to steer clear of cities. Up in Idaho, reform is still a dirty word."

"Oh, pleeze!" Josie said airily. "Coeur d'Alene is such a backwoodsy little place. I'll take a city anytime."

"Now, honey," Earp said, trying to placate her. "Why do you want to talk that way? We've done pretty good in the goldfields."

"Money isn't everything, sweetheart. A girl does like a bit of refinement now and then."

Short saw that nothing had changed between them. Earp doted on his young wife, and went out of his way to indulge her whims. His friends found it amusing, for Earp was a hard man, tall and square, with stern features and a handlebar mustache. He rarely brooked nonsense from anyone, man or woman. Josephine Marcus Earp was the exception.

On the street, Short had a carriage waiting to take them to the hotel. Earp assisted Josephine inside as the porter stowed the luggage on the rear boot. Short thought the three of them looked surprisingly fresh after such a long trip. The Earps had traveled by train from the Idaho goldfields to Denver, where they met Masterson. From there, they had proceeded on to Fort Worth.

"All right," Masterson said as the carriage pulled away from the curb. "Give us the lowdown on the reformers. Are they trying to close your club?"

"Not yet," Short said. "They're still mainly concerned with Hell's Half Acre."

"What's the problem, then?"

Short recounted the brief history of the reform movement. He began with the shootout at the Empress Saloon, which led to the formation of the Law and Order Association. When he related the crucifixion of Velma Banks, Josephine caught her breath in a sharp gasp. He went on to describe the courthouse rally and the subsequent raids on the Acre. There had been no further raids in the week past.

"Things have been fairly quiet," he concluded. "But I don't expect that to last much longer. The reformers will wake up to the fact that these raids were just whitewash."

"Rowdy Joe's real cute," Masterson remarked. "But like Abe Lincoln said, you can't fool all the people all the time. Somebody will catch on."

"That's what worries me," Short observed. "When they do, they'll come down twice as hard. The drive to close the Acre will spill over to the uptown clubs."

"I suspect you're right," Earp said. "How do you figure we can help you?"

"By associating your names with the White Elephant," Short replied. "The public will see the club in a completely different light—simply by virtue of your names."

Earp chuckled. "Hope we're as famous as you think we are."

"I don't think it, I know it."

Short felt he'd correctly gauged public opinion. Bat Masterson and Wyatt Earp were renowned as lawmen across the breadth of the frontier. Earp, in particular, had garnered national headlines with the Gunfight at the O.K. Corral. There, on an October day in Tombstone, he and his brothers, along with Doc Holliday, had emerged victorious from the most famous shootout in American history. His name ranked high in the pantheon of Western peace officers.

Earp, like Masterson, had traded his badge for the more lucrative occupation of professional gambler. All of which worked to the advantage of Short's plan to further distance the White Elephant from the Acre. For the next week, two of the more famed lawmen on the frontier would occupy a poker table at the club. Their names were forever linked to law and order, and by association, the White Elephant would be canonized a legitimate enterprise. The message would not be lost on the reformers.

"I owe you both," Short said. "You saved my bacon in Dodge City, and now Fort Worth. I'm obliged."

"No need for that," Earp said, brushing it off with a gesture. "From what Bat tells me, we'll be in your debt. Did he really win three thousand last time he was here?"

"That sounds about right," Short affirmed. "But whatever you win, you've still got my marker."

"Three thousand!" Josephine exclaimed, one eyebrow arched quizzically at her husband. "I must have nodded off when you and Bat had this conversation. Why didn't you tell me?"

"No reason," Earp said with a lame smile. "Guess it slipped my mind."

"Well, don't let it slip your mind when I go shopping, sweetheart. I believe I'll buy myself a whole new wardrobe."

Short and Masterson exchanged an amused glance. Earp allowed the subject to drop as the carriage rolled to a stop before the hotel. The manager and his staff were waiting, honored to have such personages staying at the Mansion. Within a matter of minutes, the Earps were ensconced in a suite on the top floor, and Masterson in one next door. Their sitting rooms afforded a spectacular view of the courthouse dome.

Not quite an hour later the reporters arrived. Short had arranged the interviews, confident that a good part of the discussion would dwell on the topic of law and order. The reporter from the *Democrat* was shown into Earp's suite, and his counterpart from the *Gazette* was assigned to Masterson. Their questions, predictably,

dealt with how lawmen turned gamblers felt about reform.

The campaign for the White Elephant would be
waged in the newspapers.

Marie and Josephine got along famously from the start.
Once the interviews were under way, they settled into
Short's suite with a coffee service and a platter of fresh-
baked cookies. Short, meanwhile, ran back and forth between the interviews. The women quickly became
confidantes.

One was married to a gambler. The other lived with
a gambler and was herself a dealer. Josephine remarked
on the similarities in their lives, and laughed. "Wyatt is
such a tightwad sometimes. But then, at other times, he's
the soul of extravagance. Does Luke treat you well?"

"Oh, he certainly does," Marie confessed. "I've
never known a man so generous. Sometimes it's embarrassing."

"Never, ever let yourself be embarrassed. How many
nights do we spend alone while our men play cards forever and a day? We deserve to be spoiled."

"Just between us—I love it!"

Josephine took a pack of the new tailor-made ciga-
rettes from her pocketbook. She tapped one out, and
with careless elegance, placed it in her mouth. Then,
with a jeweled matchbox, she lit up and held the cigarette daintily between her fingers. She exhaled a thin
streamer of smoke.

Marie was fascinated by the performance. Her grand-
mother had smoked a pipe, and she'd seen saloon girls
smoke roll-your-owns. Yet she had *never* seen a lady
with a cigarette, and particularly one who smoked with
such worldly nonchalance. She thought Wyatt Earp had
married himself a handful.

"I so envy you," Josephine said, delicately waving
her cigarette. "I wish I could talk Wyatt into moving to
a city. Coeur d'Alene is so . . . crude."

"I know what you mean," Marie said with a note of empathy. "I dealt faro in several cowtowns before I came here. Talk about crude!"

"Thank God Wyatt got the cowtowns out of his system. A mining camp is bad enough."

"Don't misunderstand, I'm happy here. But even a place like Fort Worth has its bad side. I suppose you've heard about Luke's problems."

"With the reformers?" Josephine pulled a face. "I despise people who get on their moralistic high horse. What gives *them* the right?"

Marie nodded vigorously. "The man leading this crusade was a high roller himself. He quit gambling altogether to organize the reform movement. Can you imagine?"

"Well, my dear, the world is filled with hypocrites. They delight in telling us how we should run our lives."

"Luke says the only thing worse than a reformed drunk is a reformed gambler. It's just sickening!"

Josephine exhaled smoke, her expression thoughtful. "On the way from the depot, Luke told us about the prostitute. The one that was crucified." She shuddered. "What a horrid way to die."

"Some men are such beasts," Marie said fiercely. "And the reformers were practically dancing with joy! That poor girl's death rallied people to their cause."

"From what Luke said, the red-light district—Hell's Half Acre?—should be closed. Of course, once it starts, you never know where it will end. Everyone gets tarred with the same brush."

"I worry so much about Luke. I don't know what he would do if he lost the White Elephant."

"I'm glad we came," Josephine said firmly. "Perhaps Wyatt and Bat can help salvage the situation. The newspapers just adore all their stuff and nonsense."

Marie looked confused. "Stuff and nonsense?"

"Oh, you know how men love to exaggerate. To hear

them tell it, they won the West all by themselves. King Arthur and Sir Lancelot in buckskins.''

"I love it!" Marie giggled softly. "Which one is King Arthur?"

Josephine tilted her cigarette. "I'll give you one guess.''

"Wyatt."

"And I'm Lady Guinevere."

They covered their mouths to stifle their laughter.

The club room at the White Elephant was mobbed. By seven that evening, the crowd was backed up all the way to the staircase. They were there to see Wyatt Earp and Bat Masterson.

The demand for a seat in the game exceeded anything Short might have imagined. Three days ago, when he'd made the announcement, every high roller in town had asked to be included. To treat everyone fairly, he had drawn the names by lot, five men each night for the next week. Any man who arrived late automatically lost his seat.

The table was centered in the room under a blaze of light. The crowd stood shoulder to shoulder outside the roped-off area, watching as Earp and Masterson shook hands with the men drawn for tonight. All of them had shown up early, eager to try their luck against the fabled peace officers. The buy-in for a chair was five thousand dollars.

Short had taken himself out of the game. The demand was too great, and three professionals at one table would have been unfair to the other players. As he watched, Masterson cut high card for the opening deal, and the game began. Beside him was Anson Tolbert, one of the wealthiest merchants in town, who was scheduled to play tomorrow night. A regular at the poker tables, Tolbert was there tonight as a spectator.

"Luke, you're to be congratulated," he said warmly.

"Wyatt Earp and Bat Masterson at the same table represents quite a feat."

Short grinned. "They're the talk of the town, all right."

"Too bad Karl Van Zandt turned reformer on us. He's probably drunk with regret tonight."

"You think so?"

"I've known Karl for almost twenty years. Believe me, he's an inveterate poker player. I'm sure he misses it."

Short walked him off away from the crowd. "I wonder if I could ask a favor of you?"

"Anything within reason," Tolbert said. "What's on your mind?"

"Under the circumstances, it wouldn't be appropriate to contact Mr. Van Zandt myself. Would you approach him on my behalf?"

"To what purpose?"

"A message of sorts," Short said. "I brought Wyatt and Bat here to demonstrate that the uptown club owners support law and order. We're solidly behind reform in the Acre."

Tolbert nodded. "But you're concerned you'll get caught in the backwash?"

"That's it in a nutshell. Sometimes people get carried away with good deeds."

"What would you like me to say to Van Zandt?"

"Just a simple request," Short said earnestly. "The uptown clubs shouldn't be punished for the sins of the Acre. Ask him to use his influence to make that point to the reform committee."

"I'll do more than that," Tolbert promised. "I'll remind him you're one of the biggest civic boosters in Fort Worth. You deserve fair treatment."

"That's all we want, Mr. Tolbert. As the saying goes, don't throw the baby out with the bathwater."

"I'll speak to him first thing tomorrow."

A buzz of excitement swept through the crowd. Short

and Tolbert turned back just as Wyatt Earp pulled down a large pot with a full house. By rough count, Short estimated there was over two thousand dollars on the table. But he told himself the White Elephant had already taken the largest pot of the night.

His message would be delivered directly to Karl Van Zandt.

Chapter 24

On February 2, the police again raided the Acre. Squads of officers centered their efforts on Rusk Street, where most of the bordellos were located. The wagons were loaded to the gunnels with whores.

Marshal Bill Rea stood at the corner of Tenth and Rusk. He watched with a stolid expression as two of his men carried a squawling madam through the door of her establishment. Whores always caused more trouble than the rest of the sporting crowd, fighting and scratching until they were thrown in the wagons. He idly wondered why they were so offended.

Nine days had passed since the last assault on the Acre. For a week following the raids, Rea and Mayor Smith thought the reformers had been appeased. But yesterday's newspapers had excoriated the mayor and the city council with scathing editorials. The papers denounced the previous raids as a hollow gesture with no other purpose than to hoodwink the public. The mayor was savaged for operating a corrupt regime.

The editorials were clearly the work of the Law and Order Association. The word was out that Karl Van Zandt, accompanied by several clergymen, had called on both the *Democrat* and the *Gazette*. The reformers had waited a week, skeptical that City Hall would continue the war on the Acre. Their suspicions confirmed, they had demanded that the newspapers express the will of the people, and fire a broadside. The headlines reflected their outrage.

Last night, the mayor had convened an emergency session of the city council. Under siege from the newspapers, and the aldermen from the uptown district, he'd been forced to take action. The meeting was loud and contentious, and the aldermen representing the Acre had refused to buckle beneath the pressure brought by the newspapers. But in the end, with the council at a deadlock, the mayor had finally gone with the uptown crowd. The vote was four to three to resume the raids.

Later that evening Rea had met with Joe Lowe. He was the message bearer, and the message had been received with explosive anger. Lowe went into a tirade, furious that he hadn't been consulted before the council session. In a hectoring voice, he had denounced Mayor Smith for caving in so quickly to the reformers' demands. Time was on their side, he'd shouted, and they should have waited a few days, maybe a week, rather than be spooked into action. But then, in a sudden turnaround, he had calmed down, apparently resigned to the council's decision. He'd told Rea to get on with the raids.

Tonight, thinking about it, Rea was still puzzled by the conversation. Rowdy Joe Lowe was not one to back off once he'd taken a stand. His anger was understandable, for the mayor had acted without orders. But his abrupt turnabout was uncharacteristic, and therefore something of a mystery. Rea was uncomfortable when the peg didn't fit the hole, and even more so when it involved Fort Worth's vice lord. He wondered why Lowe went from shouting mad to gruff acceptance, and he found no ready answer. That bothered him.

A wagon pulled away with a load of whores. The raid tonight was restricted to brothels and two-bit cribs in the red-light district along Rusk Street. The mayor felt that prostitutes made for bigger headlines, and he'd ordered Rea to bypass the saloons and gaming dives.

Whether or not Van Zandt and the reformers agreed remained to be seen. But Rea was certain of one thing.

Lots of men would go wanting for a whore tonight.

A block over, the streetcar clanged to a stop at Tenth and Main. Jim Courtright hopped off the rear platform and walked toward the corner. As he stepped onto the curb, he heard the shrill screech of women's voices in the distance. He turned and saw helmeted policemen on Rusk Street.

Outside the Blue Belle Dance Hall, a knot of men stood watching the commotion on Rusk. Courtright nodded to one of the men. "What's all the fuss about?"

"Damn police are raiding the whorehouses."

"Guess the reformers stirred up a hornets' nest."

"What d'you mean?"

"Don't you read the papers?" Courtright said. "All the Bible-thumpers are hollerin' for salvation."

"Goddamn 'em anyway," the man cursed. "You'd think they had better things to do."

"They're trying to save your soul, brother. You'll never get through the Pearly Gates hanging around whorehouses."

"I'd sooner go to hell, anyhow. There won't be no reformers there."

"Amen to that."

The reformers seemed to Courtright a bunch of busybodies with strange ideas. The nature of man was to gamble, and drink hard liquor, and expend his lust by rolling with whores. Otherwise the Acre would never have flourished and grown to encompass the southern half of the town. He thought the reformers were an oddball crowd, with odd notions. Worse, they were bad for business.

The concept of progress was foreign to Courtright's view of things. He still longed for the old days, a time when there was rough work for a man who was handy with a gun. His detective agency was a poor substitute, but the Acre nonetheless provided him with a passable livelihood. The reformers were hellbent on destroying what little was left of the old days, and the thought of it curdled his stomach. He wished he could turn back the clock.

The sound of whores still ringing in his ears, he turned into the Blue Belle. The inside of the dance hall was festively decorated with bunting and paper lanterns suspended overhead, which lent the place an intimate atmosphere. A wooden balustrade separated the customers from the twenty or so women who waited on the dance floor. The charge was a quarter a dance, and the men purchased tickets which allowed them through an opening at the end of the railing. One ticket entitled them to ten minutes on the dance floor.

The women were presentable if not attractive, and many of them had good figures. For the most part, they came from small towns throughout the farmlands of Texas, drawn by the lure of excitement in the big city. Their features were rouged, their mouths painted bright red, and their dresses were cut low at the top and short on the bottom. On every ticket, they received a commission of ten cents, and on a busy night a girl could earn four or five dollars. Which made them better paid than most of the men who rented their services. They were known as ten-cents-a-dance girls.

On a stage at the rear of the room, five musicians wailed away with more enthusiasm than style. The men, laborers and railroad workers, shoved the girls around the dance floor like a tribe of acrobatic wrestlers. No drinking was allowed on the floor, but there was a bar outside the railing where busthead whiskey went for a quarter a shot. Dancing was thirsty work, and between sessions, they stood at the bar, their toes tapping to the music. Hardly a man among them would end the night sober.

Courtright walked toward the ticket booth. The woman behind the counter was thin and wispy, with narrow features and a pleasant smile. She was known as Ma Holbert, a nickname earned for her motherly attitude toward the girls. She nodded as he approached the booth.

"Evening, Jim," she said. "Out and about, are you?"

"Just making the rounds," Courtright replied genially. "How's tricks with you, Ma?"

"Hard times, and that's the gospel truth. I expect the police to bust through the door any minute."

"I doubt you've got anything to worry about tonight. Way it looks, they're mostly interested in the girly trade."

"The night's still young," she scoffed. "Last time, they didn't stop with the whorehouses. Arrested me and all my girls, too."

Courtright shrugged. "Don't figure they'd hit you two times in a row. You're likely safe, Ma."

"I surely hope so. Why the devil would they raid a dance hall, anyhow? I run a clean place."

"Who knows how the police think? No rhyme or reason to it."

"Hope you're not here collecting," she said pointedly. "The night we got hauled in, it cost over a hundred dollars to bail my girls out. Times are rough, Jim."

"Not that rough," Courtright countered. "I'd like a little something on account."

"Well, don't you see, that's the problem. I'm paying you to protect me and my girls. Where's the protection?"

"You know better'n that, Ma. Way things are, nobody could put the fix in with the police. Not with the reformers raisin' holy hell."

She shook her head. "Why pay for something I don't get? Fair's fair."

"That's not smart business," Courtright warned. "You're liable to buy yourself more trouble than you want."

"Don't you threaten me, Jim Courtright! You keep

your end of the bargain and I'll keep mine. Till then, I'm not paying a plug nickel!''

They argued back and forth for several minutes. She was adamant, and Courtright finally saw that it was a lost cause. He stalked out in a temper, furious that he'd been made to look the fool. But his next three stops were more of the same, with everyone demanding protection he couldn't deliver. His threats were like water on stone.

He collected nothing for the night.

A wagon packed with whores rolled past the Centennial. Lowe and Kate stood at the window, watching with grim expressions. Neither of them spoke until the wagon turned the corner.

"You made a big mistake," Kate said in a caustic tone. "You should've ordered Smith to call off the raids. That was the move."

"You're a great one for hindsight," Lowe said sullenly. "Next thing you'll be tellin' me I ought to break his legs. Maybe sew his lips shut."

"Not a bad idea. Who's that little turd to take charge and start with more raids? He's supposed to check with you first."

"Just for a change, tell me something I don't know."

Lowe was in a foul mood. Last night, upon hearing of the mayor's decision, his first reaction had been to order the raids suspended. But then, on the spur of the moment, he'd changed his mind. The city council had already voted, and to countermand the decision would risk revolt. Something told him that Smith wouldn't go along, and he was wary of putting it to the test. So he had authorized the raids, for once employing discretion rather than force. Still, the mayor's sudden streak of independence left him rankled. He was accustomed to issuing the orders.

The other reason for his dour mood was directly across the street. Wyatt Earp and Bat Masterson had now been in town four days, and their high-stakes game continued to draw large crowds to the White Elephant. Lowe was forced to a grudging sense of admiration, for Short was playing the law and order angle for all it was worth. He thought it was a clever gambit; but he was nonetheless disgruntled at losing business to a competitor. Nor had he forgotten that it was Short who betrayed him to the reformers. He still intended to settle that score. Soon.

Jim Courtright walked through the door. He saw Lowe and Kate standing at the far window, watching as another load of whores was carted off to jail. Kate gave him a sharp glance and Lowe continued staring out the window. Courtright's features were glum as he crossed the room and stopped beside them. He jerked a thumb in the direction of downtown.

"Helluva night in the Acre," he said. "There won't be a whore left in town by the time they're through."

"You can say that again!" Kate huffed. "Why do they have to pick on working girls, anyway?"

"No mystery there," Lowe said. "Our mayor's looking to grab headlines. He's a regular showboat."

"No, dearie, he's a goddamn skunk!"

Kate turned on her heel. She waddled off in a cloud of cheap perfume and indignant outrage. There was a moment of strained silence, broken only by crowds of men on the street jeering at the whores. Courtright finally looked around at Lowe.

"What's all that about?" he asked. "You and the mayor on the outs?"

"You might say we had a little misunderstanding. Nothing important."

"Maybe you can talk to him, then. Do something about this mess in the Acre. I'll go broke if it keeps on."

"How's it hurt you?"

"I'm not gettin' paid off, that's how. All the dives are using these raids for an excuse. Dumb bastards think I ought to protect 'em from the police."

Lowe sensed opportunity. He seized on the moment, nodding across the street. "Forget the police," he said. "Your problem's right over there at the White Elephant."

"Short?" Courtright said blankly. "What's he got to do with it?"

"Well, for openers, he tied a can to your tail. Everybody knows he's never paid you a red cent."

"I'm workin' on it."

"Work harder," Lowe told him. "Short's thrown in with the reformers, and they're the ones behind these raids. That makes you look all the worse in the Acre."

"Yeah," Courtright said, swiping at his mustache. "I see what you mean."

"There's a real easy solution, Jim. Get Short to pay off and show everybody you made him back down. That'll put you in solid with the dive owners."

"You mean because he's thick with the reformers?"

"Damn right," Lowe assured him. "Short turned Judas on the whole sporting crowd. They'll line up to kiss your feet."

"I guess they might at that."

"No guesswork about it."

Courtright's thoughts went suddenly to Wyatt Earp and Bat Masterson. He envied Short the friendship with such men; but he wanted no part of gunfighters with their reputation. He nodded slowly to himself.

"I'll have a talk with Short in a few days."

"Why wait?" Lowe said. "No time like the present."

"A few days won't matter," Courtright allowed. "I'll pick my own time."

"Whatever you think's best, Jim."

Lowe congratulated himself. He'd finally touched a nerve, one that would settle the score on several counts. Where the timing was concerned, he agreed with Courtright.

A few days wouldn't matter.

Chapter 25

I so hate to leave."

"No more than I hate to see you go."

"Isn't that the way of it, though? Time flies when you're having fun."

"I wish we could do it all over again."

"Now that would be fun!"

Josephine placed a folded dress in her valise. Marie sat on the edge of the bed, watching her pack. They had become fast friends over the past week, and neither of them wanted it to end. But the days had slipped away all too quickly, and suddenly, it was February 7. The Earps and Masterson were departing on the noon train.

"Well, anyway," Marie said, nodding at the overstuffed valise. "You aren't leaving empty-handed."

Josephine laughed softly. "Wyatt says we can't afford to stay longer. He thinks I bought out the town."

"You practically did!"

"A girl has to take advantage of opportunity. God knows when I'll see a city again."

Every day for the last week they had gone shopping. Josephine, with Marie as her guide, had gleefully worked her way through every fashionable ladies' store in Fort Worth. Her valise was bursting with new gowns and frilly underthings, and several bottles of imported French perfume. Marie estimated she had spent over a thousand dollars.

"You'll definitely be missed," Marie said. "Every shopkeeper in town will remember your name."

"Honestly, I think Fort Worth has ruined me. I just dread going back to Coeur d'Alene."

"Yes, but all your new clothes will knock their eyes out. You'll be the belle of the ball."

"I have to say, that's small consolation. Idaho is still Idaho."

Josephine closed her valise. She sighed, casting a last look around the bedroom, and followed Marie into the sitting room. Masterson and Short were seated on the sofa, and Earp sat across from them in a wing-back chair. Marie took a place on the sofa and Josephine perched on the arm of Earp's chair. He glanced up at her.

"All packed?"

"Yes, unfortunately," she said in a small voice. "I regret to say I'm ready to travel."

Earp patted her hand. "Maybe we'll come back one of these days. You never know."

"Don't bank on it," Masterson said jestfully. "I think we wore out our welcome."

Their week-long poker game had treated them well. Masterson had won something over three thousand and Earp had come away with close to five thousand. The marathon game was still all the talk among the town's high rollers, and a wry editorial had appeared in that morning's edition of the *Gazette*. The editor, tongue-in-cheek, wished them Godspeed.

"You're welcome anytime," Short assured them. "You'll always find a game at the White Elephant."

Earp looked at him. "Question is, will you find a game? The reformers don't show any signs of backing off."

"Wyatt, I've got a good feeling about the future. You and Bat helped out a lot."

There had been another series of raids in the Acre last night. The reformers, with the newspapers sounding their battle cry, had again badgered City Hall into action. Yet Short was relatively sanguine about the prospects for the uptown clubs. Through Anson Tolbert, the merchant acting as his intermediary, he had received a message back from Karl Van Zandt. The leader of the Law and Order Association made no promises, but he offered encouragement. The Acre was all the fight the reformers could handle.

Short nonetheless felt that Earp and Masterson had been the turning point. Their appearance at the White Elephant had underscored the support of law and order by the uptown clubs. All that had gone before—the newspaper ad favoring reform and the donation to the reformers' war chest—had been mere prelude. The clincher, more persuasive than anything, had been two of the frontier's most respected lawmen conducting themselves in a professional manner at a poker table. Karl Van Zandt had said as much, without saying it openly, in the message delivered by Tolbert. The uptown clubs had been granted absolution.

"You're satisfied, then?" Earp said at length. "You think the do-gooders will leave you alone?"

Short nodded. "I'd say things are looking rosy. Lots more so than a week ago."

"Strange times," Masterson said in an unusually somber tone. "Never thought I'd see the day when gambling was lumped in with sin."

"These days it's called progress," Short said. "There's no room for the old sporting crowd. They're a thing of the past."

"All the same . . ." Masterson paused, shook his head. "When progress overtakes us, I think I'll look back and miss the old days. Those were good times."

"The best of times," Earp amended. "Or maybe we were just younger then. Hard to say."

There was a profound silence. The three men sat lost in thought, reflecting on the past. For them, the frontier of their youth was dwindling into mythic memory, a time when all things were possible. They were survivors, seldom given to sentiment, their eyes on the future. But for a moment they stared inward at the old days.

Josephine and Marie exchanged a glance. "My goodness, just look at yourselves," Josephine said, playfully mocking them. "Anybody would think you were a bunch of old coots with one foot in the grave. You're still young men!"

"Younger than we look," Masterson said, joshing her. "Some days I feel like a regular ball-o'-fire. How about you boys?"

Earp chuckled. "Luke's the fire-eater of this crowd. Who else would take on the reformers?"

"You know, that reminds me," Masterson said, turning to Short. "Last time I was here, you'd locked horns with the local toughnut. I forgot his name."

"Courtright," Short said. "Jim Courtright."

"How'd things work out?"

"So far so good. We've got a truce of sorts."

"What about Lowe?" Earp asked. "Do you have a truce with him?"

"More like a standoff," Short said. "Rowdy Joe tends to hold a grudge."

"Watch yourself," Earp warned. "I remember Lowe from the cowtowns. He's a dirty fighter."

"Don't worry, I'll keep my eyes open."

Some while later a bellman came to collect the luggage. A carriage was waiting outside the hotel, and Marie accompanied them on the ride to the train station. There was no more talk of the reformers, or what the future held for Fort Worth. Instead, they spoke of lighter topics, their conversation purposely carefree, dwelling on the good times shared over the past week. None of them looked forward to parting.

At the depot, Marie and Josephine got teary. They hugged each other, promising to write, and Josephine finally hurried aboard the lead passenger coach. Earp clasped Short's hand, again expressing thanks for a profitable week, and followed along. Masterson, jaunty as always, sobered a moment before he boarded. He told Short to get on the telegraph if things went wrong with the reformers. Friends, he announced with a grin, were on call in the event of trouble.

Short and Marie waved as the train pulled out of the station. They stood watching until the last coach faded into the distance. As they walked back to the carriage, she dabbed at her eyes with a hanky. She smiled sadly.

"I'm going to miss them terribly. I wish I had friends like that."

"Yeah, Bat and Wyatt are a matched pair—aces high."

Marie thought it was actually three of a kind. For the man beside her filled the hand.

All of them aces high.

Tongues of flame leapt brightly in the fireplace. Short sat smoking a cheroot, his gaze fixed on the crackling logs. In the bedroom, he heard Marie bustling about, changing clothes for an evening at the club. Yet he was only vaguely aware of her movements, or her presence. His mind was elsewhere.

For a week he had been preoccupied with Masterson and Earp. Organizing their nightly poker game, and entertaining them during the day, had distracted him from other matters. But with their departure, his concentration centered again on the reform movement, and business. He had invested himself and his bankroll in the White Elephant, and despite his optimism that morning, there was lingering concern for the future. A gambling man never took anything for granted.

Short was all too aware of the vagaries involved in any reform movement. He felt reassured by Karl Van Zandt's promising attitude toward the uptown clubs. Still, the weight of public opinion was the ultimate factor in whether the fight would be won or lost. His campaign to establish himself as a civic booster had cast him in a favorable light. Yet he was a great believer in hedging his bet, and he pondered what more could be done. Nothing particularly noteworthy came to mind.

The problem was one of appearances. He had arranged a substantial contribution from the uptown clubs to the Law and Order Association. The profits from John L. Sullivan's exhibition, generous by any standard, had been donated to the town's churches. Any further contribution might appear that he was trying to buy—or bribe—the men who influenced public opinion. Which left him stumped for some grand scheme to garner added newspaper coverage for himself and the White Elephant. Wyatt Earp and Bat Masterson were a hard act to top.

Lost in his ruminations, he hardly noticed as Marie came through the bedroom door. She moved forward and took a chair opposite him by the fireplace. He glanced around, surprised to find that her expression was downcast. She appeared somehow apprehensive.

"Why so glum?" he said. "Something wrong?"

"I've been thinking." Her eyes were troubled. "What Wyatt said about Joe Lowe . . ."

"You mean about Lowe being a dirty fighter?"

"Yes."

"Well, that's not exactly a revelation. I knew that without being told."

"But there's more to it," she said. "While I was dressing, I suddenly got afraid. Maybe he was waiting until Bat and Wyatt were gone."

Short took a pull on his cheroot. "Waiting for what?"

"Maybe he was afraid to try anything with them in town. Maybe he was waiting for them to leave."

"Let me get this straight. You think Bat and Wyatt were protecting me from Lowe? Is that the idea?"

"Of course it is," she said. "Lowe would be a fool to try anything while they were here. It makes perfect sense to me."

"Does it?" Short chuckled around a cloud of smoke.

"I've been on the outs with Lowe for a long time. What's last week got to do with anything?"

"Don't you dare laugh at me! Joe Lowe is a cold-blooded murderer. You've said it yourself, more than once. Why won't you take it seriously?"

"Believe me, I take Rowdy Joe very seriously."

"Then why are you laughing?"

"I suppose it's what you said about Bat and Wyatt. Where Lowe's concerned, I don't need any protection. I can handle it myself."

"You're just one man," she persisted. "Lowe has a dozen men on his payroll. Can you handle all of them?"

"Slow down a minute," Short said in a temperate voice. "What's got you so upset all of a sudden?"

"I couldn't stop thinking about what Wyatt said on the way to the train station. He sounded so . . . ominous."

"Wyatt was just talking friend to friend. He wanted me to be on guard."

Her face crumpled. "God, I couldn't bear it if anything happened to you." She blinked back tears, her voice hollow. "I just couldn't."

Short tossed his cheroot in the fireplace. He moved to her chair, lifting her by her arms, and pulled her into a tight hug. "Nothing's going to happen to me. Guarantee it."

She nuzzled against his shoulder. "You promise?"

"On a stack of Bibles."

A while later they emerged from the hotel. The weather was raw, with overcast skies and a blustery wind out of the north. Marie clung to his arm as they walked to Main Street and turned the corner. She had pulled herself together, but she still looked on the verge of tears. Her features were drawn, oddly leeched of emotion.

Jake Johnson was standing at the bar when they entered the White Elephant. He started forward to greet them, but Marie continued on by herself, staring straight

ahead. Short joined him at the bar and they watched as
she went up the stairs to the club room. Johnson cocked
his head in a quizzical look.

"What's wrong with Marie?" he asked. "She didn't
even say hello."

Short made an empty gesture. "She thinks I'm about
to get myself killed."

"What gave her that idea?"

"We got to talking about Joe Lowe. She's convinced
he'll have some of his bully-boys punch my ticket."

"Well, now that you mention it . . ." Johnson offered
him a lame shrug. "I haven't said anything because it'd
just get you hot under the collar. But the word's
around."

"Oh?" Short held his gaze. "What word is that?"

"The sporting crowd's laying ten-to-one odds Lowe
will kill you. I don't have to tell you they're rooting for
Lowe."

"I always fancied being the underdog. When did this
get started?"

"Couple of weeks ago," Johnson said. "Just after
we ran that ad supporting the reformers. Word got out
pretty quick how Lowe busted in here and threatened
you."

"Ten to one," Short said in a musing tone. "What
about you and the other club owners? Any odds on
you?"

"Everybody knows you were the one behind that ad.
You'll remember I warned you about Al Lynch. He let
the cat out of the bag."

"So it's just me?"

Johnson nodded. "Sort of looks that way."

"Not bad odds," Short said with some amusement.
"How would you bet it, Jake?"

"Don't kid around about a thing like that."

"I'm trying to give you some good advice."

"What d'you mean?"

Short grinned. "Take the odds."

Chapter 26

A branch rattled against the window like the bones of a skeleton. The tree was bare of leaves and stood framed against a dingy sky. Late afternoon slowly faded to a cold, wintry dusk.

Courtright's mood was as bleak as the weather. He sat slumped in a chair, staring out the parlor window. His eyes were dull, and he watched vacantly as a keening wind battered at the tree. The naked branches whipped against the side of the house.

From the kitchen, he heard a garbled monotone of voices. The children were acutely sensitive to his moods, and never bothered him when he sat lost in a funk. After returning home from school, they had retreated from the parlor and joined their mother in the kitchen. The smell of freshly baked bread wafted through the dining room.

Outside, the tree continued to thrash in the wind. Courtright's gaze clung to the branch that tapped against the window, the beat like a scratchy metronome. All afternoon he had sat, locked within himself, brooding on problems that were rapidly spinning out of control. The police raids in the Acre last night had left him reeling and dumbfounded, at a loss as to how he could restore his name among the sporting crowd. He felt like a man sinking ever deeper into quicksand.

Elizabeth came through the door of the dining room. She moved hesitantly into the parlor, fearful of unsettling him further. Since late that morning, when he'd awakened from a drunken stupor, he had sat staring out the window in glum silence. She knew his nerves were frayed, and suspected that his dark mood was somehow linked to the troubles in the Acre. For almost two weeks now, when the police raids first began, he had steadily become more withdrawn, wrapped in a sullen torpor. She stopped beside his chair.

"Supper's almost ready," she said gently. "Wouldn't you like to get washed up?"

Courtright stirred listlessly. "I'm not hungry."

"Jim, you hardly ate anything for breakfast. You've got to have food in you."

"Maybe later."

She tried to keep her voice neutral. "You can't go on like this. Drinking all night and not eating enough for a sparrow. You'll kill yourself."

"Humph." Courtright grunted a sour laugh. "Wouldn't be much of a loss."

"For mercy sakes, Jim! What's the matter with you? Why do you talk like that?"

She moved around the chair, facing him. He motioned her off. "You're in my way."

"What?"

"I want to see that tree."

"Tree?" She turned, glancing out the window. "What's so important about that tree?"

The branch scratched against the windowpane. Courtright waved her aside. "I have to see if that branch breaks off."

"Why would you care about a silly old branch?"

"Maybe if it lasts, I will, too. Some things break and others don't."

Elizabeth studied him for a long moment. His words made no sense, and she felt a stab of fear that he'd lost his mind. A sudden vision of the insane asylum flashed before her eyes, and she saw him wandering the halls with the other crazy people. She took his face in her hands.

"Jim," she said softly. "Jim, look at me."

Courtright reluctantly tore his gaze from the branch. She saw that his eyes were clear and he appeared lucid. Her heart skipped a beat with relief. "Please, Jim, please talk to me. What's wrong with you?"

"Why, I reckon that's pretty simple, Betty. I've lost it all. Everything."

"I don't understand. Lost what?"

"My business," Courtright muttered. "What with these raids, my customers are refusin' to pay. Last night just made it worse."

"You worry too much," she said, trying to downplay it. "Things like this come and go. It won't last."

"You're wrong there. Damn reformers aren't about to quit. They'll wreck everything."

"I'm sure it's not as bad as you make it sound."

"No?"

Courtright pulled a thin wad of bills from his pocket. He motioned for her to hold out her hand, and slowly counted the money. He closed her fist on the bills.

"Twenty-three dollars," he said with an air of finality. "That's all we've got between us and the poor house. You'd better hang on to it."

Elizabeth was shocked. The desperate cast of his features shook her even more than the poverty of their circumstances. She attempted to put the best light on it. "We've had hard times before," she said brightly. "One way or another, things always work out. We'll manage somehow."

"No, we won't! That's what I'm tryin' to tell you. They've ruined my name."

"What are you talking about? Who ruined your name?"

"Short and the reformers," Courtright said bitterly. "The little runt wouldn't pay up, and then he tossed in with the reformers. They made a laughingstock of me in the Acre.''

''I can't believe that,'' she said, shaking her head. ''You have too many friends, all over town. They wouldn't turn on you.''

''Turned out the joke's on me. I don't have any friends, Betty. Never did, the way things look.''

Elizabeth heard defeat in his voice. In all their years together, she had never known him to lose heart. His steadfast spirit, for all his faults, was one of the reasons she loved him still. She refused to believe he'd fallen so low. She wouldn't accept it.

''You're no quitter,'' she said with some feeling. ''You've got to get hold of yourself and show them you won't be beat down. Do you hear me?''

''Yeah, I hear you.''

Courtright stared at the branch. He saw that it was still there, still tapping against the window, and he took that as a good omen. He told himself that his wife was right, that he was no quitter. He was down but not out.

Elizabeth moved aside as he rose from his chair. He walked to the wall pegs by the door and strapped on his gun belt. Then, after clapping on his hat, he shrugged into his mackinaw. She hurried across the room.

''Where are you going?''

''Downtown.''

''But you haven't had supper.''

''I'll get something along the way.''

''Jim—''

''Don't worry about it.''

Courtright went out the door. When it closed, she rushed to the front window and watched him walk off into the gathering dusk. She felt a moment's guilt and wondered if she'd done the right thing, provoking him with stern words. But then, on second thought, she realized there were no good options, given the situation. There was only what seemed best at the time.

She turned back toward the kitchen.

*   *   *

Lowe stood at the bar. He lifted a schooner of beer and took a long, gulping swallow. Foam stuck to his mustache, and he wiped it away with a swipe of his hand. His cigar had gone out and he struck a match on his thumbnail. He lit up in a wreath of smoke.

The Centennial was starting to fill with the evening crowd. Kate was off somewhere backstage in the theater, browbeating a new song-and-dance team that had performed poorly in rehearsal. Lowe didn't envy them the experience, but neither could he work up any great sense of sympathy. He had troubles enough of his own.

Last night's raid seemed to him the handwriting on the wall. The reformers' war on the Acre was gaining momentum, and he couldn't find a way to sidetrack them. Despite his threats, Mayor Smith had bowed to pressure from the newspapers and ordered the police to conduct yet another sweep through the sporting district. His one consolation was that Smith would be dumped from office come election time. He planned to throw the swing vote to another candidate, any candidate. One who would follow orders.

Lowe saw Courtright come through the door. His simmering anger went up another notch, and he puffed sullenly on his cigar. He'd begun to think of Courtright as one in a chain of nettlesome disappointments, all of them somehow involving Luke Short. The reformers, the mayor, his loss of influence with the uptown club owners, all part and parcel of Short's crafty handiwork. Yet almost a week had passed since he had last put the goad to Courtright, and nothing had changed. Short was still walking the streets.

"Evenin', Joe," Courtright said, leaning into the bar. "How about one on the house?"

Lowe signaled a bartender. "I'm starting to think Kate's got you pegged right. You're turning into a freeloader."

"Hard times, that's all."

The bartender poured a shot and Courtright downed it neat. He knuckled his mustache. "Matter of fact . . ." he paused, averting his eyes. "I was wonderin' if you might advance me next month's fee. I'm stone broke."

"Don't come crying to me. You've got nobody to fault but yourself."

"You know damn well that's not so. The reformers are the ones that—"

"Horseshit!" Lowe exploded. "You can't lay it off on the reformers. Your problem's over there at the White Elephant." He drilled Courtright with a hard stare. "When are you gonna do something about it?"

"Any day now," Courtright said, stung by the sarcasm. "I was waitin' for them glory-hounds to leave town. Three to one's not good odds."

"Are you talking about Earp and Masterson? Hell, they wouldn't have interfered. It's between you and Short."

"Who knows whether they would have taken a hand? I wasn't willin' to run the risk."

Lowe fixed him with a look. "You're a joke all over the Acre. Everybody thinks you've lost your balls."

"Goddamn lie," Courtright said, his features flushed. "I'd like to have somebody say that to my face. We'd clear it up real quick."

"There's only one thing that'll lay it to rest. You've got to brace Short."

"Joe, I just told you that's what I aim to do."

"I mean *now*." Lowe leaned closer, dropped his voice. "You've either got to collect from Short or kill him. Otherwise you're through in this town."

Courtright nodded, his eyes suddenly cold. "Guess it's time to fish or cut bait. Him or me."

"Now you're finally talking sense."

Lowe ordered a round of drinks. He'd heard something in Courtright's voice, and he was confident now that the matter would be brought to a head. For his part, though he couldn't stop the reformers, he felt certain the

account would be settled with Short. He told himself it
would have to do.

Half a loaf was better than none.

Late that night Courtright wandered into Stewart's Saloon. The establishment was at Fifteenth and Main, a
couple of blocks from the train station. For a decade or
more, it had been a hangout for railroad workers.

Courtright was drunk. All evening, he had cadged
drinks throughout the Acre, and he was listing slightly
from the effects of the alcohol. Yet he was still able to
navigate, though by now his speech was slurred. He was
not a happy drunk.

The whiskey had further darkened his mood. He
glowered at John Stewart, the proprietor, who stood behind the bar. Stewart knew him to be a troublemaker
when under the influence, and frowned as he crossed the
room. But he suddenly veered off and walked to a table
where two men were seated. He dropped into a chair.

"Howdy, Tom," he said to one of the men. "Let's
have a drink."

Tom McCarty was superintendent of the railyards. He
had known Courtright for many years, and considered
him a friend. The other man at the table was Arnold
James, the stationmaster of Union Depot. Like many
men, he was a nodding acquaintance with Courtright,
and on occasion, they'd shared a drink. McCarty signaled a barkeep for a clean glass.

"Out on the town?" he said to Courtright, pouring
from a bottle on the table. "Damnable weather out there
tonight. Looks like it's gonna rain."

Courtright tossed off the drink. "That's the story of
my life. Always gettin' rained on."

"Yeah, I know what you mean," McCarty said. "I
heard about your troubles in the Acre."

"Hell, you don't know the half of it. Goddamn Short,
he's caused me a world of grief."

"Luke Short?"

"Who else?" Courtright mumbled, sloshing a shot of whiskey into his glass. "Thinks he's Mr. Big anymore. Him and his fancy ways."

"I saw him today," James commented. "He put Wyatt Earp and Bat Masterson on the noon train. I heard they won nine or ten thousand between them."

Courtright grunted. "Good riddance to bad rubbish. Couple of nobodies with overblown reputations. Short's not any better."

"Overblown?" McCarty repeated blankly. "I don't follow you, Jim."

"Like folks say, God made men, but Sam Colt made them equal. Short's liable to learn that the hard way."

"Strong talk," McCarty said. "What've you got against Short?"

"Whole bunch of things." Courtright motioned with a loose, sloppy gesture. "Little bastard don't show the proper respect. Gave people the wrong idea."

"About you?"

"Who the hell else we talkin' about? He's the one that got everybody in the Acre down on me."

"I thought that was caused by the police raids."

Courtright knocked back his drink. "Wasn't caused by nothin' but that little pissant. I'm gonna fix his wagon for it, too."

McCarty and James exchanged a glance. The braggadocio of drunken men was usually written off to whiskey-talk. But Courtright was a different matter, someone notorious for resorting to a gun. McCarty took it a step further.

"What is it you've got in mind?"

"Rowdy Joe had the right idea," Courtright said, reaching for the bottle. "I'm gonna brace Short up at the White Elephant. If he don't pay, then he pays." He paused, looking at them with a drunken leer. "Get it?"

McCarty and James both got it. But the introduction of Joe Lowe's name altered the tone of the conversation. Neither of them wanted any part of a matter involving

Fort Worth's vice lord. Finally, after a prolonged silence, McCarty shrugged.

"Too late tonight to do anything. Don't you think so, Jim?"

"Tonight, tomorrow night," Courtright muttered. "I got lots of time."

"Sure you do," McCarty agreed. "Sleep on it and you'll likely change your mind. Things always look different in daylight."

"You wanna know something, Tom?"

"What's that?"

"I've done slept on it too much."

They watched as Courtright poured himself another drink.

Chapter 27

A biting wind drifted in from the northwest. Early that morning, the skies opened in a cold drizzle that had lasted all day. The sidewalks were still wet, glistening beneath the glow of streetlamps.

Short and Marie came out of the hotel as a murky dusk settled over the town. She hugged his arm, her breath frosty in the damp chill. Up ahead, a wagon rounded the corner of Main and splashed through a puddle at curbside. She shivered, clutching his arm tighter.

"I just hate it when it rains."

"Look on the bright side," Short said. "We'd be up to our knees in snow if it was any colder. I'll take the rain."

Neither of them had been outside all day. They had lounged around the suite, with a cheery blaze in the fireplace, under no compunction to brave the dreary weather. Their meals were ordered from room service, and after the maid tidied up following breakfast, they had returned to bed and made love. They got dressed only when the dinge of twilight darkened the windows.

"I suppose you're right," she said as they turned the corner. "If it had snowed, we probably wouldn't have any business tonight. How's that for the bright side?"

"Spoken like a professional," Short said wryly. "A gambler looks to the play first, last, and always. The game's the thing."

"Oh, I don't know," she said with a mischievous smile. "You had a different game in mind this afternoon. Feeling pretty frisky, weren't you?"

Short chuckled. "I seem to recall I was the innocent party. You're a brazen woman."

"Brazen!" she protested. "I am no such thing."

"What would you call it, then?"

"Well, maybe a little—spontaneous?"

"Let's settle for wanton."

Arm in arm, laughing, they walked into the White Elephant. Philipe Bordeaux, the maitre d', greeted them as they came through the door. Short thought the name was wholly invented, along with the sophisticated airs Bordeaux employed to impress their patrons. He suspected the maitre d' had taken lessons in New Orleans.

"Good evening," Bordeaux said in a suave manner. "You are the very picture of a happy couple."

"Thank you, Philipe." Short glanced around the restaurant. "Jake in the office?"

"No, he asked me to inform you he will be a bit late this evening. A business matter, I believe."

"Business," Short said archly "—or pleasure?"

"One never knows with Mr. Johnson."

"And one would never tell even if one knows, correct?"

Bordeaux feigned ignorance. "There's a man here asking for you." He discreetly ducked his head across the room. "The portly gentleman at the end of the bar."

Short inspected a heavyset man who stood in profile, nursing a beer. "Who is he?"

"He offered no name and I was reluctant to ask. He did say it was important."

"Definitely not a high roller," Short decided, turning to Marie. "I'll find out what's so important. See you upstairs."

"I'll be there," she said saucily. "The game's the thing, you know."

Short grinned, watching as she moved toward the

staircase. He nodded to Bordeaux, removing his hat, and crossed to the bar. The heavyset man, who was standing alone, saw him approaching, and placed his beer mug on the counter. Short stopped a pace away.

"I'm Luke Short," he said. "You asked for me?"

"Yessir, I'd know you anywhere. Seen your picture in the paper often enough."

"You have the advantage of me."

"Arnold James," the man said hastily. "I'm station-master down at the depot."

"What can I do for you, Mr. James?"

"I was hoping we could talk in private."

Short glanced over his shoulder. "We're not likely to be overheard. What's on your mind?"

"Well . . ." James lowered his voice, eyes darting along the bar. "I'd need your word this won't go any further, Mr. Short. I can't have my name involved."

"Why is that?"

"I'm not anxious to get myself killed."

"You make it sound like you're at some risk, Mr. James."

"No, sir, you are."

Short looked at him. "All right, you have my word."

"That's good enough for me." James cast another glance down the bar. "Last night, me and a friend were having a few drinks at Stewart's Saloon. Who walks in but Jim Courtright. Drunk as a lord."

"Are you friends with Courtright?"

"No, not by a longshot. But he's on a first-name basis with my friend, Tom McCarty. So, anyway, he sits down with us."

"Go on, I'm listening."

"Like I said, he was drunk," James went on. "Got talkative, and turns out he blames you for all his troubles in the Acre. He threatened your life."

"You heard it yourself?" Short asked. "He threatened to kill me?"

"Yeah, in so many words. Something about if you

don't pay, then you'll pay. He means to braee you for protection money."

"And if I don't pay . . ."

"Way it sounded, he'll kill you. 'Course, there's more to it."

"More to what?"

"Courtright let it slip," James said, his eyes furtive. "Joe Lowe's the one that gave him the idea. I got the feeling Lowe put him up to it."

"You couldn't be mistaken?" Short insisted. "He actually used Lowe's name?"

"Yessir, I heard it with my own ears. You've got yourself some powerful enemies, Mr. Short."

"So it seems."

"None of my business," James said. "But it's probably got something to do with you backing the reformers. Word's around on the grapevine that Lowe popped his cork."

"I'm curious," Short said in a speculative tone. "We've never met, and it's not like you owe me anything. Why tell me all this?"

"Well, that's pretty simple. Anybody who could bring Wyatt Earp and Bat Masterson to town gets my vote. I felt obliged to warn you."

"I appreciate your concern," Short said, grasping his hand in a firm grip. "Not many men would have the sand to come here tonight."

"Don't think I didn't try to talk myself out of it. Guess I'm just stubborn."

"Whatever the reason, you have my marker, Mr. James."

"I'm glad to have been of service."

James walked toward the door. Short watched after him a moment, mentally assessing everything he'd been told. From the start, he had suspected that Lowe was behind Courtright's demands for protection money. Nor was there any question in his mind that Lowe wanted him dead. So all the pieces had now fallen into place.

Courtright would call him out, maybe tonight. Force it to a fight.

One of the bartenders wandered over. "Get you something, Mr. Short?"

"No, Bob," Short said. "I'm not drinking tonight."

"Not feeling off your feed, are you?"

"Ask me that at closing time."

After collecting his hat, Short moved across the room. As he started up the staircase, a sudden thought went through his mind. He wondered when Courtright would show.

Jake Johnson rounded the corner from Third onto Main. He was feeling chipper tonight, his stride brisk, a satisfied smile on his face. He hardly noticed the dreary weather.

Usually once or twice a week, Johnson visited a lady friend on the east side of town. Opportunity was key to their secret liaison, for she was the mistress of Mayor Smith. When the mayor spent an evening with his family, Johnson slipped by for a tryst with the woman. She'd put ginger in his step tonight.

Officer Wally Tucker was standing beneath a streetlight on the corner. A wiry man with knobby joints, he was idly swinging his nightstick. Johnson considered him one of the more reliable policemen on the force, tough and even-handed if not a mental giant. He nodded with a pleasant smile.

"Evening, Wally," he said. "Think it's stopped raining?"

"Sure hope so," Tucker said, his helmet bobbing. "Leastways, the wind's dropped off a mite. Not so cold."

"No raids in the Acre tonight?"

"Nope, and I aim to tell you, that's fine with me. I'm plumb wore out wrestlin' whores."

"I wouldn't doubt it," Johnson said. "What do you hear around City Hall? Will the raids continue?"

Tucker shrugged his shoulders. "Guess that depends on the reformers and the newspapers. Every time they yell frog, the mayor squats."

Johnson was amused by the image. Still, having just entertained himself at the mayor's expense, he restrained a laugh. "Nothing like the steamroller of democracy," he said dryly. "In the end, the people usually get their way."

"All the same, I sure do miss the good old days. Things was lots easier then."

Tucker was still shaking his head when Johnson walked away. A few doors downstreet, the crack of a rifle sounded from the shooting gallery. Johnson saw two men of casual acquaintance, Will Allison and Bud Herring, standing at the counter with rifles. Ella Blackwell, who operated the gallery, looked around as Johnson stopped to watch.

"Hello there, Jake," she said engagingly. "Care to join the contest?"

"No, I'll have to pass," Johnson told her. "I'm surprised you're open tonight."

"Well, you know, a girl's got to make a living. Soon as it quit raining, I opened up. A nickel here, a nickel there."

Herring fired, dropping a metal duck off the trolley. He glanced around. "How's things, Jake?"

"Never better, Bud," Johnson replied. "Who's the best shot?"

"I'd say we're about neck and neck. Loser buys the drinks."

"That'll be Bud," Allison said, pausing to sight on a pinwheel. "He's never beat me yet."

Herring laughed. "I've got your number tonight."

"Tell me that when you pay for the drinks."

Johnson walked off as the gunfire resumed. He entered the White Elephant and found that Philipe Bordeaux had everything under control. As he started toward the office to drop off his hat and coat, Short came down the stairs. He thought he'd never seen such a cold expression.

"Something wrong, Luke?"

"Let's go back to the office."

Short led the way down the corridor. Inside the office, he closed the door as Johnson shrugged out of his top-coat. His features were stolid. "Do you know a man named Arnold James?"

"Yes, I do," Johnson said. "He's the Union Depot stationmaster."

"Is he trustworthy?"

"I've never known him to be otherwise. Why?"

"Mr. James says Jim Courtright intends to kill me."

Johnson's face went slack. "Where the devil did he get that?"

"From Courtright himself."

Short went on to explain. He related the gist of the conversation with Arnold James. His manner was cool and collected, and his tone of voice seemed almost detached. He ended on a somber note.

"I think it's only a matter of time. I'd guess sooner rather than later."

Johnson heaved a sigh. "Maybe it was just the whiskey talking. Courtright tends to go off half-cocked when he's drunk."

"I take it as the straight goods," Short said firmly. "He dropped Joe Lowe's name, and that's the clincher. He's been primed to put me under."

"How would Lowe convince him to kill you?"

"I've been thinking about that. They're pretty thick, and Lowe plays him like a ventriloquist. Kill Short and all your problems are solved in the Acre. That's probably what Lowe got him to believe."

"Jesus," Johnson said on an indrawn breath. "I wouldn't doubt but what you're on the money. Courtright's just dopey enough to fall for it."

A knock sounded at the door. Bordeaux stuck his

head into the office. "Someone to see you, Mr. Short. His name is Bud Herring."

"Herring?" Short repeated. "I don't know anyone by that name."

"I do," Johnson said. "I saw him a few minutes ago at the shooting gallery. Let him in, Philipe."

Bordeaux ushered Herring into the office and closed the door. Johnson greeted him with a bemused smile. "What can we do for you, Bud?"

"Nothing for me," Herring said. "I've got a message from Jim Courtright."

"Courtright?"

"Yeah, he broke in on me and Will at the shooting gallery. Got a little tough about it, and I don't mess with the likes of Courtright. He sent a message for Mr. Short."

Short stepped forward. "What's the message?"

"Well, it's sorta odd," Herring said. "Courtright wants to see you outside. Don't know why he sent me. He could've come himself."

"I appreciate you taking the time," Short said. "Tell him I'll be out directly. Sorry if you were inconvenienced."

"No, it wasn't nothing like that. Glad to be of help."

Short saw him to the door. A moment passed in leaden silence before Johnson finally collected his wits. He wagged his head. "You can't go out there, Luke."

"Why not?"

"One of you will get killed."

"And you're afraid it'll be me."

"Courtright's no slouch with a gun."

"Neither am I."

"Look . . ." Johnson spread his hands, clearly flustered. "Let me try to talk sense with him. Maybe he'll listen."

"For how long?" Short asked. "Lowe can spin his head like a top. He'll just be back tomorrow night."

"What's the harm in trying? Who knows what'll happen between now and tomorrow?"

"Jake, it won't change a thing."

"At least let me try."

Short deliberated on it a moment. He thought it was a waste of time, postponing the inevitable. But on the other hand, he preferred not to kill Jim Courtright. He finally nodded.

"All right, but don't give him an inch, Jake. No money, no promises. Nothing."

"I'll get him to listen to reason somehow. You just wait here."

"I'm not going anywhere."

Johnson hurried out of the office.

Chapter 28

Courtright was waiting near the shooting gallery. Between shots, Bud Herring and Will Allison watched him with guarded looks, still unsettled by his gruff manner. Ella Blackwell watched them all with an air of puzzlement.

Johnson came through the door of the White Elephant. He spotted Courtright standing at curbside, and caught the curious glances of the men from the shooting gallery. Upstreet, on the corner, he saw Officer Wally Tucker idly twirling his nightstick. A policeman within hailing distance somehow eased his nerves.

As he approached, he observed that the former lawman was in an agitated state. Courtright kept shifting from foot to foot, and the muscles in his jaws were knotted tight. His jacket was brushed back, and the reversed grips of his pistols jutted from their holsters. Johnson gave him a quick nod.

"Evening, Jim," he said pleasantly. "What can I do for you?"

"Forget the soft soap," Courtright grated. "I sent for Short. Where's he at?"

"Luke's busy just at the moment. Was there something you wanted?"

"Goddamn right there's something I want. Why else d'you think I'm here?"

"I don't know."

Johnson detected no odor of alcohol. He thought Courtright appeared remarkably sober, and he took that as a dangerous sign. He'd never known Courtright to be so belligerent except when drunk.

"What's the problem?" he said, still trying to defuse the situation. "Maybe we could talk about it."

Courtright snorted. "I've had all the talk I care to hear. Short owes me money."

"Come on now, Jim, we've covered that ground before. You know he won't pay protection."

"Then tell him to trot his little ass out here *muy pronto*. Time to square accounts."

"What's that mean?"

"What the hell you think it means? I'll have my money or I'll have satisfaction."

"Good God," Johnson said. "You'd call him out over a few measly dollars?"

Courtright's features twisted in a grimace. "Don't play thick with me, Jake. We're not talkin' about money."

"Then just what are we talking about?"

"I won't be made a fool, especially by a goddamn runt. You should've warned Short who he's dealin' with."

Johnson struggled to mount an argument. All Courtright had left was his pride, and that had been savaged by gossip among the sporting crowd. Everyone in the Acre was laughing about the little man at the White Elephant running a sandy on the town's big pistolero. There was no skirting the insult.

"How long have we been friends?" Johnson said earnestly. "Going on ten years, isn't it? Maybe more."

Courtright shrugged it off. "So what?"

"Jim, I'm asking you as a friend. There's no sense pushing things this hard. Let it lay."

"Don't go pullin' friendship with me. You should've made Short pay up when you had the chance. Who owns the White Elephant, anyway?"

"You know he's my partner in the gaming club. I couldn't go against him once he had his mind set."

"You went against me," Courtright said sharply. "Time to pay the piper, Jake. I've come to collect."

Johnson ruefully wagged his head. "I'm asking you again to let it drop. No good will come of this."

"Send him out or I'm coming inside. That's my last word on it."

"Will you at least listen to him? Not go off half-cocked and start a fight."

"Why, sure I'll listen," Courtright said with a wolfish grin. "I'm not one to pick a quarrel."

"All right, I'll see what he says. You just wait here."

"Tell him it's here or inside. His choice."

Johnson hurried back into the White Elephant. Despite the cold, he felt a sheen of sweat on his forehead. He warned himself not to believe what he'd heard.

Jim Courtright was spoiling for a fight.

Short stood at the bar. He struck a match, lighting a cheroot, and exhaled a thin plume of smoke. Waiters scurried back and forth from the kitchen serving a room full of diners seated at the tables. But he scarcely noted their passing, or the murmur of conversation. His eyes were on the door.

Marie came down the staircase. He turned, watching her descend the last few steps, and caught motion out of the corner of his eye. Johnson rushed into the restaurant as she crossed the room to the bar and stopped beside Short. She looked from one to the other, on the verge of speaking, when Johnson halted before them. His features were haggard.

"Luke, it looks bad," he said in a tinny voice. "I tried, but he won't listen to reason."

"Who?" Marie interrupted. "What's going on?"

Short waved his cheroot. "Courtright showed up a while ago. He wants to see me outside."

"Outside?" she repeated. "What does he want?"

"Well, Jake, you heard the question. What's he got to say for himself?"

Johnson grimaced. "Either we pay him off or he wants satisfaction. Those were his words."

"Satisfaction." Short carefully flicked an ash off his cheroot. "Sounds like I'm being challenged to a duel. Courtright must fancy himself a Southern gentleman."

"You've made him look the fool in front of the town. It's all come down to a matter of pride."

"And if I don't meet him outside?"

"Then he'll come in here," Johnson replied. "He was pretty plain about that. Told me to tell you it was your choice."

"Not much of a choice." Short smiled, motioned around the restaurant. "We can't have him spoiling these folks' supper. Just wouldn't be polite."

Johnson and Marie exchanged a glance. There was a trace of mockery in his tone; but neither of them saw any humor in the situation. After a stilted silence, Johnson made an offhand gesture. He tried to sound reasonable.

"There's a better way around this, Luke. I know how you feel, but it's gone too far. Why not pay him off and have done with it?"

"No," Short said flatly. "I don't pay extortion."

"I understand," Johnson said. "But doesn't that put you in the same boat as Courtright? Maybe it's your pride talking."

"Jake's right," Marie broke in. "If you go out there, someone's certain to get killed. Does the money really matter that much?"

"That's not the point," Short told her. "I won't be threatened by any man. We're not talking about money."

Johnson snorted derisively. "That's exactly what Courtright said. Damn near word for word."

"Then we seem to be in agreement. Courtright's got his principles and I've got mine."

"Think about what you're saying, Luke. Are you willing to get yourself killed over honor?"

"I can't think of a better reason," Short remarked. "On the other hand, it's a moot point. Nobody's killed me yet."

"Listen to me," Johnson persisted. "Courtright intends to get you out there and let the whole town see it. He's determined to force a fight."

"Jake, I've never been one to keep a man waiting. When the fiddler plays, everybody dances."

"Luke . . ." Marie touched his arm. "You don't have to do this. There must be some other way." Her eyes pleaded with him. "Please don't."

"Some things can only be done one way. No need to worry yourself. I'll be back directly."

Short walked toward the door. Johnson gave Marie a helpless look, then followed along. She waited a moment, torn by indecision, and finally hurried after them. Yet she couldn't bring herself to go any farther than the front of the restaurant. She took a position by the window.

Outside, Short turned upstreet. As Johnson trailed behind, he moved toward Courtright, who was standing by the shooting gallery doorway. Herring and Allison paused, lowering their rifles as he rapidly closed the distance. Ella Blackwell followed their gaze, her forehead wrinkled in a frown, watching him with an apprehensive expression. He halted a pace away from Courtright.

"I understand you're looking for me."

"You understand right," Courtright said coarsely. "Took you long enough to work up the nerve."

Johnson hastily intervened. "Jim, let's not get off on the wrong foot. You said you were willing to talk things out."

"So talk," Courtright said, his eyes locked on Short. "You ready to pay me what you owe me?"

"I don't owe you anything," Short informed him. "We settled that a long time ago."

"Not by a damnsight!"

"You're a gambling man, aren't you?"

"What the hell's that got to do with anything?"

"Tonight's not the night to press your luck."

Short hooked his thumbs in the armholes of his vest. Courtright stiffened, his eyes suddenly alert. "Don't you pull a gun on me!"

"Take it easy." Short fanned the lapels of his coat aside. "I'm not heeled."

"Like hell you're not!"

Courtright was primed for a fight. He knew Short habitually went armed, and when the gambler spread his coat, that was all the pretext needed. His arm a blur, Courtright reached for his right-hand gun, smoothly performing the reverse draw. The barrel cleared leather.

Short was a beat behind. His hand dipped to his rear pocket and came out with the stubby Colt. The men were not three feet apart, and he saw the long barrel of Courtright's pistol swinging into position. But then, incredibly, the sight on Courtright's gun snagged on the watch chain looped low across his vest. He yanked, struggling to untangle the barrel, and the watch popped out of his pocket. Short fired.

The slug all but severed the thumb on Courtright's hand. He grunted with shock and attempted to shift the pistol to his left hand. Short fired again, the report deafening at close range, and the bullet struck Courtright in the shoulder. He staggered backward into the doorway of the shooting gallery, badly wounded but still game. As he tried to switch his gun from one hand to the other, Short got off a third shot. A starburst of blood appeared on Courtright's vest, and he slammed sideways into the gallery doorway. Ella Blackwell and her customers dove for cover.

Short triggered two more shots in the span of a heartbeat. The slugs pocked Courtright's vest over the breastbone and just below his shirt collar. His legs buckled and he collapsed at the knees, falling backward through the doorway. He hit the floor, the pistol still clutched in his right hand, his chest a welter of blood. A last rush of air rattled in his throat, and his eyes rolled upward in his head. One boot heel drummed the sidewalk in an afterspasm of death.

There was a numbed moment of silence. Short stood over the fallen man, gun still extended, staring down at the body. Then Ella Blackwell screamed, and in the next instant, Officer Wally Tucker sprinted downstreet from the corner. He slammed to a halt before the gallery, looking from Short to the bloodied lump in the doorway, his mouth slack-jawed in amazement. After a time, finally gathering himself, he glanced back at Short. He held out his hand.

"No trouble now," he said. "You'll have to give me that gun."

Short palmed his pistol, extending it by the butt. Tucker took it, inspecting the loads, and looked up with an odd expression. "You emptied it," he said vacantly. "Why'd you shoot him so much?"

"Why?" Short appeared bemused by the question. "I suppose it seemed like the thing to do. He was trying to kill me."

A crowd began collecting on the street. Marie rushed out of the White Elephant and hurried to where Short and Johnson stood by the gallery. Her eyes teared when she saw that Short was unharmed, and she clutched his arm. He gave her a strange smile, and neither of them spoke, unable to summon words. Across the way, Lowe and Kate emerged from the Centennial, clearly surprised that Short has survived the shootout. Their features were set in a hard cast.

Some while later Marshal Bill Rea arrived on the scene. He first examined the body, which now lay puddled in blood. Then he spoke with Short and Johnson, listening without comment to their account of the fight. Afterward, he questioned Herring and Allison at some length, and separately talked with Ella Blackwell. All the time, Short was loosely guarded by Officer Tucker and another policeman, John Pemberton. Rea finally walked back to where Short waited with Marie and Johnson at the curb.

"Short, you're under arrest," he said solemnly. "I'll ask you to come along peaceable."

"On what charge?" Short demanded. "It was self-defense."

"Some of the witnesses tell a different story than your version. We'll have to let a court sort it out."

"You still haven't told me the charge."

Rea's eyes flicked past him across the street. Short turned and saw Joe Lowe in the crowd, nodding with a broad, gloating smile. As he looked back, Rea seemed to have arrived at a decision. "For now, you're charged with murder," the lawman said. "You'll have your chance before a judge in the morning."

"Jake, get me a lawyer," Short said over his shoulder. "I think I'll need a good one."

Marie stifled a cry with a hand to her mouth. Before Johnson could reply, Officer Tucker took Short by the arm and marched him toward the corner. Rea left Pemberton to await the undertaker, and followed along behind. Short kept his gaze straight ahead as the crowd parted to let them through.

He told himself he'd been drawn into a rigged game. A game engineered by Joe Lowe.

Chapter 29

Court convened at ten o'clock the next morning. Johnson and Marie were seated in the front row, and directly behind them were reporters from the *Democrat* and the *Gazette*. The room was packed with spectators, drawn by the sensational nature of the shooting. The morning newspapers had carried the story with banner headlines.

A door opened to the rear of the jury box. Short, flanked by Sheriff Walter Maddox and Marshal Bill Rea, was escorted into the room. The sheriff, as the chief law enforcement officer in the county, had taken Short into custody last night. But Rea, as the arresting officer, was unwilling to surrender the spotlight. He insisted on accompanying the prisoner into the courtroom.

Short had spent the night in the county jail. That morning, he'd been allowed to shave, and brush his clothing, and he looked reasonably presentable. He smiled at Marie and nodded to Johnson as the lawmen got him seated at the defense table. He appeared confident and unconcerned, though he was all too aware of the gravity of the charges. A night in jail had given him time to assess the situation.

Rowdy Joe Lowe, in his view, was the man pulling the strings. Had Courtright killed him, Lowe would have cleverly dispensed with a rival who supported the reform movement. The fact that he'd killed Courtright, and now stood charged with murder, sullied his reputation and might yet place him on the gallows. Either way, Lowe was the winner, all of it accomplished from behind the scenes, with the adroit touch of a puppet master. He was convinced as well that Lowe had enlisted Marshal Rea into the scheme. The idea was to kill him or hang him, which amounted to much the same thing.

Overnight, Jake Johnson had arranged for a lawyer to represent him. Alex Stedman was a skilled trial attorney, versed in matters of criminal law. Somewhat stout in build, fleshy and rumpled, his appearance belied a quick legal mind. Late last night, he'd met with Short at the jail and devised a strategy for today's hearing. He greeted Short now with a reassuring smile, and they got themselves seated at the defense table. The bailiff called the court to order.

Judge Wilbur Furnam took his place on the bench. He was an imposing man, with a thatch of white hair and a sweeping walrus mustache. From a handwritten document, he read aloud the purpose of the hearing, an inquest into the death of one Timothy Isaish "Jim" Courtright. Then he glanced at a man seated at one of the two tables directly before the bench.

"Are you ready to proceed, Mr. Bowlin?"

County Prosecutor Ned Bowlin rose to his feet. He was slim and dark-haired, and as an elected official, he represented all criminal matters for Tarrant County. He nodded. "We are prepared, Your Honor."

Furnam glanced toward the other table. "Good morning, Mr. Stedman. Are you representing Mr. Short?"

"Yes, I am, Judge." Stedman stood. "We are prepared to move forward as well."

"Let the record so indicate," Judge Furnam said, nodding to the prosecutor. "Call your first witness, Mr. Bowlin."

Doctor Andrew Phelps, who served as the county coroner, took the stand. Under questioning from Bowlin, he testified that the deceased, commonly known as Jim

Courtright, had sustained five gunshot wounds. He went on to state that a bullet to the heart had been the cause of death.

Officer Wally Tucker was the next witness. He testified that upon arriving at the scene, he had found Luke Short standing over the deceased with a gun in his hand. He further related that Short had admitted to the killing. "So I asked him," Tucker went on, "Why'd you shoot Courtright so many times?"

"And his response?" Bowlin prompted.

"Something about it seemed like the thing to do. He said Courtright was trying to kill him."

"Where was the deceased lying at this time?"

"Just inside the door to the shooting gallery."

"Was he armed?"

"Yessir, he was," Tucker said. "Found one gun in his right hand. Had a second holstered on his left hip."

"I see." Bowlin paused a beat. "Had the gun in his hand been fired?"

"No, sir, it hadn't."

"In your time as a police officer, how many gunfights have you witnessed?"

"Well, I've been on the force close to five years. I'd say ten or twelve shootings, anyway. Maybe more."

"Ten or twelve," Bowlin repeated. "Have you ever known of an instance where one man got off five shots and the other man fired none?"

"Nope," Tucker said. "Never even heard of such a thing."

"Jim Courtright was known to be fast with a gun. Do you think he could have been beaten that badly in a fair fight?"

Judge Furnam peered down from the bench, waiting for Stedman to object. The question clearly called for an opinion, but Stedman made no move to interject. Tucker was quick to answer.

"I don't think there's a man alive that fast. With an

even draw, Courtright would've at least got off one shot.''

''No further questions.''

Bowlin walked back to his chair. Stedman rose and approached the witness stand. ''Officer Tucker, you seem to be an unusually observant man. Was there anything peculiar about the deceased's right hand—his gun hand?''

''Sure was,'' Tucker said. ''His right thumb was near tore off.''

''How do you explain that?''

''Way it looked, it was done by a bullet.''

''So Mr. Short's *first* shot could have struck the deceased in the thumb. Is that correct?''

''Not too likely. That'd mean Short beat him on the draw. I'd say it was Short that pulled first.''

''Would you?'' Stedman appeared pensive. ''Doctor Phelps testified that the bullet struck Courtright's thumb, ricocheted off his pistol, and penetrated his lower right rib cage on a straight line. For that to happen, where would his gun hand have been? In what position?''

. . ''Objection!'' Bowlin interrupted. ''Calls for speculation.''

''Overruled,'' Judge Furnam said. ''Answer the question.''

Tucker's brow screwed up in thought. ''Well, I don't rightly know. Somewheres around belt level, I guess.''

''To his front,'' Stedman added. ''His pistol pointed at Mr. Short. Isn't that correct?''

''Yeah, maybe so.''

''And if any of the other wounds had happened first— the shoulder, the chest, the heart—the deceased could never have brought his pistol to bear so high, so far out. Isn't that true?''

''I suppose it might've happened that way.''

''Which means . . .'' Stedman hesitated, playing for effect. ''The deceased could have drawn first and Mr.

Short was simply faster. Otherwise, there's no logical explanation—is there?''

"I dunno." Tucker sounded befuddled. "I was up on the corner when the shootin' started. I didn't see it."

Stedman walked away. "Nothing more for this witness, Your Honor."

The prosecution next called Bud Herring. After being sworn, he related how Courtright had sent him into the White Elephant. He went on to describe the sequence of events after Short and Johnson came outside, and the exchange of harsh words. His impression, from where he was standing at the shooting gallery, was that Short had drawn first. He based his conclusion on the fact that Short had fired the first shot. He thought it impossible that Courtright had pulled first, and lost.

Will Allison followed him to the stand. Under questioning by Bowlin, he told essentially the same story. His contention, stated in adamant terms, was that no man could beat Jim Courtright on an even break. Ella Blackwell, who testified next, believed that it was Short who had provoked the fight. She recounted Courtright's words to the effect "Don't pull a gun on me," and her opinion was based on that statement alone. She was convinced that Short had made the first move.

On cross-examination, Stedman went after them with the tenacity of a bulldog. He forced each of them to admit that Courtright's back was to them during the opening moments of the confrontation. He then extracted the admission that Courtright blocked their line of sight, and as a result, they had no clear view of Short. Finally, he got them to concede that they could not swear under oath as to who drew first. One by one, they admitted that Courtright could have started the fight. They simply didn't know.

The prosecution then called Jake Johnson to the stand. Bowlin was quick to establish that Johnson and Short were not only business partners, but also close friends. His questions were phrased in such a manner as to imply that Johnson would twist his testimony to benefit Short. Johnson angrily denounced the smear on his integrity, and stated that he had been friends with Courtright long before Short became involved with the White Elephant. Bowlin ignored the outburst, confident he had made his point. He moved on to other matters.

"Tell us, Mr. Johnson," he said. "How close were you to Short and the deceased when the fight began?"

Johnson stared at him. "I was within a couple of feet. Off to one side, facing them."

"So you had an unimpeded view. Isn't that so?"

"I did."

"Think carefully now," Bowlin instructed. "Who went for his gun first—Short or Courtright?"

"Courtright," Johnson said without hesitation. "I was standing right there. No doubt of it."

"Indeed?" Bowlin arched one eyebrow in a skeptical look. "We have heard testimony that Courtright shouted, 'Don't pull a gun on me.' Why would he say that if he drew first?"

"Luke hooked his thumbs in his vest. Courtright took that as an excuse to start the fight."

"In other words, Short deliberately made a movement that led the deceased to believe he was in danger. Isn't that true?"

"Just the opposite," Johnson said. "Luke even told him he wasn't heeled. Tried to head off a fight."

"Which was a lie!" Bowlin announced loudly. "Short was carrying a pistol and he used it to deadly effect. True or not?"

"Only after Courtright pulled his gun."

Bowlin grilled him at length, trying to impeach his testimony. But Johnson refused to be rattled, and doggedly stuck to his story. Finally, frustrated at every turn, the prosecutor stumped back to his chair. Stedman approached the witness stand.

"Let's clear the air here," he said firmly. "You were

acting as a peacemaker in this situation, were you not, Mr. Johnson?''

"I tried my best," Johnson acknowledged. "Courtright wouldn't listen to reason. He had his mind set on trouble."

"And what was the source of the conflict?"

"Courtright demanded protection money, and Luke wouldn't pay. He called it extortion."

"What form did those demands take? How were they expressed?''

"Courtright said he'd have the money or he'd have satisfaction."

"Did he clarify what he meant by satisfaction?"

"Just came right out and said it. Either we paid him off or he'd push it to the limit. Force Luke to fight."

"So Courtright was the aggressor? The one who resorted to violence?"

"No two ways about it. He came there to kill Luke."

"Thank you for your candor, Mr. Johnson. You are excused."

Johnson walked back to the spectator benches. County Prosecutor Bowlin had exhausted his witness list, and he rested the state's case. Stedman then opened the case for the defense, confounding everyone in the courtroom by calling two surprise witnesses. Arnold James and Tom McCarty recounted their drinking session with Courtright on the night before the shootout. They related Courtright's open threat on Short's life, and their impression that the idea had been planted by Joe Lowe. Bowlin, seething with frustration, was unable to shake their testimony on cross-examination. Their story set the tone for the final witness.

Short took the stand. After he was sworn in by the court clerk, Stedman went straight to the point. "You had prior knowledge that Jim Courtright would make an attempt on your life. Is that correct?"

"Yes, it is," Short said. "Arnold James told me the night before."

"Knowing that, why did you accede to Courtright's demands and meet him outside the White Elephant? Why not hide, or send for the police?"

"Courtright would have just caught me at another time or another place. I thought I could talk him out of it."

Stedman faced the spectators. "But he wouldn't be dissuaded, would he?"

"No," Short said simply. "He drew his gun while I was still trying to talk."

"We've heard the opinion expressed that no man could beat Jim Courtright to the draw. How did you accomplish that, Mr. Short?"

"The barrel of Courtright's pistol got tangled in his watch chain. That gave me time to get my own gun into play."

"Let me understand," Stedman said, turning back to the witness box. "Courtright took you off guard and drew first. Only by a fluke were you able to avoid being killed. Is that a fair statement?"

"Fair and accurate," Short commented. "Luck was on my side."

"So you killed him only as a last resort. Only when you were forced to defend yourself. Correct?"

"I meant Courtright no harm. I fired on him when there was no other choice."

"Indeed so." Stedman walked away. "No further questions."

Bowlin warily approached the stand. He made one last stab at reversing the situation. "Correct me if I'm wrong," he said in a caustic voice. "You shot Jim Courtright in the thumb. You shot him in the shoulder and the chest and the neck, and at some point, in the heart. You shot him to pieces, emptied your pistol. Why, Mr. Short? Why?"

"Because I had to," Short said calmly. "He was trying to kill me."

"Why five shots, though? Why not two, or three? I

submit you intended to kill him, that it was premeditated. You went out there last night determined to murder him—and you did!''

''Courtright was trying to switch his gun to his left hand. I kept firing until he went down. Until he was out of the fight.''

''And that took you five shots? *Five shots!*''

''Courtright was game to the end. He was a brave man.''

Bowlin looked as though he'd been socked with a rock. He shook his head, dazed and defeated, and turned away with disgust. Stedman immediately jumped to his feet.

''If it pleases the court,'' he said, addressing the bench. ''I move for a ruling of justifiable homicide. Mr. Short was clearly acting in self-defense.''

''Motion granted.'' Judge Furnam paused, and looked down at Short. ''For the record, Mr. Short, you should never have been charged in this matter. I deplore shootings, but you were entirely within your rights.'' He hammered his gavel with a sharp rap. ''This court stands adjourned.''

Marie squealed with joy. She rushed to the defense table and threw her arms around Short's neck. He grinned, looking past her shoulder, and exchanged a warm handshake with Stedman. Across the way, he saw Bowlin and the sheriff and Marshal Rea huddled in a glum conference. Bowlin appeared to be lecturing them in harsh terms.

Short was distracted by Johnson and Marie. Their exuberance at the verdict reminded him that he'd emerged with his reputation intact. Yet he told himself the celebration was premature. A token victory.

There was still the matter of Joe Lowe.

Chapter 30

Early that afternoon Short stepped out of the bathroom. His features were ruddy after a long soak in the tub, where he'd scrubbed off the grime from a night in a jail cell. He felt refreshed and clean, almost his old self, if not exactly chipper. His mood was still thoughtful, oddly withdrawn.

A cloud of steam followed him into the bedroom. Marie had laid out fresh underwear and a shirt, and a charcoal-gray suit hung on the door of the armoire. She turned as he entered the room, and gave him a quick kiss on the mouth. Her eyes were bright with happiness.

"Just look at you!" she said gaily. "You're positively glowing."

Short smiled vaguely. "I stayed in there so long, I almost scalded myself."

"Well, really, it's certainly understandable. What a horrid thing, locked away in that jail."

"I'd have to say I've had better accommodations."

She heard something strange in his voice. At first, when they'd returned from the courthouse, she had thought it was the aftereffects of the killing and the ordeal of the inquest. But she sensed now that he was brooding on something else, his thoughts turned inward. She gave him a quizzical look.

"You seem a little down, sugar. I thought you would be clicking your heels."

Short stepped into his trousers. "Not down, just have a couple of things on my mind. Didn't mean to rain on the parade."

"Don't be silly." She watched as he shrugged into his shirt. "Do you want to talk about it?"

"We've had enough trouble for one day."

"Not if it's going to spoil your mood. What kind of trouble?"

"Joe Lowe."

"What about him?"

"Nothing's changed." Short finished buttoning his shirt. "I'm a thorn in Lowe's side and he wants me dead. He'll try again."

"No, he wouldn't dare!" Her voice rose an octave. "Everyone knows he was the one behind Courtright. How would he dare try anything else?"

"Rowdy Joe doesn't give a hoot about public opinion. He plays by his own rules. Dirty rules."

"But he couldn't hope to get away with it. I bet the police would be on him in an instant."

"You'd lose that bet." Short began knotting his tie, and glanced at her in the mirror. "Our esteemed town marshal is in Lowe's hip pocket. Bought and paid for in full."

She sat down on the edge of the bed. "What about the sheriff? He's not on Lowe's payroll."

"Nobody would ever pin it on Lowe. He'd use one of his strong-arm boys, or some dimwit gunman with no better sense. The same as he did with Courtright."

"Good Lord, you're right, he would. How can you stop him?"

"I haven't decided just yet."

"But there has to be a way . . . doesn't there?"

"I'm thinking on it."

After Short was dressed, they left the suite. Marie's mood was now as dreary as his own, and as they emerged from the hotel, her features were downcast. But they proceeded on toward the corner, for they were expected at the White Elephant by three o'clock. Jake Johnson was planning an informal celebration during the afternoon lull, and Short was the guest of honor. They were going to toast his victory in court.

A small crowd greeted them as they came through the door. Nat Kramer and the other uptown club owners were present, as well as the dealers and croupiers who worked the White Elephant gaming room. Someone shouted congratulations, and the whole group broke out in lively cheers. Johnson hurried forward and affectionately threw his arm around Short's shoulders. He faced the well-wishers with a broad grin.

"The man of the hour!" he proclaimed grandly. "A high roller who knows how to win when the chips are down. Let's hear it for Luke!"

Champagne corks popped. Waiters moved about, pouring fluted glasses to the brim, and Johnson led the crowd in a toast. Short accepted their kudos with a wide smile, raising his glass to everyone in the room. Marie's spirits brightened for the moment, and she sipped champagne as men pressed forward to shake Short's hand. When the other club owners drifted off, Nat Kramer lingered behind. His manner was affable, his smile cordial.

"Luke, you lead a charmed life," he said with genuine warmth. "The betting around town was that we would be celebrating your wake rather than your triumph. I'm delighted you overturned the odds."

"No more than myself," Short said with some irony. "I just suspect there's no celebration in the Acre. The sporting crowd's probably crying in their beer."

"I wouldn't doubt it for a moment. After Courtright's untimely demise, they thought for sure you would end up on the gallows. You've disappointed them greatly."

"That's only the start of it, Nat. I intend to throw some heavy support behind Van Zandt and his reformers. Maybe I'll run another ad in the newspapers."

Kramer's expression turned sober. "Your friend across the street would take that as a personal affront. I assume you know you're not done with him yet.''

"Never thought otherwise," Short remarked. "Lowe works a grudge like a dog gnawing on a bone. He never quits."

"How do you plan to handle it?"

"You're a better judge of Rowdy Joe than most. How would you handle it?"

"In the most expeditious manner," Kramer said levelly. "Get him before he gets you."

On the opposite side of the room, Marie stood talking with some of the dealers. Short watched her for a moment, then looked around. "Funny thing," he said, holding Kramer's gaze. "I've given it a lot of thought since last night. I came to the same conclusion."

"I suspected as much," Kramer observed. "Which leaves you with a rather sticky problem."

"What's that?"

"Lowe very likely realizes he's not in your league with a gun. How do you propose to force him into a fight?"

Short smiled, his mouth a hard straight line. "Rowdy Joe has a weakness. When he loses his temper, he's like a bull with a red flag. He goes loco."

"All well and good," Kramer said. "But first you have to goad him into losing his temper. Do you have a red flag?"

"I've got one with his name on it, Nat. He'll fight."

"You sound confident."

"I am."

The celebration got louder as waiters continued to pour champagne. Kramer wandered off to join the other club owners, who were congregated around Johnson at the end of the bar. Short moved through the crowd, shaking hands and accepting congratulations, slowly making his way toward the front of the room. There, he paused beside Marie, who was still engaged in conversation with several of the dealers. She turned, smiling at him, and her eyes suddenly shifted to the window. Her face went ashen.

A hearse, drawn by four black horses, rolled slowly past the front of the White Elephant. The sides of the hearse were framed in glass, and an ornate casket was visible, burnished wood gleaming beneath a westerly sun. Directly behind the hearse, Elizabeth Courtright and her three children rode in an open carriage, their features stark with grief. A hundred or more mourners, most of them members of the sporting crowd, followed along on foot. Up and down the street, passersby paused and the men removed their hats. The funeral procession was enveloped in a dirge of silence.

Elizabeth Courtright turned her head as the carriage came abreast of the White Elephant. Her face was gaunt, her features pale against the somber black of her dress. She stared straight at the window, and it was as though the fire in her eyes burned holes through the glass. On the other side, watching her, Short felt the intensity of her hatred, and knew it was directed at him. Then her head turned again to the front, and she sat stiff with the dignity of a bereaved widow. The carriage disappeared down the block.

"I should've warned you," Johnson said, appearing at Short's elbow. "The funeral was held over at the Methodist Church. They're burying him at Oakwood Cemetery."

"That's on the edge of town," Marie said uncertainly. "Why would they bring him by here?"

"I don't know," Johnson muttered. "I just don't know."

Short knew. For a moment, he had looked into Elizabeth Courtright's eyes, and he'd seen her soul consumed by fury and loss. She had brought the body of her husband past the White Elephant as a final, symbolic damnation of the man who'd put him in a coffin. Had she accosted Short on the street and vented her wrath, her message could have been no less clear. She wanted him to live with the memory of the man he'd killed, and a woman widowed too young. She had, in her own way, branded him a murderer.

A dark mask came over Short's features. His gaze went across to the Centennial, and something in his mind snapped. The man who had actually murdered Jim Courtright was over there now, probably amused by the drab spectacle of the funeral procession. All day, Short had restrained himself, suppressed his own anger, determined to await the right time and place to confront Joe Lowe. But the sight of the hearse, and the brittle hatred he'd seen in Elizabeth Courtright's eyes, pushed him beyond the bounds of whatever was rational or cunning. He turned toward the door.

"Luke!" Marie cried out in alarm. "Where are you going?"

"I've got some unfinished business."

Short twisted away when she clutched at his arm. He went out the door, a sense of calm finality in his pace, and crossed the street. On the opposite side, he pushed through passersby clogging the sidewalk and burst into the Centennial. His eyes scanned the bar, searching for Lowe, and he started toward the staircase leading to the club room. Frank Meade, the house manager, was coming down the stairs, and they met at the landing. Short drilled him with a look.

"Where's Lowe?"

"Gone."

"Gone where?"

"I don't know." Meade hesitated, weighing the risk. He decided it wasn't worth getting himself shot. "Joe and Kate are catching the evening train. He knew you'd come for him."

"Don't hand me that," Short said brusquely. "Lowe's got too much at stake in Fort Worth. He wouldn't just quit and run."

"I'm tellin' you the God's honest truth. He left Roy Tutt in charge of things while he's gone. Don't ask me how long, because I don't know. He didn't say."

"Who's Roy Tutt?"

"The Tivoli Saloon," Meade said. "One of Joe's dives down in the Acre. Tutt's the manager."

"You're sure about the evening train?"

"That's what he told me, Mr. Short. I wouldn't lie about it."

"You damn well better not."

Short checked the clock on the far wall. He turned, leaving Meade on the staircase, and rushed out of the Centennial. On the street, he commandeered a carriage for hire, ordering the driver to the train station, and peeled off twenty dollars from his roll. The driver whipped his horse into an ungainly lope, and they went tearing down Main Street, dodging wagons and scattering pedestrians at every intersection. Some minutes later, they skidded to a halt in front of Union Station.

Twilight lurked at the edges of afternoon as the sun dropped below the horizon. Short jumped out of the carriage, brushing past people waiting at the curb, and ran around the side of the depot. The evening train, bound for points south, was slowly gathering steam, pulling out of the station. He saw Lowe and Kate on the observation platform, at the rear of the last passenger coach, and realized they'd only just made it aboard the train. He cursed, shouting Lowe's name, and hurried forward. They turned as the train picked up speed.

Lowe raised his arm in an obscene gesture. Kate brayed a vulgar laugh, screaming something that was lost to the wind. Short reacted on reflex alone, drawing the Colt in a fluid motion. He thumbed the hammer, centering the sights on Lowe, and feathered the trigger. At the last instant some deeper instinct took hold, and he found himself unable to kill in cold blood. He raised the sights and fired, and a lantern dangling from the roof of the observation platform exploded in a showery flame. Lowe and Kate tumbled over one another scrambling through the coach door.

The train rapidly vanished into the wintry dusk. Short grinned, holstering his pistol, and walked back around the depot. Five minutes later, at the corner of Main and Fourteenth, he entered the Tivoli Saloon. One of the bartenders directed him to a small office off the hallway at the rear of the room. He went though the door without knocking and found Roy Tutt seated at a battered desk. Tutt started out of his chair, his face contorted in a mix of shock and fear. Short pulled the stubby Colt.

"Keep your seat," he said, wagging the snout of the pistol. "I just saw your boss off at the train station. We waved good-bye."

Tutt kept his hands flat on the desk. "What's that to me?"

"Well, it's like this, Roy. I'm told you're running things now. So I'm here with a message."

"You're the one holdin' the gun."

"I am at that," Short said dryly. "Wherever Lowe's gone, get word to him to stay there. He's worn out his welcome in Fort Worth."

"Says you." Tutt's beady eyes narrowed. "What about all the dives he owns in the Acre? You think he's just gonna toss 'em over?"

"Lowe took off because he knew I'd kill him. Play it smart and you could probably buy him out at a pretty price. All those dives aren't worth a plug nickel to a dead man."

There was a moment of deliberation. Tutt finally nodded, his mouth set in a tight smile. "You've got a good idea there, Short. Maybe I'll make him an offer."

"Tell him I said he'd be smart to accept."

"I'll do that."

"One other thing, Roy."

"Yeah?"

"A word to the wise." Short fixed him with a cold stare. "I'd lay odds Rowdy Joe told you to have me killed. Don't try it."

"Wouldn't think of it," Tutt said readily. "I might

just wind up ownin' the Acre. Maybe you and me will do some business.''

''Keep away from uptown and we won't have any trouble.''

''What if I make a deal with Lowe on the Centennial?''

''I'll buy it from you at a profit.''

''See?'' Tutt bobbed his head with a crafty look. ''I knew we could do business.''

''Never doubted it for a minute, Roy.''

Short holstered his pistol. He walked back through the saloon and emerged onto the street. Outside, he caught the trolley car and took a seat, confident he'd solved the problem for now. Whether or not Roy Tutt ended up owning the Acre was a matter for another time. Tomorrow would take care of itself.

Uptown, he hopped off the trolley car at the corner of Third and Main. When he came through the door of the White Elephant, Marie and Johnson were standing at the far end of the bar. Their features were taut with worry, and they seemed wrapped in a cone of silence. He was halfway down the bar when Marie happened to glance around, and she gave a little yelp. She rushed forward and threw herself into his arms.

''Oh, Luke!'' she cried. ''We saw you run out of the Centennial and we didn't know where you went. I was just terrified.''

''Nothing to worry about,'' Short said with an ironic shrug. ''I had to put Rowdy Joe and Kate on a train.''

''Train?'' she echoed. ''You mean they're gone?''

''Way it looked, they bought a one-way ticket.''

''Are you saying they won't come back?''

''I seriously doubt it.''

Her eyes went round. ''You clever devil. You're telling me it's all through, aren't you? It's ended!''

Short smiled. ''I think it's just begun.''

They popped the cork on another bottle of champagne.

For decades the Texas plains ran with the blood of natives and settlers, as pioneers carved out ranch land from ancient Indian hunting grounds and the U.S. Army turned the tide of battle. Now the Civil War has begun, and the Army is pulling out of Fort Belknap—giving the Comanches a new chance for victory and revenge.

Led by the remarkable warrior, Little Buffalo, the Comanche and Kiowa are united in a campaign to wipe out the settlers forever. But in their way stand two remarkable men...

Allan Johnson is a former plantation owner. Britt Johnson was once his family slave, now a freed man facing a new kind of hatred on the frontier. Together, with a rag-tag volunteer army, they'll stand up for their hopes and dreams in a journey of courage and conscience that will lead to victory...or death.

BLACK FOX

A Novel by
MATT BRAUN

Bestselling author of *Wyatt Earp*

In 1889, Bill Tilghman joined the historic land rush that transformed a raw frontier into Oklahoma Territory. A lawman by trade, he set aside his badge to make his fortune in the boom-towns. Yet Tilghman was called into service once more, on a bold, relentless journey that would make his name a legend for all time—in an epic confrontation with outlaw Bill Doolin.

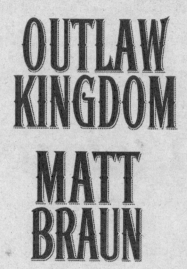

OUTLAW KINGDOM
KINGDOM
MATT BRAUN

CAMERON JUDD
THE NEW VOICE OF THE OLD WEST